What You Don't Know

Also by David Belbin

Bone and Cane

What You Don't Know

David Belbin

**Tindal
Street
Press**

First published in 2012
by Tindal Street Press Ltd
217 The Custard Factory, Gibb Street, Birmingham, B9 4AA
www.tindalstreet.co.uk

A CIP catalogue reference for this book is available
from the British Library

ISBN: 978 1 906994 33 4
Ebook: 978 1 906994 88 4

Typeset by Tetragon

Printed and bound by
CPI Group (UK) Ltd, Croydon, CR0 4YY

For Don and Jo-Anne Freeman

PROLOGUE

June 1998

'Sarah, can I have a word?' the Home Secretary asked.

'Of course.' Sarah followed her boss out of the debating chamber, expecting him to congratulate her on the speech she'd just made. The riot at Wormwood Scrubs had ruined her weekend, but it was over and, as prisons minister, she had come out of the situation with her reputation enhanced.

'There's somebody who needs to speak to you urgently,' he said when they were alone. 'Could you go with Sir Robin?'

The senior civil servant was standing, discreetly, by a large bookcase filled with the biographies of Sarah's fellow MPs. He led her into the depths of the Commons estate.

'Can you tell me what this is about?' Sarah asked.

'I'm afraid not. It's an informal interview, but I would advise you to be very careful about what you say.'

Sarah was worried now. 'An informal interview with whom?'

The question was ignored. Sir Robin knocked on an unlabelled door. He ushered her inside but didn't join her, which was probably for the best, as this office had barely enough room for the two people already there. Sarah suspected that the space was normally used for storage. The desk that the suited men sat behind was shabby and utilitarian. There were no windows or pictures on the walls.

The men introduced themselves as police officers. Sarah was too flustered to take in names, but she got their ranks: a detective chief inspector and a detective superintendent. As a former police officer herself, she knew immediately how serious this was. The DCI asked the questions.

'We need some sensitive information, Minister.'

'About what?'

'Your relationship with Paul Morris.'

'I see.'

'How would you describe your relationship with Mr Morris?'

'A professional one. We serve on some of the same committees.'

'Perhaps, to save time, I should show you an item we found in Mr Morris's flat. Can you confirm that these are yours?'

He held up an evidence bag containing a pair of pale blue knickers with a small navy ribbon bow. Sarah tried to keep her voice neutral.

'Possibly. I do own some underwear like that.'

'And can you confirm that you left Mr Morris's King's Cross apartment at twenty-five to eight last Friday morning?'

They must have a witness. Stupid to lie. 'Yes, I did.'

'I take it you weren't there for a business meeting.'

'No, I wasn't.'

'Can you tell me what state Mr Morris was in when you left that morning?'

'Angry. I'd just dumped him. So from then on our relationship became purely professional, which is why I characterized it in that manner just now.' Should she have explained her earlier obfuscation? Too late, she'd blurted it out.

'You're sure that he was the angry one, not you?'

'I never get angry, Inspector, except for effect. Maybe angry's not the best word for the state that Paul was in. He was miffed, insulted, eager to change my mind.'

'Change your mind about what?'

'About my not seeing him again.'

The men exchanged glances. The superintendent spoke. 'And you won't be seeing him again, will you?'

'Not outside our professional relationship, no. But I don't understand what you're getting at. What has Paul done?'

'Just to reiterate, he was in good health when you left him?'

'He was. Very good –' Sarah stopped herself. 'Wait. Are you telling me that . . .'

The superintendent took over. 'Paul Morris was murdered, Minister. Some time on Friday morning, according to the pathologist. You were seen hurrying down Pentonville Road with what passers-by referred to as a "distracted air" at around twenty to eight the same morning. Is that accurate?'

For the first time, Sarah hesitated. 'Before we go any further,' she said, 'I think I'd better consult my solicitor.'

I

October 1997

You have nice clothes, top trainers and great hair. Twice a week you're late back from school. Once you were spotted getting out of his car.

'Was that your trick dropping you off?' a girl from the hostel asked. 'Likes the uniform, does he?'

It's not the uniform, he says. He likes what's underneath.

You meet after school. Mid-afternoon suits him best. He doesn't want you to waste time going home, getting changed and made-up. He wants your pale white skin against his, as often as time allows. In the back of the car, in rented rooms and back alleys. Weekends are a no-go. He gives you nice stuff and, occasionally, money. But never a set amount. You're not a whore. Loads of girls give it away to older guys. You know why, and you know where it leads. Your guy doesn't give you drugs, and he always uses protection. All he asks is you don't go with anybody else.

You've got exams next year and your school is shit. You never have the same teachers from one term to the next. Only a couple can keep order in the classroom. After four years, you're sick of it. You showed him your report. He knows how smart you are. He wants you to be all the things that you want to be. He'll help. At fifteen, he says, everything is still possible.

Tonight he takes you to the out-of-town multiplex. On the way, you talk about your week. He likes it when you ramble on. He never tells you what he's been up to: he says it's boring. You've chosen an old grey jumper that got you funny looks from mates in class. Makes it look like you've got no boobs. He likes to get you in at the child's rate. It excites him. You've picked a film that's been out a while, so the screen is nearly empty: you have a row to yourselves at the back. You're well away from the aisle. He slips his hand down your knickers during the trailers, fingers you in the opening titles. Sometimes you'd prefer to enjoy the film, but that's not why you're here.

By the time the film starts, it's his turn. You go down on him until he lifts your head and kisses you on the lips. He doesn't come. That happens later, in the disabled toilets, where he takes you from behind, over the sink. This bit is always quick. Afterwards, he cleans up, shoves some cash in your pocket, leaves before you do. You watch the rest of the film, then take a taxi home. You wait for him to call again.

You're not allowed to be in love. Love is for those who can afford it. Love is a luxury, sex a necessity. He says you have to wait until your life's sorted before falling in love, laying yourself open like that.

Whatever he wants to call it, you're his. You'd carry a child for him. You'd kill for him. After him, the smelly boys who hang around the hostel, with their cheap drugs and cheaper clothes, have nothing to offer you. Your only worry is he'll get bored. You're jailbait now, but you won't be for ever. Your boobs are still growing. Your thighs are getting thicker. You're getting taller. He says you'll always be his princess. Always.

He'd better not be lying.

The meeting was at Hambleton Hall, a country house retreat on Rutland Water, an hour's drive from Nottingham. The round table in the private dining room held eight people, as long as they sat just a little too close together. Sarah was the only woman and the only MP. Eric Turnbull, the chief constable, was on her right. Now and then his left thigh brushed her skirt. Deliberately, she assumed. He had form in that area.

They were here to discuss the city's long-term drug strategy. Compared to the rest of the city, Nottingham West, Sarah's constituency, didn't have a drugs problem. It was relatively well-off, a former Conservative seat. Her constituents didn't need to commit crimes to pay for the drugs they used. So she had been surprised when Eric asked her to come along, calling in a favour that made it impossible for her to refuse.

Eric, it turned out, knew something she didn't. Two years ago, Nottingham's Crack Action Team had been established to deal with the addiction epidemic that crack cocaine had created in the city. In its short lifetime, the CAT had been deemed to be very successful. Until today.

'How is it possible?' Sarah asked the meeting. 'Are you seriously telling me that the head of the team you set up to deal with the crack epidemic is also the city's biggest crack dealer?'

'It's looking that way,' the chief constable said.

'We're going to be the laughing stock of the country.'

'Only for a day or two,' said Paul Morris. 'What we have to discuss today is damage limitation.'

County councillor Paul Morris had a legal background and was highly articulate, but these weren't the main reasons for his election as chair of the police committee. He'd been given the nod because he was black, with parents born in Guyana. Thing was, the city's police needed a figurehead to help counter its reputation for racism. A justified reputation. For the first couple of meetings, Paul gave the impression that he was out of his depth. Soon, however, it became clear that he wasn't afraid to take risks, talk tough and tell things the way they were.

Frank Davis, head of the Crack Action Team, had also been given his job largely because he was black. Sarah had never met him, but people said he was forceful and charismatic. Davis spoke at anti-drug conferences up and down the country.

It wasn't long before rumours started to circulate about him and his ten-strong team. City politicians were quick to dismiss these as racism or paranoia. Until this morning, when Davis was arrested for possession of several thousand pounds' worth of crack cocaine.

For half an hour, the round table discussed the fiasco, which would be all over the papers in a day or two. Two years ago, when the city's other MPs gave the CAT their backing, Sarah wasn't asked for her support. She wasn't expected to survive this year's general election. By-election gains usually reverted to the original party. However, thanks to Labour's landslide victory, Sarah had hung on to her seat, albeit with a decreased majority. When Eric insisted that she come today, he hadn't told her that none of the city's other MPs had been invited. As chief constable, he would have known that Davis was about to be busted. And he would know that the police authority would need a politician with national status and clean hands to spin this story to the national media. Sarah had been stitched up, good and proper.

Paul Morris was the first to move the agenda on in a positive way.

'This is a PR disaster, but we have to salvage something from the wreckage. We have to show that we have a replacement ready.'

'That would take months to set up,' Eric pointed out.

'Not if we expand an already existing organization.'

'This is premature,' John Wood, the County Council leader said. 'Let the dust settle. Otherwise whatever replaces the Crack Action Team will be tarred with the same brush.'

'We can't afford to let that happen,' Sarah argued. 'We need to help vulnerable young people and we need to be seen to help them.'

'I agree with Sarah,' Paul Morris told the meeting. 'We can't just give up. The demand for crack is still there and the problems it generates are getting worse. We have a pilot operation that police and politicians can get behind. The Power Project. I took Eric there the other day.'

He handed over to the chief constable. Eric explained that, while the Power Project had been set up to help long-term drug users, its remit could be expanded to help young people too.

'Could we divert some of the better CAT workers to this Power Project?' Sarah asked him.

'No. We don't know for sure which of those workers are involved in the drugs trade. There was a rash of accusations and counter-accusations. Therefore, in order to isolate the new body from the old body, no drugs workers – no matter how squeaky clean they might appear – should be employed in the new unit.'

'Who's in charge of the Power Project?' Sarah asked.

'Kingston Bell. Do you know him?'

'I know *of* him. We've not met. But he sounds like a good choice.'

Sarah knew that Bell was a community activist with church connections. The *Nottingham Evening Post* had done a story on him recently, when he was awarded an MBE for services to the community. He had been brought up in a children's home and was now on the board of several city institutions that looked after kids in similar situations.

'To conclude,' Eric said. 'We want to give the Power Project a big boost. I'd like everyone to do their bit by talking the place up.'

*

Over dinner, Sarah discovered that Paul Morris had excellent taste in food. Like her, he ordered the scallop ravioli, following it with roasted French partridge with ceps. The food was exceptional, as was the wine, which Eric chose. When the final plates were cleared, a waitress poured generous brandies and left the bottle on the table. Cigars were lit. Several separate conversations broke out at once.

'Rumour has it you're moving on,' Sarah said to Paul.

'You're well informed. Yes, I'm giving up the council seat, heading for the capital. An offer too good to refuse. I've only told Eric. Did he . . .?'

Sarah shook her head. She had no intention of giving away her source, the Home Secretary. 'Congratulations. Is Annette looking forward to living in London?'

'She's going to stay in Nottingham for the time being. You know how it is, with the kids settled at their schools.'

'I expect we'll see each other on the train.'

'I hope so,' Paul said, then leaned in closer. 'There was a favour I want to ask of you. It's about the Power Project. Thing is, Suraj Hanspal persuaded me to be on the management board, but carrying on isn't compatible with my new role. The project needs somebody weighty to reassure the agencies concerned that there'll be proper scrutiny.'

Sarah, experienced in such matters, got in her refusal before he could take it any further. 'I don't think so, Paul. You know how busy the Home Office keeps me. And how marginal my seat is.'

'It'd be worth votes. And we're talking one meeting a month, half of which you can skip. Six afternoons a year and a couple of press conferences. I'd be forever in your debt.'

'Many men have said that to me,' Sarah replied, with a wry smile. 'Not one's paid up yet. I prefer payment in advance.'

'Name your fee,' Paul said, with a cheeky smile.

Eric stood up. 'I'd like to propose a toast,' he said. 'To a departing friend.' And then he turned to Paul and smiled.

'Did you know that Eric was going to let the cat out of the bag about your new job?' Sarah asked Paul later, in the drawing room. The cigar smoke had got too much for her, and Paul, gallantly, had escorted her to this elegant but cosy room, with its heavy curtains, wood fire and array of easy chairs and sofas. Earlier, Eric had not been able to spell out the nature of Paul's new job, only hint at its importance. Sarah knew that Paul was to head up a hush-hush policy research unit at the Home Office.

She sipped her third brandy, conscious that she was a little drunk, hence dangerously indiscreet. 'Got a place in London yet?'

'Hotel. Looking to buy. I don't like wasting money on rent.'

'And you call yourself a socialist. What happened to "property is theft"?'

'Proudhon would have been the first to change his mind when economic circumstances changed.'

'I expect you're right,' Sarah said, standing. 'Must get to bed.'

'Me too.' Paul followed. 'I'll get you those papers about the Power Project.'

'It can wait until morning,' Sarah said, already at the stairs.

'I'm taking off before breakfast. It'll only take me a minute.'

'Whatever. I'm in here.' There was a boyish twinkle in his eyes, so she added, as she unlocked the door, 'No funny business.'

'Last thing on my mind,' he said.

She kicked off her shoes and waited for him to return. This was the Noel Coward room, which was said to have been regularly used by the famous playwright. It was large, with an expansive double bed and two armchairs on either side of the TV. Sarah went into the bathroom and checked her make-up. She heard a gentle knock on the door.

'It's not locked.'

She wasn't going to sleep with Paul, but maybe she'd offer him a nightcap while she glanced at the papers, made up her mind about the project. She would rebuff any pass politely, with just a hint that in London, during the week, she might one day behave differently. She wouldn't, but Paul was gorgeous. She enjoyed his attention. And she hadn't had sex for – count them – seven months. A girl had to remind herself how to flirt or she might lose the facility. The door opened.

'I hoped you'd like some company.' It wasn't Paul. It was Eric. The recently separated chief constable swayed slightly. He held a bottle of Armagnac, two thirds full, in his left hand. 'You look fantastic tonight, by the way.'

'And you look pissed. Eric, what are you doing here?'

'You know how long I've . . . I thought that, now I'm free, well . . .'

There was another knock on the door.

'Answer it, would you?' Sarah said. 'Or would you prefer to hide in the wardrobe to make the bedroom farce complete? I think it's big enough.'

Her suitor turned to the wardrobe in question and appeared to contemplate the suggestion.

'It's open,' Sarah called.

'I brought you those papers about that project.' Paul Morris had a folder in one hand and a bottle in the other. Sarah swore under her breath. Paul's eyes met Eric's. Each wore a sheepish yet defiant expression: schoolboys who had been found out. Sarah took the folder from Paul, then held the door open.

'Looks like you boys are set to party all night,' she said. 'Try not to wake me when you come up to bed. I have to be bright-eyed and bushy-tailed for my surgery tomorrow.'

She locked the door behind them.

2

Nick's flat was above a locksmith's on the run-down Alfreton Road. The entrance was on a side alley, via a cast-iron stairway that doubled as a fire escape. He did not get casual visitors. He didn't get many callers, full stop. The postman. His brother Joe. That was about it.

At first, he ignored the knock on the door. It was quarter past seven and he was about to go out, didn't want to be late. He hadn't been sure that Nancy would agree to meet him for a drink. She was going to do him a favour, although she didn't know it yet.

The knocking resumed: masculine, insistent. Nick buttoned his shirt, then opened the door. The guy standing there was thirty-ish and slight. His smile was familiar, but Nick couldn't place him.

'Nick. My man. I heard you were out.'

Hearing his voice, Nick remembered how they knew each other. 'Wayne. You'd better come in. But I've only got a couple of minutes.'

'Smart shirt. Hot date?'

'It's kind of a professional thing. What can I do for you, Wayne? I'm not in the supply business any more.'

'I know, I know. It was all over the papers nearly, what? Six years ago. How long did you do?'

'I did five, got out in April.'

'Keeping body and soul together?'

'I'm here, aren't I? Don't want to be rude, but I am in a hurry.'

Wayne glanced around Nick's Spartan flat, made instant judgements. 'Some of your old friends, they thought you might be looking to make some proper money again. People liked you, Nick. You were always very trustworthy, reliable. When you got busted, you didn't name names. Things like that don't get forgotten.'

'Nice of you to say, but . . .' Nick hesitated. He had no intention of getting involved in drug dealing again. It was only happenstance, an unlikely opportunity provided by a cave network beneath his old flat, that took him into the game in the first place. For more than a year, money had poured in, but every penny had cost him, several times over. 'Thing is, I'm on probation. I have to keep my nose clean or I'll be sent back to serve three more years. So it's good of you to think of me, but . . .'

Wayne shook his head, as if in wonderment. 'I understand your situation. It's just that a vacancy has arisen and my employer wants to make you an offer. You wouldn't grow, just supervise the guys who look after the grow houses. Serious money for virtually no risk. Sky's the limit – that's the message I was told to give you. Will you at least think about it?'

Nick didn't ask who 'my employer' was. Probably a guy he used to supply. Six years ago, Wayne was a runner for one of the bigger dealers in the Meadows estate. He was bound to have been promoted several times since then.

'I'll think about it,' Nick said.

Wayne scribbled his number on a bus ticket, which Nick stuffed into the back pocket of his black Levi's. 'Going into town? Let me walk you there.'

'Best we're not seen together,' Nick said.

'Already thinking like a pro. Call me soon.'

'I said I'll think about it. But if I don't call, don't contact me again. Understood?'

'Understood,' Wayne said, and let himself out.

Nick checked his hair and looked at his watch. Five to. The bar was nearly ten minutes' walk away and he didn't want to work up a sweat. He gave Wayne a minute, then left. Into the first bin that he passed, Nick threw away the bus ticket. You could never be too careful.

He got to the Fat Cat late, but needn't have worried. Nancy wasn't there yet. He examined the cocktail menu. Six years ago, Nick could have afforded to drink here all night. Then the most exotic drink on offer would have been a glass of bad wine. Nancy had suggested the venue. He hoped she'd be happy to move somewhere cheaper after a drink or two.

Here she was, nearly six years older than when he'd seen her last, in the public gallery at his trial. She was lightly tanned, despite the time of year. He stood to greet her with a kiss on the cheek. She pressed her heavy breasts against his chest.

'You've changed,' Nancy said. 'Filled out. I like your hair short.'

'It's not that short.'

'No, but people started to grow it longer while you were away.'

Nancy was always a straight talker. He liked the way she acknowledged his imprisonment up front. For a few minutes, they discussed her latest boyfriend, whom she described as 'a guitarist'. He doubled as a supply teacher, which was how she'd met him. Once she'd got the issue of her unavailability out of the way, Nancy gave Nick a quick summary of the comings and goings at the comprehensive school where he used to teach. She didn't talk about herself except when asked a direct question. Nick admired that in her.

'How are you getting on with teaching?' he asked, after a while. 'I remember how exhausted it used to make you.'

'Some things get easier. Class control, preparation. People say I should go for promotion, but I don't want more paperwork. I want a life.'

Six years had made Nancy more womanly and less anxious, dissipating some of the nervous energy that used to make people awkward around her. She was slender, with skinny legs, a flat bottom and a chest almost too prominent for her frame. She wore her dark, straight hair in a bob that set off her finely boned face, with its intelligent, deep blue eyes and perfectly proportioned nose. Only her chin, a little pointed, prevented her from being drop-dead beautiful.

'The kids still talk about it, you know,' Nancy told Nick, lighting a Silk Cut. 'How one of the teachers got busted for growing tons of dope in a cave. You're a school legend.'

'No chance of them hiring me back, then?'

'That's what you were after? I'd ask the head, only . . .'

'I'm kidding. Stoneywood's the last place I'd want to work if I went back into teaching. Not that anywhere would have me.'

'I owe my job to you,' Nancy said.

'Nonsense.'

Seven years ago, Nancy had been a teaching student at Stoneywood, Nick her mentor. After she qualified, he went part-time to tend his hydroponics operation, freeing up a half-time job for his protégée. Not long after he was arrested and forced to resign, she'd taken up the job full-time.

'I really thought you were writing a novel,' Nancy said, as though she'd just read his mind. 'That was your reason for going part-time when we started working together. Have you got any ideas? A prison novel, maybe?'

'I spend as little time as possible thinking about prison.'

'There must be lots of good stories there.'

'Not much good goes on inside, believe me.'

'People are interested in prison stories. There's this great TV show –'

He and Nancy always used to talk about what they watched on TV. Nick remembered her as having better taste than that. 'You mean *Prisoner: Cell Block H*?' Nick asked.

'No, that's over. This one's about a men's maximum security prison, very realistic, very bleak: *Oz*. On Sky. Have you got Sky?'

'Can't afford it.'

Nancy winced slightly and stubbed out her cigarette. 'I could tape it for you, if you're interested.'

She looked away as she said 'if you're interested' and Nick didn't reply. He rolled himself a slim cigarette, remembering the crush she'd had on him during teaching practice. That was a vulnerable time for anyone, working all hours, under huge pressure to perform. Then, she was too immature for him. He'd only have been interested in the sex. Not that he had been above such behaviour, back in his drug-fucked days, but even at his lowest he wouldn't have taken advantage of someone he was meant to be caring for. Six years on, the age gap was immaterial. Nancy was staring thirty in the face and still seeing blokes who had no intention of settling down.

He remembered getting mildly agitated at school when she described the men she went out with, thinking she deserved better. The only one he met was an actor with a small part in a Shakespeare at Nottingham Playhouse. He'd had an inflated ego, a weak voice, no chin and no feel for iambic pentameter. They took a class to see the play and even the kids took the piss out of him afterwards. But Nancy had been devastated when he dumped her.

Nick lit his cigarette.

'You're not interested?' she said, turning to look him in the eye.

He let himself fall into her blue gaze for a moment before he remembered what she was asking him about. 'No, thanks. Too close to the bone, most likely.'

'I'd like to hear what it was like some time,' Nancy said.

'I'll tell you some time, when it's further behind me.'

'And you never tried to write a novel?'

'Not a sentence. I hardly read books now. They remind me of being inside, where there was fuck all else to do.'

'You wrote me some great letters that first year you were inside,' Nancy said. 'I'm sorry I stopped writing back. The guy I was with at the time got jealous. You know how it is. I'm really glad you got in touch.'

'Me too. Actually, if you don't mind talking shop for a bit, I wanted to pick your brains about teaching English before the vodka kicks in.'

Nancy affected disappointment. 'I figured you must have had an ulterior motive for meeting me.'

Nick explained how, as a convicted felon, he couldn't get a job in a state school, but was allowed to give private tuition for GCSE and A-level students. He needed up-to-date subject knowledge, particularly on exams. Nancy told him what he needed to know. Nick made notes, and bought her a second, overpriced drink. When a bell went for last orders, he was relieved that she had to catch the bus. He accompanied her to the stop. He liked to watch her walk in her short brown leather skirt.

'So that's it, then,' she said, as he waited with her at the bus stop. 'You'll call me for another drink when they next change the GCSE syllabus?'

'Not at all. I've really enjoyed seeing you. It'd be nice to do it again.'

'Let's.' The bus pulled in. It would take her home, going past his flat, which was only a ten-minute walk away. 'Getting on?'

'No.'

'Come on,' she said, grabbing his hand. 'I'll pay your fare for the pleasure of your company.'

She knew he was short of cash. Nick almost said he preferred to walk, but pride was a foolish thing. He followed her. When she'd paid their fares, Nancy took his hand again. Although his was a short journey, she led him to the upper deck, then to the very front.

'Sure you want to be seen out with me?' Nick teased.

'You've nothing to be ashamed of,' she said, squeezing his thigh. 'You've paid your penalty. More than paid it, I'd say.'

'Thanks.' He squeezed the hand that was squeezing his thigh. Nancy took this as a signal to move her pretty head towards his: not to kiss her would have been incredibly rude.

'That was nice,' she said, breaking away a little earlier than he would have liked, then giving him a coquettish grin. 'But I think this is your stop. I'd invite you back to mine, but I really am going out with Carl – at least until I get a better offer.'

Nick stood and pressed the bell, then leaned down and kissed Nancy on the forehead. 'I'll call you,' he said.

The bus ground to a halt. Downstairs, he thanked the driver and got off. That was one thing about Nottingham that hadn't changed while he was away. It was a hard city, but passengers always thanked the driver.

A fine rain had begun to fall on the Alfreton Road, a strip of shabby stores that, if you followed it far enough, joined the motorway north, towards Sheffield, where Nick was born. He'd thought about moving back when he got out, but had nothing to return for. His only family was in Sherwood, a couple of miles away, where Nick's kid brother, Joe, had his own taxi firm.

Nick pulled a loose brick from the wall halfway up the iron staircase that led to his flat. That was where he kept his small stash. Too dangerous to leave it inside. The hash was brittle and needed heating before he could crumble it onto the tobacco.

He'd recently switched from Samson to Drum Milde, looking after his lungs.

In prison, he'd exercised regularly – there wasn't a lot else to do – but he'd never managed to give up smoking tobacco. He'd stopped smoking dope after getting caught out on a random drugs test, losing three months of his remission, then started again as soon as he got out. His brother always had a good supply.

Dope made some people paranoid, but it had the opposite effect on Nick. It helped him to chill out, to feel centred. It prevented him from dwelling on the past.

The hash, on top of the booze, took the edge off the frustration he'd felt since leaving Nancy. He slept easily, dreaming that Nancy was a schoolgirl and he was her teacher. He kept telling her that, if they did what she wanted to do, he'd be sent back to prison.

'I'm worth it,' she told him.

Then another of his prison nightmares started. He snapped awake with an ashtray throat, sank half a pint of tepid water that he kept by the bed, then tried to go back to sleep. But sleep wouldn't return. He thought about Nancy. He'd not been surprised when she stopped writing to him. Prisoners expected to be forgotten. It made life easier all round.

Inside, Nick had spent a lot of time thinking about the women in his life. There had been many, but only two with whom he might have stayed for good: Nazia, whom he'd nearly married. She had left him for a dentist. And Sarah, his first real love. They had lost touch soon after splitting up, fourteen years ago. While he was away she had become an MP. If Sarah hadn't been re-elected earlier this year, they might have got back together. The old flame was still there. They'd spent a lot of time in each other's company in the spring, but hadn't spoken since two days after the election. Sarah had scraped back in, then been made prisons minister, a job that made it absolutely impossible for her to associate with him.

He missed her.

3

Sarah's parliamentary office was in Norman Shaw House, the old Scotland Yard, part of the Commons estate. She could get to a vote in two minutes. This space was three times the size of her stuffy room at the Home Office, where she spent more of her time. She came here because it was important to be seen on the estate, to keep up connections with fellow MPs. On Monday evenings she went to parliamentary Labour party meetings. She also hung around on Wednesday afternoons, following Prime Minister's Question Time. This used to be a twice weekly, fifteen-minute slot, but Tony Blair had changed it to thirty minutes on a Wednesday. This meant he only spent one morning a week preparing for any question that might come up.

As a junior minister, Sarah could not ask questions, but she was expected to be present. It felt a bit like being a prefect at school. She and other juniors stood at the front side, near the speaker's chair, since they did not need to catch her eye. The new Conservative leader was no match for Tony Blair. Five months into New Labour, the government was still in its honeymoon period.

On her way out of the chamber, Sarah was cornered by Pete Rugby, the East Midlands party whip.

'Having a little trouble with the lone parent benefit issue. Like you to talk to one or two of the new girls, bring them into line.'

Sarah hated being put on the spot like this. This was one issue she'd been hoping would go away.

'Actually, Pete, I just signed a letter to Gordon, asking him to rethink the whole thing. So I'm not the best person to ask. Must rush.'

She hurried away, but not before she'd registered the whip's frown. There was no chance that Gordon Brown, the Chancellor of the Exchequer, would change his mind about the welfare cuts. He had committed the government to sticking with the outgoing government's spending plans for its first year in office. A needless promise, given that the economy was in a better state than Labour had expected, but Gordon rarely changed his mind. Sarah was convinced that the cuts being proposed for single parents were mean, destructive and unnecessary. However, as a member of the government, she had to vote for them, or resign from the Home Office.

Sarah went to the Tea Rooms, which were close to the voting chamber. Despite the change of government, Labour MPs still congregated at the same end of the long, narrow room. The green leather sofas were all full. She cast a rapid eye around the low tables, each of which sat four MPs. Alison Blythe, one of the new Labour intake, gave her a small wave. They had stood together in the 'Blair's Babes' photo taken back in May. Ali, as she was to her friends, had a mop of short blond hair and a mark in her nose where she had recently removed a stud. She had escorted Sarah on a prison visit in her Birmingham constituency. The two of them had hit it off, kind of. Both thought of themselves as being on the left of the party, but not the hard, ideological left. Sarah could use some friends in the new batch of women MPs. She waved back, deposited her bag on the free chair next to Alison, then got herself a drink.

'Has Pete been onto you?' Ali asked, when Sarah sat down.

'Just now. I told him I'd signed that letter. Did you?'

'Yes. Over a hundred signatories, I heard. Will he back down?'

'You don't know Gordon. It'll make him more stubborn. It's Harriet I feel most sorry for.'

They discussed the health and social security minister, who was currently stuck between a rock and a hard place. The word was that she'd been given a choice between cuts to disability benefit or the single parent benefit. Either would hit Labour's heartland vote.

'There's somebody over there trying to catch your eye,' Alison pointed out.

On the other side of the partition, Sarah saw Andrew Saint. Her old friend was sitting with Gill Temperley. The former Conservative minister had let her blond hair grow since leaving office.

'I'd better go over and say hello,' Sarah said. 'Excuse me.'

'Will you join us? We're celebrating.' Andrew stood and kissed her on the cheek. They used to be the same height but, since university, he had become taller than her by at least two inches. Did he have lifts in his shoes? 'You're looking great,' he said.

'Running on pure adrenaline. What are you celebrating?'

'Gill's my public face,' Andrew said. 'She's going to help me take Saint Holdings to the next level.'

'First move,' Gill said. 'Find a better name. Thank you so much for putting the two of us together, Sarah.'

'My pleasure,' Sarah replied. No point in letting Gill know that this was a job she had been offered and might have taken, had she failed to be re-elected. The two women's positions had reversed. Sarah was now the Home Office minister; Gill, the back-bench MP with time on her hands.

'How do you two know each other?' Gill asked.

'We were at university together in Nottingham,' Andrew told her. 'I helped win Sarah's first campaign, to be union president.'

He hadn't helped much. More often he'd whinged about how much time Nick Cane, his best friend, spent on Sarah's campaign, when they could be going to gigs, getting out of their tree and talking metaphysical mush – the way heavy stoners are prone to do. Still, to be fair, he had come to a few hustings, asked the questions Nick had planted to help show Sarah in a good light.

How had Andrew made his money? Nick might know how his best friend had become a millionaire, but Sarah had never got to the bottom of it, not even when Andrew was offering her a well-paid job. *Saint Nick*, the two of them used to be called at uni. She wouldn't be telling Gill any of this.

'I'm glad I've run into you,' Gill said, 'because I wanted to invite you to a party. It's short notice. Jeremy wanted to surprise me.' Jeremy was her husband, a Tory Euro MP. 'Then he realized that there might be a few guests – like Andrew here – who I'd want to invite, but he didn't know about. It's at the London Planetarium, a week on Friday. Do say you'll come.'

'I'd love to.' Sarah had to think of a quick get-out. The last thing she wanted to do was give up a Friday night for a party full of Tories. 'Oh, but I'm tied into something else, a police authority thing. The chief constable twisted my arm. I owe him a favour.'

'It always does to keep in with the police,' Gill said. 'But you could come to me afterwards. We tend to party very late.'

'Do,' Andrew said, as though he were hosting the party, rather than the MP's husband.

'I'm afraid it's in Rutland. Hambleton Hall.'

'Very nice place,' Gill admitted. 'Luxurious. Almost worth putting up with dull company for.'

Gill had been a minister since the 1983 election, when she would have been the same age that Sarah was now, thirty-six. The party, therefore, was for her fiftieth, but she looked much younger. Was Andrew interested in her as more than a well-placed consultant? It wasn't an impossible combination. Andrew was on the short side, but taller than Gill. A dark, tightly trimmed beard hid his chin, which had always been wobbly. He was hard-faced, not really handsome, but rich and clever with a rough charm. Even so, the idea of an affair was far-fetched. Like Gill, Andrew liked them young. At uni, he always went for first years. Before that, according to Nick, he was prone to the sixth-form girls who served at formal dinners in their hall of residence.

Excusing herself, Sarah returned to Alison, who was trying to work up the courage to rebel against the Labour whip.

'Maybe it won't come to that,' Sarah said. 'I don't understand why these cuts are necessary. The single parent benefit cut only saves sixty million quid next year, less than two hundred million by year three.'

Alison blinked and said nothing. Such numbers still seemed huge to her.

'Are you going to sign the letter to Gordon?' Steve Carter asked Sarah later. Both were waiting for a ministerial car to take them back to the Home Office. Steve was her closest friend in parliament and, like her, had been made a junior minister in the new government, covering transport.

'I already have,' Sarah said.

'Mistake. You'll just piss him off. We're in government now. We have to support everything the government does, right or wrong.'

'My mum was a single parent for most of my upbringing,' Sarah reminded him. 'This is personal.'

'You only reel out that detail when it's convenient,' Steve teased her. 'Otherwise, as I recall, you had a rather happy childhood. After your dad pissed off, there was a wealthy knight of the realm in the picture, making sure nobody starved. He'd have told you all about collective responsibility.'

Steve was referring to her grandfather, Sir Hugh Bone – as he had become after he left parliament, where he was a Labour minister.

'Collective responsibility only applies to the cabinet,' Sarah said, pretty sure that this was true. 'We're not in the cabinet. We didn't get to discuss this.'

'Do you think the cabinet did? I doubt it.'

'And the decision hasn't been made yet.'

'On your head be it. Should please your local party, anyway.'

Sarah's local party had its share of hard-left activists, who would have liked it if she had joined the Campaign Group, which comprised fifty or so left-wing MPs. But Nottingham West was the least active, most right-wing of the Nottingham constituency Labour parties. Usually, Sarah could persuade her members to back whatever stance she took. Indeed, there were probably a few who would support slashing benefits to single mums by up to twenty pounds a week. After all, there were parallel cuts being made in income support, jobseeker's allowance and council tax benefit. But it was worse for single parents. Many claimants would be between five and ten pounds a week worse off. That was a significant amount of money when you were scraping to get by.

She'd heard all the arguments in favour: there was usually a man somewhere in the picture, not living up to his responsibilities. Young mothers allegedly saw having multiple children as an easy career choice. But those stories didn't fit with Sarah's experience. Polly Bolton, for instance, was bringing up four children, two of them not her own, and worked every hour she was allowed to before it cut into her benefits. Sarah hoped a deal would be reached to water down the cuts. The vote was still weeks away.

You don't know what he does for a living. You don't want to know. The first time you saw him, over a year ago, he was visiting the home. You never found out why. Everyone else was at Goose Fair. You were the only girl there. Alice introduced him. She had to go, so you offered to show him round. He asked how old you were. When you said fourteen he acted surprised, made a joke about how he'd better behave himself. The look he gave you was knowing yet hungry, the same look you get from older lads at school: pure lust. Made you feel warm down there. Made you reckless. You asked if you could have his number 'for when I'm a bit older'.

'Not too much older,' he said. Then he asked what time you got out of school and checked the coast was clear before squeezing your bum. A week later, his car was waiting at the top of the road.

He's had you a hundred times since. But he's not been round much lately, says he has to work a lot. You're starting to think he's gone off you until this afternoon, when he shows up and takes you to a hotel room on Mansfield Road. He's brought you special stuff to wear. While you're in the bathroom, changing, he takes a call on his mobile. You listen, wanting to hear how he is with his wife, if he has a wife. But it's business. He keeps his voice low, talks big numbers. You don't understand what he's up to.

The call finishes. You open the door. He says you look tasty in black rubber. Fantastically fuckable. He's been working up to this. You know what he wants tonight and you know that it's going to hurt. You don't mind, just as long as he's with you.

An hour later, he gives you a lift home, says you both have to cool it for a while, shoves a hundred quid in your hand and kisses you on the cheek.

Next time you try his mobile number, it's disconnected. Takes a good week for you to figure it out. He will never call again. You've been dumped.

4

Dave Trapp, Nick's probation officer, had gradually reduced their regular sessions to a few minutes once a month.

'And the flat? Comfortable? You've been there, what? Six months? It must be hard, getting by on the money you scrape from private tuition.'

'It's better than the dole,' Nick said.

'There's a job advertised,' Dave said, pulling a sheet of cream-coloured, headed A4 from his top drawer. 'The Power Project. Drugs rehabilitation and all the rest. Might be up your street.'

'Didn't know I had a street.'

'You're still volunteering at the drop-in, aren't you?'

'I'm on tonight,' Nick said.

'You should be able to get a reference there. You'll need two. If there isn't anybody from your teaching days, I'll be happy to write one for you.'

'I expect I'll be okay,' Nick said, glancing at the details. 'Can I keep this?'

'Be my guest. Let me know how you get on.'

Nick hadn't heard of the Power Project, but had followed news stories about the disbandment of the Crack Action Team, with all the rumours flying around about it being a front for dealers. The story had broken just after his visit from Wayne. Was Wayne's offer related to the CAT arrests? Probably not. Anyway, Wayne hadn't been in touch since.

When he got to the drop-in centre at Victor House, three hours later, Nick showed the job spec to his supervisor, Rob. Rob was one of two full-time, paid workers who supervised the volunteers.

'Dave says I might be in with a shout.'

'Fourteen grand a year!' Rob said. 'That's more than I get paid. Maybe I'll apply.'

'Know anything about this Power Project?'

'I've heard of the bloke in charge, King Bell. Religious. Respected figure in the Afro-Caribbean community. He's about your age, forty or so, maybe a bit older.'

'I'm thirty-six!' Nick pointed out.

'Sorry. Everyone over thirty looks the same age to me.' Rob grinned. He was about twenty-five, with a social work qualification. 'You thinking of applying for it?'

'I'd need a reason not to.'

Rob reread the form. 'It says ex-offenders are welcome to apply. You don't often see that on job specs.'

'You'd do me a reference?'

'No problem.' He looked over Nick's shoulder. 'There's a queue outside. We'd better start letting them in.'

Nick glanced at the men waiting to enter the former church. Badly dressed, with worse haircuts, they were a poor advert for hard drugs. Most had smack or methadone habits. Nick had never been tempted to experience the escape that heroin provided. Nor crack, which, from what the guys in the nick said, gave a heightened coke buzz that wore off in minutes and was addictive as fuck. These days, the haze from hash and grass was enough for Nick. His younger brother, Joe, liked skunk, the killer form of grass that had dominated the market since Nick went inside.

Nick wasn't a fan. He liked a mild, spacey buzz, not being wasted for hours.

At first, when Dave suggested that he volunteer at this centre, Nick had been dubious. For obvious reasons, he hadn't told his probation officer that he still smoked dope. He thought he'd feel like a hypocrite, advising people not to take drugs. Then he went for a chat with Rob. He admitted to having had a bit of a problem with coke, mentioned having talked to a lot of users in prison, even helped a couple of them when they were in withdrawal. He didn't say how he'd lost three months' remission for failing a drugs test. Cannabis stayed in your system for a month or more, unlike heroin. Later, when they knew each other better, Nick mentioned the test. Rob didn't have a problem with it. Nick's fuck-ups actually gave him cred for this new role.

There wasn't much training. At first, he had to make it up as he went along. Then he managed to get on a two-day cognitive behaviour therapy course. He used to hate courses when he was a teacher, thinking that he could get the same information over in half the time. That was true of the CBT one, to a degree, but the pointers he picked up were useful when used as a loose guide, rather than a fixed mantra. Clients had to accept that they had a problem, then a drugs worker could help them find the tools to deal with the problem. You had to identify the triggers that set off cravings for the drug and, where possible, eliminate them. Trouble was, for a lot of clients, the only hope of escape was to stop hanging out with their drug-using friends. That required serious motivation.

Sometimes, people came to the drop-in centre because their parents had pushed them into it, or a partner was bugged by their drug use and was threatening to leave. But that never stopped people using. Nick saw how families wanted advice agencies to focus on the moral arguments against drugs, but he didn't think drugs were a moral issue. People had to accept that the drugs they took were causing them problems and want to change. If their only drug problem was that their drug of choice was illegal, good luck to them.

Nick had a sit-down with Shug, a teenage crack addict who was waiting to go on trial for a dozen shoplifting offences. Shug's main concern was how he'd cope with his habit inside. Depending on where he was sent, chances were Shug would be on smack within a week, which he would pay for by renting out his arse. Nick could only see one way forward.

'You need to cut down steadily,' Nick told him. 'Reduce your dependence before you go in. You can get anything in most prisons, but they do random tests and a positive will cost you a lot of remission.'

'Cut down steadily,' Shug repeated. 'What the fuck does that mean?'

Talking to junkies sometimes felt like dealing with special needs kids in his teaching days. Except most junkies had less incentive to listen and the drugs they were on depleted their already limited attention spans.

But not all of them. Blond, willowy Alice came in, glanced in Nick's direction, then went to the drinks table. According to Rob, Alice only showed up evenings Nick was working. Nick was pretty sure the lad was teasing him, although Alice did seem keen. She used to have a bad habit, but was now maintaining on next to nothing, with occasional relapses, and holding down a steady, responsible job.

'Come and see me next week,' Nick told Shug, dismissing him as he once would have done a pupil. Some clients might take offence, but Shug was near enough to his school days to think he deserved to be treated this way. 'Cut down on the crack.' He tried a joke. 'See if you can develop a nicotine habit instead.'

'Nicko what?'

'Cigarettes.'

Shug shook his head. 'That shit'll kill you.'

Alice wore black Paul Smith jeans and a dusty blue T-shirt with an FCUK logo. She worked in a hostel for teenage girls. Nick watched her spoon three sugars into a polystyrene cup of weak tea. When she joined him, she stood closer than was strictly necessary. Her hair smelled good.

'How's it going?' Nick asked.

'Could be better.'

'Seen Jerry today?'

Nick's only source of income at the moment was GCSE tutoring. He currently had five teenagers he helped with their English. Jerry was one of them. Jerry lived in the hostel where Alice worked, and Alice had put her on to Nick.

'No. Why do you ask?'

'She seemed a little low the other day, said something about not being able to afford as many lessons.'

'She didn't offer to . . . you know?'

Nick shook his head vigorously. 'She's a smart kid. I can't imagine that she works the streets.'

'Me neither. But she's got at least one generous regular, that's what the other girls say.'

Nick shook his head. 'She barely looks fourteen.'

'She'll look sixteen soon enough, and her price will go down,' Alice said, with a sad look. Nick remembered she hadn't come here to talk about her job.

'You said things weren't too good,' he said, softly. Alice had been addicted to smack since a boyfriend turned her on to it when she was seventeen. She was twenty-four now and had been trying to stay clean for more than a year.

'Two wraps yesterday,' Alice admitted.

'Trying to keep it down to one today?'

'That's why I'm here.'

*

Beany wants to run you. That goes without saying. He's already running Shaz, and a couple of girls a year older. They have their own flat. Beany's all right. Lots of lads hang around the hostel. Most of them are stupider than him. He's mixed race, nineteen or twenty, with good clothes and a shaved scalp. You suspect that, some of the time, he lives with his mum. Compared to other guys who hang round here, he's clean and healthy-looking.

Beany mainly comes to the hostel to see Shaz. Shaz calls him her boyfriend, even though everyone knows she turns tricks for him. But Beany will ignore Shaz and talk to you whenever he gets the chance. Because, before he makes you turn tricks for him, he wants to fuck you.

'I can't believe you're only fifteen, girl, you look like a woman. You're the fittest girl here, you could be a model.'

No, you couldn't, you're not tall enough, but you like it when grown men take an interest in you. You don't mind when teachers try to get a glimpse down your top. You appreciate it when Beany shares a spliff with you, giving you the front bit where there's always the most grass. He thinks it might persuade you to give it up for him and, if your lover stays away much longer, you just might. Shaz says he's fantastic in bed. He eats her out and everything. Most black guys won't do that. But Shaz is on your case.

'What were you looking that way at Beany for?' she says on Saturday afternoon, when you've gone back to the hostel. 'I saw you.'

You're stoned. You can't deny that you were looking at him, considering his offer. Shaz probably saw him whispering in your ear, saying how fine you are, how he'd like to make you his princess. But you're not going to tell Shaz that.

'He got me stoned. I don't know what I was looking at.'

'You'd better not be trying to steal him off me.'

'I don't steal.'

'All I'm saying is, don't even think about it.'

Shaz is stupid sometimes. The way Beany works, she will be number one for a few months, then he will move onto someone else, still taking most of what Shaz earns. He'll move Shaz on from weed to crack, which she's already tried. She says it's nice but 'too strong to do a lot of'. That'll change.

'If you fuck Beany,' Shaz says, 'I'll fuck you up.'

And you decide, whatever happens, you're not going to give it up for her pimp. Beany might treat you nice for a while, but he won't if you refuse to fuck his friends when he asks you to. Next you'll be expected to service sad, middle-aged tossers in a scummy flat off Woodborough Road. It's not too bad if you have a drink first, Shaz once told you, when she was pissed up.

You lean forward. 'Listen,' you tell her. 'Between you and me, I don't like boys Beany's age. I like men. And I've got one. But he could get done for doing me, so I keep it quiet.'

'Who?'

'Nobody you know. What kind of fool do you think I am? I like smoking Beany's dope, but I've got my eye on a bigger prize. We're mates, right? Can we help each other here?'

Shaz sees how sincere you are and fakes a little cry. Then it's all, *We're mates, we're mates, I've never had a better mate, I come to you for advice, nobody else* and things are all right between you again. You know that, sooner or later, probably by tomorrow, what you've told her will work its way back to Beany. So Beany will know that you're not a virgin and try even harder. But he'll also think that you've got someone, which might make him hold off.

You miss your lover. You want to kill him for not coming to see you. You could find out where he lives, but you promised not to. You don't want to know about his other life. You're afraid that, if you confront him about the future, he'll say that you haven't got one. It's over. And you couldn't bear that.

5

Winston, Sarah's agent, collared her on Sunday morning. He thought that she ought to join the Power Project management committee.

'They're having a press conference. Just local TV, aimed at creating goodwill after all the recent bad publicity. It would be good timing if they could also announce that you were on board.'

'I don't want to be on another management committee.'

'You don't have enough links with the black community, Sarah, which could make the difference between victory and defeat next time.'

'Are you telling me that drugs are mainly a black thing?'

'I'm telling you that the Afro-Caribbean community suffers most from everything to do with shitty street drugs. You go to one management committee a year, send your apologies to the rest.'

'If I take on a job, I do it properly.'

'We've got a local councillor on the committee, Doug Hay. If there's anything you need to know, he'll tell you.'

She knew Doug: a family man, who was deputy chair of housing. A little slow, but dependable. 'When's the press conference?'

'Tomorrow afternoon.'

'See if you can clear it with Hugh,' she said, referring to her diary secretary. 'But I want to take a look at the place. Set something up for Friday.' Sarah put the phone down and turned on the midday news.

'More on New Labour's first big scandal . . .'

She groaned. Soon after the election, the new government had banned tobacco advertising and all cigarette company sponsorship for sport. It was the right thing to do. After all, tobacco was the most dangerous legal substance in the world. Then, this month, after being lobbied by the people behind Formula One, the government had made an exception. Formula One. Trouble was, it turned out that a Formula One owner had donated at least a million pounds to the party before the election, and had promised to donate a million more.

'I'm a pretty straight sort of guy,' the prime minister was telling the BBC, trying to ride his charm. He would get away with it, Sarah reckoned, but he'd have to give back the money. The shine was starting to come off their landslide victory. The PM's popularity had kept growing since the election, peaking a couple of months ago after the death of the Princess of Wales in a car crash. Then, he had shown a sure touch. Today, he looked rattled.

Jerry was hunched up on the carpet watching *Countdown* when Nick showed up.

'No homework?' he teased her.

'It's English, kind of? Vocabulary.'

Nick conceded that it was. He'd seen too much daytime TV while he was inside. The sight depressed him, brought back images of dull men in uncomfortable chairs, farting and smoking while their brains putrified. He got out his Arden edition of *Macbeth* and flicked through the second act.

'Did you get that video of Polanski's *Macbeth* that I suggested?' he asked.

44

'No. Shop didn't have it.'

Alice appeared at the door. 'Want a brew, Nick?'

'Please. How much longer is this on for?' he asked Jerry as the adverts began. She shrugged.

'I'll come back in fifteen minutes,' he told her. 'Do us a favour and dig out your essay plan while the ads are on.'

Jerry pouted, then left the room. On her return, she handed him the plan without a word and spread herself out on the cheap carpet again. Straight, dirty-blond hair fell over her pale, sullen face. When she chose to smile, she could look very pretty. One day, Nick suspected, she would be devastating. Compared to the other girls in the hostel, she already was.

Nick joined Alice in the hostel kitchen.

'Is she getting her work done?' Alice asked.

'Just about. But she's the boss. I don't mind waiting.'

'Time's money.'

'Maybe, but I'm not that busy. You don't have any more waifs and strays who want help with their homework, do you?'

'Not ones who'd pay for it.'

Alice had put Jerry onto Nick when the girl had complained about never having the same English teacher two weeks running. Jerry had decided that, if she was going to pass her exams, she had to help herself. Neither adult was exactly sure where Jerry got the money to pay Nick. Maybe there was a guilty parent lurking in the background, though Nick doubted it. Alice said that nearly all of the girls were alone in the world; he shouldn't be surprised that most had pimps and habits to feed by the time they left care. The other girls assumed that Jerry was working. She had the figure and face to charge top dollar. Alice, however, was pretty sure she didn't have a pimp.

Nor was she on crack. According to Jerry, she was happy with a few ciders and the odd spliff. By Alexandra Park standards, that made her a goody two shoes. She treated Nick with more respect than the other kids he tutored, who were being pushed by their parents. Jerry was as bright as the brightest kids Nick had ever worked with. But that was no guarantee of success. For now, she was motivated. But without a decent school or family behind her, there was no way of telling how long her motivation would last.

'You down the centre tonight?' Alice asked, lighting a roll-up.

'No. I'm next on Thursday, six to nine. Keeps me out of mischief.'

'Doesn't pay, though, does it? You ought to do a job like mine.'

'All that human misery? You can keep it.'

'Hey!' Jerry called from the next room. 'King's on the telly.'

She'd changed the channel. A slender black man with close-cropped hair was on Central News talking about the damage that drugs were doing to the East Midlands. His voice was deep, resonant.

'And that's why we called it the *Power* Project. People have the power to change their lives, but they need support. This project will empower them, show them where to go – in the community, in the medical services – it will teach them how to say no to dealers.'

Jerry stared hard at the screen.

'You know this guy?' Nick asked, then was distracted. Sarah Bone appeared on the screen, outside the Houses of Parliament, while a red banner bearing the words *Local MP, Home Office Minister* unfurled across the bottom of the screen.

'I like her,' Alice said. 'I voted for her.'

'I was delighted to hear the project has got full funding,' Sarah told the cameras, 'and I look forward to working with Kingston Bell on the management committee. We'll be hiring more top-quality drugs advice workers over the next few weeks. The Power Project has the potential to have a major impact on the drugs problem in Nottingham.'

'Skanky ho,' Jerry said, a purpose-built put-down for any successful woman who looked like she might still have a sex life. 'I'll bet the stuck-up bitch wouldn't know a spliff if you smoked one in front of her.'

Nick, who had last shared a joint with Sarah the night she got re-elected, changed the subject. 'You know Kingston Bell?' he asked Alice.

'He visits sometimes. Not for a while. The kids like him. It's good, you know, gives them a positive role model.'

'Come on,' Nick told Jerry, as he made a mental note to call Sarah. 'Let's go over this essay plan.'

Jerry turned down the sound. 'I think Alice likes you,' she said. 'Why don't you ask her out?'

'Because my girlfriend wouldn't like it,' Nick said. Wondering if the fib would get back to Alice, hoping that it would.

'You're a one-woman man, are you?'

Nick opened *Macbeth* without replying.

'Thought not. No such thing, is there?'

'Anything urgent?' Sarah asked her diary secretary when she got to the Commons after a long day at the Foreign Office.

'Nothing that can't wait,' Hugh replied. 'The chief whip wanted assuring that you were on the right side of the single parent benefit vote after you signed that letter to the Chancellor. Oh, a guy phoned this morning – said he was an old friend. Nick Kern?'

'Cane. What did he want?'

'To know if you could meet. Said he had a favour to ask.'

'He wouldn't say what?'

'Not at first. I insisted it would save time if he gave me some idea before you got back to him. Turns out he wants you to give him a reference.'

'A reference?'

'That drugs centre you were talking about on Central News.'

It hadn't occurred to Sarah that Nick could work at the Power Project. But the moment she considered the idea she realized that, yes, it could be a good fit for Nick.

'Tell him sure.'

'He wants to meet, discuss the application.'

'No,' Sarah said. She didn't trust herself to meet Nick, for several reasons. 'Tell him my weekend diary's too full to meet him one-on-one.'

'He offered to come to a surgery.'

Since becoming a minister, Sarah no longer held regular walk-in surgeries. They were a waste of time since local councillors could deal with most of the issues raised. The last thing Sarah wanted was to be ambushed by constituents with a grievance. These days, therefore, constituents were told to ring for an appointment and a councillor would try to deal with the matter on the phone. If it was an issue that only Sarah could handle, she dealt with it on the phone herself. Only in extreme cases did she see individuals in person. But it would be safe to meet Nick at a surgery. No risk of bad publicity, no opportunity for them to misbehave, as they so nearly had when he spent the night in her bed on the evening of the general election.

'Where am I on Saturday?'

'You've got a couple of meetings at Stoneywood Library, World War Two veterans, single parents against cuts in benefits. Should be fairly short.'

'Okay, see if you can fit him in between those.'

Hugh made the call. Sarah listened. She could have phoned Nick herself. She could find time to meet him for a drink. But a Home Office minister needed to keep a professional distance from an ex-con. If she'd lost her seat in May, she might be with Nick now. There'd been nobody else since Dan, her social worker ex, whom she'd split up with back in March.

Fifteen years ago, she'd lived with Nick for two years, the longest she'd been with any man to date. They were both children back then, scarcely out of their teens. She missed what they used to have: the companionship as much as the passion. But she didn't want to put herself in the way of temptation. There was no space in her life for a full-time relationship. Affairs, even discreet ones, demanded too much energy, too much risk. Career came first. Still, if she could help Nick get a job, she would.

6

Kingston Bell, often known as 'King', was of Jamaican origin, a little under six foot tall and looked anywhere between thirty-five and forty-five. Sarah had read his CV, so knew he was almost fifty, old for a project that required street cred. But he was qualified. His CV showed a wide range of experience – community work, fund-raising for his church, promoting gigs, drugs counselling and running a benefits advice centre for the council.

'What do you think of the place?' King asked, his preacher's voice mild, barely audible above the drilling and hammering beyond. She looked around the dust clouds and debris that covered this part of the Lace Market building. 'We're remodelling,' he added. 'Can't move offices, but we can make it feel like a different place.'

'I'm sure it'll be great,' Sarah told him, 'but I get dust allergies. Why don't we go over to my office, where we can hear ourselves?'

'I know somewhere nearer.'

He took her to a café – George's – in the next street, opposite Broadway Cinema. It only opened in the evenings, but one knock on the door and Kingston was let in. A woman Sarah's age, wearing torn Levi's and a Madonna tour sweatshirt, abandoned cleaning the floor. She ushered Kingston and his guest to the back of the café, out of sight from the street.

'Lovely to see you, King, lovely to see you.'

They ordered cappuccinos, which, when they arrived, were strong and creamy. Kingston, wearing chinos and T-shirt despite the autumn chill, was not so well dressed as Sarah might have expected, less suave than his post demanded. Only when the caffeine hit did he become garrulous.

'The staff is the key thing. I've got people from the street, people who really know how to turn lives around, people who can go up to a fifteen-year-old who's selling his arse for crack and talk him out of it.'

'That's great,' Sarah said, then chose her words carefully. 'As long as you follow equal opportunities practice. The new jobs have to be advertised properly and, if any of them go to people you know, you have to be able to show that they were the best candidate for the job.'

'Some of the qualifications we're talking about, they're not conventional ones.'

'I understand. People who do this work often have untidy stuff in their past. Fine, as long as they're clean and declare what they've been convicted of. The board's keen on rehabilitation. But all appointments must follow the proper procedures.'

'Understood. You want to be in on the interviews?' There was a slight glint in his eyes. He was calling her bluff.

'I'm hands-on,' Sarah said, 'but not that hands-on. I ought to let you get back to the renovations. Is there anything else I can do for you?'

She wouldn't have used that phrase with some of the middle-aged men she met. They would take it as an invitation to flirt. But King wasn't the type to make an unwelcome advance. He had a slightly churchy tone that was just the right side of sanctimonious. 'Look forward to working with you,' he said.

*

Stoneywood Library had mixed associations for Nick. Seven months ago, when he was driving a taxi, off the books, he'd picked up a woman here, Polly Bolton. He ended up sleeping with her the same evening, beginning an affair that hadn't ended well. The library reminded him of prison, without the smell. The walls were painted a turgid yellow. He waited on an uncomfortable plastic seat next to an old woman in a coarse, patterned overcoat. She pointed at the photo of Sarah.

'She's a good'un,' the woman told Nick. 'She'll sort you out. I saw her grandad speak once. He were a man. Bet you've never heard of him. Cabinet minister. Lord, he ended up.'

Nick, who had spent a weekend with Sir Hugh Bone fifteen years before, didn't comment. He knew that the Labour veteran had never become a lord, although several cabinet ministers from his generation had done so. And Sarah, to her credit, had never used her grandfather as political capital.

More women arrived, and a couple of doddery men. They were ex-Navy, veterans of the Arctic convoy that escorted merchant ships to the Eastern Front during World War Two. Sarah was trying to secure medals for them. When Nick's turn came, the previous meeting had already overrun by fifteen minutes. A large group of women came out, some hauling kids along with them. Nick went in. Sarah had her head down, making notes. A young man in a cheap sports jacket, probably a city councillor, was sitting alongside her at the Formica desk, notebook in hand. Sarah looked up.

'This is a friend,' she said, turning to her aide. 'Mike, go outside, butter them up for me. We'll be really quick.'

She gestured that Nick should sit down. 'I'm sorry to be so rushed. A lot of very angry single parents, who are about to lose a chunk of benefit.'

'Good of you to see me when you're so busy. You're looking great.'

'Thanks,' Sarah said, holding on to her professional manner until her words stumbled out, displaying her unease. 'You look well, too. I'm sorry we haven't . . . you know the way it is. How have you been?'

'I've been fine,' Nick said, drinking her in. Sarah had perfect hair, brushed back but fuller than it had been a few months ago, and immaculate make-up. Soberly dressed, in grey jacket and skirt, she looked, if anything, older than her thirty-six years. 'How is it, being a minister?'

'Exciting. Thrilling, when you feel history's breath on you – if that doesn't sound too soppy. But I don't get much spare time.'

'You're on the board of the Power Project,' he pointed out.

'I had my arm twisted. They only need me for the occasional meeting. And the project's a good thing. You've applied for an advice worker job?'

'I've already put in the application. Deadline's Monday. I hope that's okay. The bloke I spoke to, Hugh, said –'

'I can't think of anyone better,' she interrupted. 'Only . . .'

He could still read her mind. 'Am I clean? Yes. Unless you count the odd spliff.'

'Nobody minds about that, long as you don't indulge at work.'

Their eyes met and he thought of the things he wasn't saying, stories he could tell her that weren't his to share.

'You're still working as a tutor?' Sarah asked.

'Yeah, and I've been volunteering . . .' He rattled off his good works and Sarah took a few notes.

'I'll give you a strong reference. I won't be on the interview panel, but I'd say you have a fighting chance.'

'Thanks. I mean that more than I can say. Thanks a lot.'

Sarah's agent, Winston, opened the door, keen to hurry Nick out. Sarah's eyes met Nick's once more, in what seemed a sad acknowledgement of the distance between them. But perhaps he was only projecting this.

54

'Take care,' she said – that one-size-fits-all, kind but meaningless injunction.

'You too.'

Outside the library, Nick unlocked his bike. Or, to be more precise, his brother's bike, which he had borrowed several months before and not returned. Joe, still only thirty, was running to fat. That was what happened when you stopped playing football and sat in an office or behind a wheel all day. The only exercise Joe used to get, chasing after women, was off limits since he became a dad. At least, that was what Nick assumed. Caroline, Joe's wife, had just gone back to her teaching job, so could no longer keep tabs on Joe's every spare minute.

Nick was halfway down the street when he heard someone call.

'Hey, Nick!'

It took him a moment to locate the source of the voice, outside Stoneywood Fruit and Veg. Nancy Tull, in jeans and leather blouson. She was arm-in-arm with a dopey-looking bloke her age or younger. He had a square jaw, shaggy hair and a combat jacket.

'What are you doing in my neck of the woods?'

'Out for a bike ride,' Nick lied.

'This is Carl. Carl, this is Nick, who I used to work with.'

Carl grunted something and went into the greengrocer's.

'He doesn't talk much,' Nancy said, with a coquettish shrug.

'Are you two living together?' Nick asked, cutting to the chase.

'He has his own place, but spends a lot of time at mine.' She smiled, as though the guy was doing her a favour, rather than the other way round. Which was probably how Carl thought of it, too. In Nick's experience, most rock musicians were arrogant sods, who got away with taking people for granted. 'I enjoyed the other night,' Nancy went on. 'We ought to do it again.'

There was something different about her, Nick thought. She wasn't wearing much make-up, if any. Her hair was ruffled in the late-morning breeze. She had a lazy, triumphant air, redolent of sex. Nancy looked around. Carl was being served. She leaned forward and whispered in Nick's ear.

'I think of you when I'm with him.'

She turned away before he could react and joined her boyfriend in the shop.

7

Sarah briefed her boss carefully, thoroughly, with none of the passion she'd expended on Commons speeches covering this subject when they were in opposition. She'd waited months to set up this meeting about her pet project. The Home Secretary heard her out without any change in his languid expression.

'We're still in the business of first impressions,' he said when she was done. 'Tough on crime and its causes. Not soft on condoms.'

'HIV isn't part of their punishment,' Sarah argued.

'Then they shouldn't share needles, or bugger each other. Can you imagine what the *Daily Mail* would say if we put this forward?'

'We're in power. We got a landslide. We don't need to keep the right-wing tabloids on our side.'

Her boss rose slowly from his red leather chair. 'This isn't a four-year project,' he told her, not for the first time. 'The next election campaign is already underway.'

He was showing her out, but Sarah remained seated. 'If we're sticking to the last government's spending limits and not offending the Tory tabloids, it feels like we didn't win the last election.'

'The whips are putting pressure on you about the lone parent benefits vote.'

Sarah nodded. She'd had several phone calls. Tony Bax, her constituency chair, had been phoned by the party whips. He, in turn, had called to ask how she intended to vote. She'd told him she was undecided.

'We'll support you,' Tony Bax had said, 'whatever you do. It'd be a pity for you to throw away a ministerial career so early on but, personally, I think the government is dead wrong.'

'I'm not clear,' Sarah told the Home Secretary, 'whether this is about us keeping to Tory spending plans or whether it's part of something bigger that I'm missing.'

'I have another meeting,' her boss said. 'Maybe you'll find that you have a meeting that can't be moved on the night of the vote.'

Sarah got the message, but wasn't sure if she dared act on it.

Nick was expecting the kind of formal interview he was used to from teaching: a panel consisting of the boss, members of the management committee. Instead he found himself on the first floor of an old Lace Market building, in a narrow, dusty space with frosted windows, the kind you get in a bathroom. Or a toilet. The Power Project manager sat at a table covered with files and cardboard coffee cups, neither opposite nor alongside Nick.

'This MP, minister, whatever. How well do you know her?'

No pussyfooting around Nick's drug counselling experience, which Bell seemed to take for granted.

'We were at university together. Belonged to the same political groups. I managed her campaign to be student union president.'

The look on Bell's face said that he had never set foot in a university his whole life and regarded such institutions with suspicion. Nick played his only card.

'We won the election, so I suppose you could say she owes me.'

The information registered with a slight narrowing of the eyes. Then Bell turned to the back of the form, where Nick had made his criminal record declaration.

'You served just over five years on an eight-year sentence. That's not full remission. What did you do wrong?'

'Failed a drugs test,' Nick confessed.

'Spliff?'

Nick nodded, then fibbed. 'I haven't used anything stronger since 1992.'

'You got a problem with anything else? Booze, pills?'

'No.'

'You're okay with the unsocial hours?'

The job information hadn't spelled out what the hours were, but now was not the time to ask.

'Suits me fine. I did unsocial shifts working as a taxi driver. I'm used to being alert in the early hours, if you need me to do outreach work.'

Bell re-examined Nick's application form. 'The taxi driving, that's not in your application.'

Nick decided to risk the truth. 'I was off the books. My brother runs a cab firm.'

'Cane Cars? That your brother?'

'Joe, yes.'

'You don't mind doing a little driving, then?'

'Not at all. I don't own a car, but I can borrow one when I need it.'

There was nothing about needing to own a car in the job spec, but Nick would act as Bell's chauffeur if that was what it took to make fourteen grand a year and get Probation off his back. He waited for the questions about the skills he could bring from school teaching, what he had learned about addiction in prison. But they didn't come. Kingston didn't give him an opportunity to shine, or to ask questions of his own.

'I've got all I need to know,' Kingston said, standing. Nick stood too. The interview had lasted barely ten minutes. When Kingston didn't offer his hand to shake, Nick decided not to offer his. Nick had no idea how he had done. Best, perhaps, to risk one question.

'When will I hear?' he asked, as Kingston led him out into reception, the one area of the first-floor office that was fully carpeted and painted.

'You start next Monday. There'll be a contract in the post.'

Nick didn't know what to say. 'Thanks. I'm . . .'

'Thank your minister friend. She pays people back. That's good to know.'

Nick stepped out into unanticipated sunlight that made him sneeze. After seven months on the out, he had a job, a good one. It paid only half what he might be making if he'd been able to teach again, but it was enough to live on. Decently. He was only qualified for the job because he had served a prison sentence for drugs offences. His luck, magically, had turned. He wanted to tell someone. His first thought was Sarah, but he would never get through to her. Then he thought of Joe, but at this time of day he would be driving. Nancy Tull would be teaching.

So Nick went home and smoked a single-skin spliff to celebrate.

8

Nick rang Nancy's number, hoping that Carl wouldn't answer. 'I was just thinking about you,' she said.

'Can you talk?'

'He's in the bath. I'll give you my mobile, if you're paranoid about him picking up.'

He wrote down the number. Mobiles cost a fortune to ring, but Nancy was worth it. He told her about his job. 'I thought we could celebrate.'

'I can't do tonight, but he's playing a gig down south tomorrow. Late ones, I always make him go back to his so he doesn't disturb me. Why don't you come here, bring a takeout?'

'Chinese or Indian?'

'Indian. Anything but prawns. I'm allergic. I'll get some booze in. About eight.' She told him where to find her.

Next, Nick rang his brother.

'Excellent,' Joe said, when Nick told him about the job. 'Who did you say your boss was again?'

'Kingston Bell. Know the name?'

'Not that I recall. We should have a drink to celebrate. Tomorrow?'

'I've got a date.'

'Not Sarah, by any chance? Bet she had a hand in your being hired.'

'She'll be in London,' Nick said, not denying her help. He'd planned to call Sarah at home on Friday, when she'd be back in Nottingham. She'd know about the job by then. He could call before, but didn't want to speak to her snotty secretary. What was he called? Hugh. Same as her revered grandad. Nick wondered if the name was why she'd hired him. Also, what the guy looked like. These casual jealousies did him no good, no good at all. Sarah was out of his league.

At Prime Minister's Question Time, Diane Abbott ambushed the prime minister about the lone parent benefit cut. Surely, the Campaign Group MP argued, there would always be mothers who were not able to work. Why should they suffer?

'I have to say frankly to you,' the prime minister began, a trace of irritation undermining his oh-so-sincere expression, 'we were elected as a government because people believed we would keep tight control of public finance and we said that clearly before the election.'

That was rubbish, Sarah knew. They were elected because the previous lot were unelectable. There was no need to water down socialist policies, but they had done.

He went on. 'What is important is to get as many people as possible off benefit and into work.'

The prime minister sounded no more convinced by these arguments than Sarah was. People said he was distracted by the Formula One affair. But this debate wasn't going away. Over the weekend, the whips had begun to spin a new line, that the cuts weren't about keeping to Tory spending limits, as previously suggested, but were part of a wider welfare reform initiative. Sarah would find this easier to believe if it weren't for the rumours she'd heard from the cabinet. Word was that the two ministers in charge of social security couldn't agree on a single policy.

'Sarah, have you got a moment?'

Sarah turned to see Ali Blythe. She remembered the brief conversation about the benefits cuts they'd had two weeks ago.

'How are you planning to vote tonight?' Alison asked.

'I still haven't made up my mind. I'm under a lot of pressure to vote "yes", but I may abstain and hang the consequences.'

'Can you abstain and not be sacked?'

'No, but I'm damned if I'm going to resign.'

One junior minister had already resigned in protest against the cuts. Sarah admired him, but knew that in a year or two nobody would remember his protest. If she was going to have her ministerial career ruined, the least she could do was make sure everybody noticed. 'What about you?'

'I can't bring myself to. You know I'm . . .'

Of course, Alison had a child herself and wasn't with the father. What was it called? Sarah, who had never wanted children, had trouble remembering the names of her friends' and colleagues' offspring, a deficiency in a politician.

'Vote against,' she told Alison. 'You'll be okay. Lots of others will, too.'

'I had phone calls at the weekend. The whips told me my career would be finished before it was started if I voted against. They phoned my constituency chair and she phoned me, said they told her to threaten me with deselection.'

'They phoned my constituency chair, too. It goes with the territory.'

The whips were trying to prove a point, Sarah figured. Obedience was all. She was beginning to wish she'd taken her boss's advice and found an urgent, conflicting appointment tonight, preferably one in another country. Then she could have got a civil servant to put in a slip and avoided this test.

'You have to think of this as a blooding,' she told Alison.

'I don't like hunting metaphors,' Alison told her. 'Pete Rugby told me it was time to lose my virginity.'

'The whips shouldn't talk like that,' Sarah said, without conviction. 'What do you think you'll do?'

'I won't if you won't.'

Was Alison lobbying her for the 'no's'? The young MP wasn't a member of the Campaign Group, but that didn't mean she was willing to sacrifice her principles. Yet. Sarah shook her head.

'I'll decide after I've heard the debate. Maybe you should do the same.'

They parted uncomfortably.

'I won't be able to come round as often,' Nick explained. He'd gone to the hostel after knocking off work at five. 'And we might have to make it later next time. After six.'

'I was going to cut back a bit on the lessons anyway,' Jerry said, crossing her long legs and smoothing down her navy blue school skirt.

'Why's that?'

Jerry gave him a frank look. 'Less money coming in.'

Nick didn't know what to say. He didn't want to know where her money came from.

'How frequently were you thinking?'

'Every two or three weeks?'

'That's doable. If you're sure you can keep up in the meantime.'

Jerry gave him a what-choice-have-I-got shrug. They arranged a session in a fortnight's time.

'You did well today,' he told her. 'I'm not just saying that because you pay me. There's no reason why you shouldn't get a top grade.'

'I want to go to university,' she told him.

That was a big statement for a girl in care.

'You're clever enough to,' he told her, honestly.

'D'you think? I was wondering . . .' She hesitated. Then Alice knocked on the door. Jerry looked embarrassed, for some reason. He said goodbye and had a quick chat with Alice before cycling home.

On his way out of Alexandra Park, Nick passed a four-by-four with shaded rear windows. Before he went inside, the only four-by-fours you saw were driven by farmers. The guy he glimpsed behind the wheel looked like Kingston Bell. Did King live round here? Alexandra Park wasn't as posh as Mapperley Park, but it was fairly upmarket. Maybe Kingston lived in one of the big old houses they'd converted into flats.

Nick cycled home and got changed for his date with Nancy. He walked to the Vegetarian Pot, further down Alfreton Road, and bought pakoras, aubergine bhaji, dal, chick-pea stew and chapattis, then flagged down a taxi. Not one of Joe's. Those guys could gossip.

Nancy's maisonette was in one of the smarter streets in a shabby area dominated by seventies council housing. When she didn't answer the door, he thought he'd come to the wrong place. Then a light came on and he heard footsteps. Nancy opened the door wearing a pale blue dressing gown.

'I forgot you were coming. I was in bed.'

'Are you ill?'

'Took the day off. You remember what it's like. Get hammered at the weekend. Struggle into school on Monday because you don't want people to know you have a hangover, then go under big time because your system's so run down.'

'I remember it well,' Nick said, though his school teaching days seemed to belong to another lifetime. 'This might make you feel better. Indian home cooking.'

He held up the brown paper bag. Nancy dipped her whole head into it and inhaled like someone snorting a line.

'Smells wonderful. Come in.'

Her place was bigger, funkier than he'd been expecting. One wall was painted purple. A lava lamp stood on the mantle over an art-deco-style fireplace. The thick, off-white shagpile carpet had seen better days.

'I've got red wine,' she said. 'Or beer. I prefer beer with Indian. You?'

'Great.' He cleared an ashtray and magazines from a glass table then went for plates. She really had forgotten that he was coming. And he'd thought she was gagging for it.

'I didn't know I was hungry until I smelled this,' she said. 'I haven't eaten all day.'

They shared a large bottle of Pilsner Urquell. Nancy ate hungrily at first, then slowed down to occasional mouthfuls, between which she gossiped about teachers, some of whom he remembered, most of whom were after his day, none of whom he was interested in. She didn't ask about his new job but, when she'd given up on the meal, passed him an old Golden Virginia tin, its bright green borders battered and scratched.

'Skin one up, would you? Helps my head.'

The big lump of hash was so fresh it didn't need warming. He crumbled plenty into a three-paper spliff. Probably from Carl. Musicians always got good dope. Nick took a couple of hits before passing it to her.

'Are you sure you should be having that, Mr Drugs Counsellor?'

'No more than you should, Ms School Teacher.'

'It's good for my migraine,' she said, before taking a deep pull, holding it in for a few seconds. 'I have some strong medication, but it takes a day to kick in. Dope softens the edges, makes me sleepy in a nice way.'

Nick felt his stone coming on. It was quality stuff, much headier than the hash he got from Joe, yet not brutally strong.

'Why don't you choose some sounds?' she said.

A CD tower, half concealed by a tall rubber plant, stood beside an old hi-fi.

Nick looked at her albums. 'Which of these are yours?'

'All of them,' Nancy said. 'Let a bloke move in his music, he thinks he's in control.'

There was a lot of techno, some jazz, nothing more mainstream than the Chemical Brothers. No Britpop. He had missed the rise of Britpop while he was inside, although his brother had introduced him to Pulp, who were from Sheffield, their hometown, and he played their last two albums a lot.

'Old school taste. I'm impressed.' Nick put on *Kind of Blue*.

'Why don't you come and sit with me?' Nancy said. She pushed herself up on the sofa so that there was room for him to sit upright with her head rested against his. He stroked her hair.

'Poor you,' she said. 'You thought you were up for a celebratory shag, didn't you?'

'The thought had crossed my mind,' he admitted, as she passed back the joint.

'I'm not sure what Carl would think about that. You've got someone too, haven't you? A bloke like you's always got someone.'

Someone ought to do a thesis on the way that strong dope acted as a truth drug, Nick thought. 'There was someone, for a while,' he said. Despite the truth drug, he decided not to go into specifics about Polly, or about how he'd tried to rekindle his relationship with Sarah. 'But it's over. Completely.'

'I really like you,' Nancy said. 'I've had the biggest crush on you since . . . well, since I met you, really. But I don't want to ruin things after we've waited so long. Let's wait. It's cruel to dump someone just before Christmas. We can be each other's new year resolution. How does that sound?'

'It sounds very good.'

Soon, she fell asleep. Would Nancy remember what they'd agreed? Did stoned conversations count? He wanted her tonight, wanted her something rotten. But he could wait. By the end of this month, he could be in a situation better than he'd dared imagine when he was inside. A respectable job, a girlfriend with a profession. A worthwhile life.

9

Sarah struggled to stay awake during parts of the debate. She had slept badly the night before. She usually managed seven solid hours, but today's vote kept playing on her mind. She was a decisive person, painstakingly so. Trouble was, she'd known for some time what she had to do.

And she hated it.

The secretary of state was marooned on the front bench of the government side of the chamber. Not a single member of the cabinet sat alongside her to offer support. The prime minister was nowhere to be seen. The rebels had put forward an amendment to restore the single parent benefits. A Lancashire MP said what Sarah would have liked to say.

'It has been turned into an insane loyalty test in which my colleagues are being invited to support the government, when they know in their hearts that what the government is doing is wrong. That grieves me, because I want the Labour government to succeed.'

The debate lasted several hours. The division bell for the vote on the amendment to Clause 70 didn't sound until twenty to eleven. Sarah entered the 'no' lobby with Steve Carter.

'This is the worst night since I got into parliament,' he told her.

'I've thought about abstaining,' she replied.

'We've all thought about abstaining, but it's no different to voting "yea". We've got to bathe our hands in blood up to the elbows, show loyalty.'

'You're right,' Sarah admitted. The principled thing would be to vote for the amendment. The sensible thing would have been what her boss suggested – organizing a series of prison visits that kept her well away from the Commons and gave her an excuse not to vote in person. But by doing that she would be effectively backing the government. By abstaining she would be asking to be sacked. This vote, she told herself, had little to do with single mothers like the ones who had harangued her at Stoneywood Library a few days ago. It was a hard lesson in politics for the new boys and girls. If Sarah deliberately failed the loyalty test, she would lose all the opportunities to do good that came with her ministerial job. And she would consign herself to a career on the back benches.

'Come on,' Sarah told Steve. 'Let's get this over with.'

Ali Blythe was heading in the same direction as them, shoulders hunched. What had changed her mind? Tories cheered the Labour members who walked into the 'no' lobby, their heads low. It was the first time that Sarah had seen the opposition look happy since they lost the general election.

The Lib Dems voted with the Labour rebels and the Tories with the government. Forty-seven Labour MPs voted against their own government. Not as many as had signed the early-day motion protesting the benefit cut, but a huge rebellion nonetheless. The amendment was lost by 457 to 107. Abstentions were not recorded.

Kingston Bell was about to be in the news. He was due to speak at a conference organized by the *Independent*. So he had called an after-hours meeting to talk through how the Power Project should present itself. This was the first time that Nick had seen the whole staff together in one room. All eight of them. King asked everyone but Chantelle to speak. Crip was laconic, his words trailing off senselessly. Leonard muttered something about reducing a habit being better than failing to abstain. The others all managed to find something relevant to say about what they were doing. Nick spoke last.

'I've been working in liaison with the safe sex clinic on George Street, handing out condoms, talking about STDs and intravenous drug use. Most of these kids claim not to be bothered by selling their bodies on the street, but the risk of catching HIV puts the fear into them.'

King frowned. 'I'm not sure that's our scene.'

'It's all part of the same problem. At the least, fear of AIDS is a first step towards them realizing that shooting smack is a problem.'

'Smack's not at the top of my agenda,' King said. 'You were the big dope grower. Give me arguments about why legalizing dope is good news.'

'When did you last hear of a schoolkid selling his body to buy grass?'

'But all these kids, you ask them, first thing they tried was dope.'

'Exactly,' Nick argued. 'And when they found out that smoking dope was fun, and safe, better and cheaper than booze, they thought, *What other drugs are the adults lying about? I think I'll try E. Hey, that's fine too. So what's wrong with crack and smack? Oh, I seem to need an awful lot of this. I don't seem to have anything else on my mind except where I can get the money for more . . .'*

'Cannabis is only a gateway drug because it's illegal,' King summed up. 'Decriminalize it, and kids are safer. I can't be that explicit, but if I spell out the situation and let people draw their own conclusions, the message might be even more effective. Any other thoughts? Okay, meeting over.'

Nick went back to his tiny office, pleased to have had some impact on his boss. For himself, he would like to see cannabis decriminalized. It was the only drug he couldn't do without. He hadn't missed alcohol while he'd been in prison. He'd had no cravings for cocaine, even though he'd been using heavily before his arrest. But when he'd had to pack in smoking dope for two years, after failing that drugs test, it had been purgatory. He'd missed the stuff every day.

10

On Friday, Sarah checked the *Independent* to see whether coverage of the single parent benefits revolt had died down. It had. The top headline was CONFERENCE CALLS FOR CHANGE IN THE LAW ON CANNABIS.

Sarah read the piece. The conference was organized by the newspaper covering it, which undercut their making it the lead story. Sarah agreed that everyone should have the right to make their own decisions about drugs, as long as they did not harm others. The way she saw it, the idea that cannabis was a gateway drug was unprovable. What was indisputable, but never mentioned, was the tax a government could collect from cannabis if sale of the drug was legalized.

Legalizing cannabis was too controversial an area for her to get stuck into publicly. Her involvement with the Power Project was risky enough. Already she had received warnings from constituents she bumped into, with the most unlikely stories, from *I've heard that the workers there go with prostitutes instead of helping them* to *I've seen one of the workers smoking a joint at a gig. Can't you sack him?* The stories, Sarah was pretty sure, were all about the project's predecessor, the Crack Action Team. If she'd realized just how much shit would still be clinging to that fiasco, she'd have avoided the Power Project by a mile.

Sarah's local party's monthly general committee meetings were held on the last Friday evening of the month. She would have to account for supporting the government on the single parent benefit cut. Lessons had been learned, the whips had assured the MPs who had reluctantly supported the government. There would be more consultation in future and the poor would be protected.

After tonight's meeting, she had nothing much in her diary beyond Christmas socials and photo ops. Back at home, with an hour before her first appointment at the constituency office, she decided to put up her cards. An MP, even the most unpopular ones, got more Christmas cards than she could keep track of. Since she'd become a member of the government, Sarah's tally had more than doubled. The work-related ones she kept in her office, with a handful of the more important – Tony and Cherie, her boss – on display. At home, on the walls of her flat in the Park, she kept the personal ones, from friends and relatives. This number had halved during her time in Nottingham. She started to arrange them, first on a sideboard, then the edges of bookshelves. It didn't take long.

What did the paucity of cards say about her? Friendships were hard to maintain when you were an MP. Her family was a small one. Dad was dead. No boyfriend – which, at least, meant no pseudo in-laws to keep sweet. Dan, her ex, hadn't sent a card. A year ago, they were living together. Nick had sent one (she hadn't reciprocated, unless Hugh had added him to the constituents' pile, which she signed on autopilot). She'd ducked the call when he'd rung to thank her for helping him with the Power Project job. Hearing Nick's voice could still do funny things to her.

One of the personal cards was from Paul Morris, with a note suggesting a meal. She was tempted. She enjoyed his company. The chief constable had also sent her a card. It bore no family greeting, but had the address and numbers for his new flat, with a note saying that he moved in on the third of January and would love to take her for a meal when she was free. This meant he was about to leave his wife. Sarah liked Eric, but he was newly single. For him, the stakes were high. Too high for her to get involved. She picked up Nick's card, reread the note inside:

Called you to say thanks. Be great if you had time for a Christmas drink but understand if you can't. Lots of luck for 98.

She could call him. She was lonely and nobody was watching. Not the press, the party or even her constituents. Sarah Bone, junior minister, wasn't all that important. She could invite her ex round for a drink. The news wouldn't appear on anyone else's radar. A Christmas truce.

Before she had a chance to change her mind, Sarah picked up the phone. The number for Nick's Alfreton Road place was still in her address book. Once, she had stood outside his first-floor flat, not daring to ring the bell. Now she dialled the number and listened to the phone ring twice. It went to machine. Of course, he would be at work. She listened to Nick's recorded message, relished his warm, intelligent voice, with its faint Yorkshire tones, then hung up.

Nick lit a cigarette. He'd got his first month's pay and returned to Marlboro Reds after six years of roll-ups. He was already smoking too many of them. Three weeks into his new job, he had run out of things to do. The office was quiet. Reception was staffed, but nobody came in. There was no sign above the door outside, only a handwritten note announcing that this was the Power Project. Could he clear off at three on a Friday afternoon? He had been to a public meeting the night before, made notes about crime in the Meadows, so could argue time off in lieu. He felt embarrassed to ask. Not that King was in at the moment. He hadn't appeared since yesterday's cannabis conference.

Nick got to work every morning at ten. He would come earlier, but Chantelle, the receptionist, couldn't be guaranteed to open up before then and he didn't have his own keys. The others tended to arrive around midday. Nick's room was barely two metres square. It had a computer with no printer or internet connection. If he wanted to write a letter and print it off he had to put the file onto a disc and take it through to Chantelle, who might get around to it by the end of the day.

Nick's official title was 'Drugs Worker', but he didn't have many drug users to work with. Not one person had made an actual appointment to see him – not this week, or the one before. Nobody had offered him any courses to go on, or suggested contacts for him to make. Yesterday he'd seen a couple of kids from the Meadows. He'd had to seek them out at an arcade haunted by crack dealers.

The Power Project was sometimes busy. In the afternoon, there were often people hanging around, waiting to see Kingston, or wanting to hang out with one of Nick's co-workers, Lester, Helen, Crip, Leonard and Satnam. Nick, by contrast, didn't have friends who showed up. He didn't have many friends, full stop. He'd hoped to get on with his co-workers, but they seemed to view him with suspicion. Nick wasn't sure whether this was because of his past, or because they knew of his connection with Sarah and her position on the project's management board.

On day one, King had told Nick to be 'proactive' about his work. *Proactive* was a new buzz word, which meant that Nick must find ways to create work for himself. An obvious route was to speak in assemblies at local schools, but he was reluctant to face that demon. Nick had resigned from his teaching job before his case went to court. He had never been put on List 99, which held the names of every person forbidden to work in a state school. Even so, these days, people who worked with young people had to have a criminal records check. Most schools would not welcome a convicted cocaine dealer and cannabis grower.

The only way Nick could think of to get around the issue would be if he made confessing his own transgressions part of the pitch. He didn't want to do that. Not because it would be humiliating, which it would, but because the Power Project was for people who had a drugs problem and Nick didn't have a problem. Schools didn't want such honesty. They wanted headlines in black and white. Illegal drugs had to be wrong, always.

The front desk was empty. Stepping into the street, Nick heard Chantelle's loud, dirty laugh. The receptionist had an additional brief. She was meant to engage with the Afro-Caribbean teens, the street girls especially. Chantelle didn't seem far from either her own teens or her clients' lifestyle. The way she was leaning into a four-by-four with heavily shaded windscreens, parked on double yellow lines, was suggestive to say the least. A familiar voice boomed from the driver's seat.

'Yo! Nick, come over here.'

Chantelle span round and flashed Nick an insincere grin.

'Getting away early for the weekend?' Nick's boss asked.

'I was at a community forum meeting in the Meadows last night, so I thought I'd take a couple of hours off in lieu,' Nick explained, bashfully. 'Have we got a team meeting next week?' he added.

King laughed. 'A meeting in the week before Christmas? Take it easy. Have a good one, yeah?'

'And you,' Nick said.

King had no scheduled hours at the Power Project. Nick had yet to see him of a morning. That didn't mean King wasn't doing his job. There were two teenage girls in the back of his car, one black, one white, both smoking cigarettes. By talking to them, Chantelle and King were helping. Impossible to gauge how much, but they were two more people than Nick had helped today. He felt inadequate. He had to make up some moves.

It was a bright, clear afternoon. Nick decided to go for a walk, a think. Rather than heading for his bus, he crossed Lower Parliament Street, strode uphill along the right-hand side of the Victoria Centre. The walk began in a dull, traffic-heavy stretch, then turned into a meander through posh Mapperley Park's liminal zone, the wide streets where the smart shared a border with rough St Ann's. Nick had considered moving here. Crime was high, but it was both nearer work and classier, leafier than the location of his own flat. More expensive, obviously, but he had decent money coming in.

'Hey, Nick!' It was Jerry, in her school uniform. 'Finished work early?'

'S'right.' He was opposite Alexandra Park, which housed Jerry's hostel and many others like it.

'Sorry I had to cancel our lesson the other day. Something came up.'

'No worries,' Nick assured her. He had assumed, from the message she left on his machine, that Jerry didn't have the money to pay him.

'What are you doing round here?'

'I like to walk sometimes, especially on days like this, helps me think.'

'It'll be dark soon. Want to come in for a brew? I've missed you.'

She gave him an open, relaxed smile. Nick was reminded how few real friends he had. Still, he hesitated. Jerry was hardly a friend. In his school teaching days, this would have been inappropriate, going home with an attractive, vulnerable fifteen-year-old. Jerry seemed to sense his awkwardness.

'Alice will be on shift. She was only saying the other day how she hadn't seen you for ages. Come on!'

'What have you done at school today?' he asked, and Jerry told him. They entered the drive that led into Alexandra Park. A familiar four-by-four followed them in. It slowed for a moment, maybe because of the pot-holed road. Nick clocked King Bell at the wheel. Had he seen Nick with Jerry, assumed something inappropriate?

'Look who I've brought with me,' Jerry told Alice as they walked in.

The hostel worker was slumped in an armchair in the hall, a Benson & Hedges almost at the filter.

'Hello, stranger,' Alice said. 'You're a sight for sore eyes.'

While Jerry made him a drink, Nick could talk privately with Alice.

'You're still volunteering at the centre once a week, they tell me,' Alice said. 'That's neat of you, when you've already got a job out of it.'

'Haven't seen you there for a while,' Nick said, cautiously.

'It's where I meet my dealer!' Alice quipped. 'Nah, I'm doing all right. Bit of weed to keep me from going potty. I'm thinking about giving that up, too, going to Narcotics Anonymous. They'll only take you if you're straight.'

'Good idea,' Nick said. 'Is it like AA, where you have to believe in submitting to a higher power?'

'Gotta be a higher power, or what's life about?'

Nick didn't reply. He hadn't believed in God since he was twelve.

'That'd be a deal breaker for you, would it?'

Nick shrugged. 'How's Jerry getting on?'

'Doing school work, far as I can see. Stays in a lot, which is a good sign. Not many of 'em do. Complains about how crap her teachers are.'

Jerry went to the sort of school where the teaching was ninety per cent trying to keep the kids in order and ten per cent handing out basic skills information. The proportion of kids who went on to college was low. Of those, the number who ended up at university was minimal. Jerry was bright enough to get into a good uni, no question. Her ambition ought to be realistic. But the number of kids from care who went on to university was, Nick knew, virtually nil.

'Here you go.' Jerry set down a mug of tea, strong with only a little milk, the way he liked it. 'Are you going to tell us about your new job?'

'Early days. Not a lot to tell. Didn't you break up today? Got coursework to do over the holidays?'

'I didn't invite you back for a free lesson,' Jerry said, her voice rising.

'I know,' Nick said, 'but I'm still interested, if you want help.'

'All right.' Jerry gave him a surprisingly shy smile. 'My English books are in my room.'

The front door opened and there was loud laughter, loutish shouting.

'I thought it was too quiet to last,' Alice said. 'Take Nick to your room, Jerry. Don't look a gift horse in the gob. Off you go.'

The room had two beds. Posters on the wall from *Smash Hits*: Blur, Pulp.

'Roommate out?'

'Left. Got the place to myself, time being.'

He had been in the room before, but then he was being paid and it was a prearranged visit. Nick felt awkward.

'Let's get to business then.'

She unlocked one of her drawers. He glimpsed jewellery, Calvin Klein perfume, a packet of condoms. He looked away.

'I have to keep my coursework locked up or some bastard would thieve it. Not to cheat. Just to fuck me up. Sorry about the language.'

'It's okay. Tell me about the assignment.'

For the next half-hour, sitting on the edge of the lower bunk, he went into teacher mode. It was absorbing and enjoyable. He'd forgotten how fulfilling it could be, working with a gifted student. There was a knock on the door.

'I'm off,' Alice said. 'Can I have a word, Nick, before I go?'

'Course.' Nick joined Alice in the corridor. He noticed that she'd brushed her hair.

'Don't let Jerry take advantage,' Alice said. 'It was nice of you to give her a free lesson. I expect you need the money.'

'It's okay,' Nick said. 'I enjoy it. And I have a job now; it's not like I'm desperate for the private tutoring work. I've stopped advertising for new students.' He lowered his voice. 'Jerry's not working, then?'

'Don't think she ever was,' Alice replied. 'She had money for a while, was secretive about where it came from. So I just assumed . . . but it's as likely some family member crawled out of the woodwork, gave her a load of guilt money then backed away when they saw how needy she was. That kind of thing happens a lot.'

She paused. Nick knew he was meant to say something, was being given the chance to suggest a drink, or at least a social opportunity that might lead somewhere.

'Got plans for the weekend?' This was as far as he wanted to go.

'Here Sunday. I'll probably get plastered tonight and spend tomorrow recovering. You?'

'Family stuff.' This was only partly misleading. Nick would, after all, have Sunday dinner with Joe and Caroline.

'I didn't know you had . . .'

'My . . . it's complicated.'

'It usually is. Try and have a good one, anyway.'

Pleased to have knocked her back without offence, Nick returned to Jerry's room.

Jerry smiled at him. She'd undone a couple of the buttons on her shirt. The smile was more embarrassed than cheesy. Nick remembered this scenario well. Adolescent girls liked to test out their sexuality on the younger, more attractive male teachers. But then you had the rest of the class to keep them in check. Other girls would tease them mercilessly if a crush became obvious. Whereas he and Jerry were alone together. Mistake. He tried to take it in his stride.

'Do you mind if we go into the office?'

'Do we have to?' She leaned down to pick up *Macbeth*, giving him an eyeful. No bra.

'I'm afraid so.'

You've been waiting to make this play. You've seen him look at your legs, so you know he's tempted. You've always fancied him a bit but, before, you were taken, and you're a one-man woman. Your first lover might have given you the elbow, but he's left his mark on you and you miss him terribly. Once you've been with me, he warned, you won't have any use for boys. And you don't. Beany can try all he likes.

Teach says he's got a new job, but he'll keep helping you if you want. You don't tell him that you can't pay him any more, but you drop a hint. You want him to make the first move.

He leaves the room for a minute. This might be your last chance. You undo your bra and take it off the complicated way, without removing your school shirt, so as not to be caught topless if he suddenly returns. You pull the bra out of your left sleeve and bung it under the bed. Then you undo another button. Are you being too tarty? Your first lover liked you to look innocent, really young. He liked you to pretend that every time was your first time. But Teach seems less pervy.

You can't hear the words of the conversation behind the door. You can hear the tone. He's knocking Alice back. There's nothing wrong with Alice. She's pretty, nice body. Either Teach is very picky, or she's too old for him. When he comes back in, he gives you that nice shy smile, sits down on the bed. He checks out your tits. Then he panics, says you should move.

'Do we have to?'

'I'm afraid so.'

You do up a button and, after that, make sure your arms stay folded, which is hard when you have to keep turning the pages of a book. Teach keeps his distance. In a while you start to concentrate on what he's trying to tell you. Shakespeare isn't so hard.

'What does that mean? "Screw your courage to the sticking place." It sounds dirty.'

He doesn't take the bait, consults the notes. 'The sticking place is for a tuning peg on a stringed instrument. When the string hits the right note, you stick it in.'

'Still sounds dirty to me.'

This time, he gives you a fleeting, cheeky smile. After half an hour, he has to go. When you offer to pay him, he says, 'Forget it, my pleasure.' Can you really pleasure a bloke by being a good student, or is he just being soft?

I I

Nick didn't know what to do with himself during the long days off over Christmas. He refused to watch TV in the day, but went for walks, reread several graphic novels that he'd bought before he was sent down, listened to a lot of Radio 4 and Radio 1.

Today's big news story was about how an unidentified cabinet minister's son had been set up by a female journalist. She'd sweet-talked him into buying, then selling a lump of hash to her. Before the story broke, his father had frog-marched him to his nearest police station, where he was given a caution. Radio 1 ran the story at length, but nobody on the youth station seemed to think that selling a lump of dope was a big deal.

How long should Nick leave it before phoning Nancy? She'd said new year, which was four days away. Another day or two, maybe. He was thinking about this when she rang.

'Were you waiting to hear from me?' she wanted to know. Her voice was breathy, affected.

'You bet. Had a good Christmas?'

'Nothing special. How about you? Been away?'

'No. I did have Christmas dinner with my brother and his wife.'

'Get any nice presents?'

Nick wasn't used to having such polite conversation with Nancy. He mumbled something about a sweater and CDs. 'You?'

'Carl didn't give me anything interesting enough to make me reconsider. I gave him the elbow yesterday.'

'At your parents'?'

'On the phone. He wasn't the sort of boyfriend you invite to meet your parents. He was the sort of boyfriend who spends Christmas getting out of his tree with his mates, then sleeps it off until new year.'

'Sounds like you could do with some company.'

'Have you got a Christmas present for me?'

'Of course,' Nick lied.

'Then get yourself over here tonight. Eight. I'll be waiting.'

You hate Christmas most of all. Some of the others go home, or to relatives, but you have nobody, nobody who's bothered, anyway. You hate the forced jollity, the crap presents, the cheap perfume and cheaper paper decorations, the plastic Christmas tree. It's been this way since you were taken into care. You can't remember what it was like before. Worse, probably. You've blocked it out.

Then he comes. It's been over a month. You'd given up on him. You missed the attention, the affection and you missed having him inside you, your first and only lover. You were tempted to track him down at work, but he forbade that and, anyway, he claims he's never in one place for long. He won't tell you where he lives and he's not in the phone book. You looked.

He's not visiting you; he's visiting the hostel. Martine, the warden on duty, makes a fuss of him. You stay clear, let him see you're there, then go to your room. Five minutes later, he opens the door.

'I've only got a minute. They think I'm in the loo.'

He kisses you the way a lover should, then takes a phone out of his pocket.

'Merry Christmas.'

'What's this?'

'I've put twenty quid's worth of credit on it. My mobile number's on there, too. Under the name 'Man'. I'm still your man, right? There's nobody else?'

You shake your head.

'Meet me up the street in ten minutes. Don't make it obvious, okay?'

'Okay.' You nod and he grabs your bum, pulls you towards him, slips his tongue down your throat. He tastes good.

Fifteen minutes later you're doing it on the back seat of his big car. He likes to finish the dirty way. It hurts, but a girl does what she has to do to keep her man. That's what the other girls say.

'Gotta hurry, sorry,' he says, wiping himself off.

'When will I see you again?'

'When I can. You'll be easier to get hold of now. Keep it turned on, okay? Put it on mute when you're at school. I'll send you text messages. Do you know how to send a text?'

'I'll get someone to show me.'

'Okay.' He hesitates, senses that there's something you're not saying. He's good that way. 'Got everything you need?'

'I could use some money for my extra English lessons. I'm behind.'

'Sure.' He opens his wallet and counts out a hundred quid.

You check that it's clear then get out and run back to the home. He didn't once ask you what Christmas was like. He gave you the money without a second thought. Does that make you a working girl? Some of the girls in the home have mobiles. You'll get one of them to show you how to do the text message thing. Then you'll phone Teach, arrange another lesson. With luck, Teach will act like what happened last time didn't happen. Older guys are good at pretending.

*

'You haven't got either of them, have you?'

'Joe taped me the Verve album. I played it a lot inside. Great to have it on CD. I don't know this one at all. Erykah . . . how do you pronounce it?'

'Like it's spelled, Badu. Meant to be the best soul album of the year.'

'Here, I got you something too. Merry Christmas.'

'You shouldn't have.'

Nancy tried to open the album that Joe and Caroline had given Nick. He'd had no opportunity to play it, so the case was still shrinkwrapped. It was called *Curtains*. Joe had decent taste, cooler than Nick's, so this was a good bet for Nancy. The cover detail reminded Nick of the curtains his grandparents had had in their front room. Nancy passed the CD back to him.

'Do this for me, would you? I don't want to mess up my nails.'

He tore the plastic film and put the album on. Nancy snuggled up to him on the sofa. The music was lugubrious, intense but laid-back, Bryan Ferry with a touch of Leonard Cohen, backed by a fifties orchestra.

'This is good,' Nancy said. 'I like this lot.'

'Me too. They're from Nottingham.'

'I saw them once, when they were called Asphalt Ribbons. Their first album's great. It must have come out while you were away. How did you hear about them?'

'I keep my ear to the ground,' Nick said.

They undressed each other hungrily, then fucked on the sofa. Nick couldn't remember a first time as good. Only one drink, no drugs, just a coal-effect gas fire, the right music and a full-length sofa.

Nancy put the Verve album on. It was the first time he'd seen her standing upright, naked. You could never be sure what a woman would look like naked. There was always some surprise involved. The dark nipples on her full breasts were upturned.

Her arms were thin but strong, as he'd just discovered. Her skin was very pale. He'd not been with a woman who shaved down there before.

When Nick came back from the bathroom, he found Nancy half dressed, carving two fat lines of coke on the kitchen table.

'I didn't know you indulged.'

'Carl left some behind. I was thinking of saving it for New Year's Eve, but I don't know where I'll be then.'

Nick nearly refused. Coke had bad associations for him. He wouldn't sleep later if he had some. That aside, sex on coke could be great, and probably even better when you were both on it. He'd told himself that, given his new job, he should stick to spliff from now on, but, fuck it, there were no drug tests on the out. It would be rude to refuse.

He did the whole line in one go, up his right nostril. Nancy followed suit. Then she took the Verve off and replaced them with the Chemical Brothers. She had put on a bra and knickers that were almost completely see-through. When she danced for him, he could feel himself getting excited again. Coke lets you live in the moment, and the moments rushed by. He began to dance opposite her. She ground her body against his, in rhythm with the music. The big beat was so loud that he didn't hear the door open, only saw the alarmed look on Nancy's face.

'What?'

'Slut!' Her ex-boyfriend's voice cut through the music. Northern, high-pitched, no longer the cool, long-haired guitarist. Nick forced himself to unclench his fist, turn the music off. He was still on probation. He couldn't get into a fight.

'What do you want, Carl?' Nancy asked.

'How long have you been fucking this guy?'

She could hardly deny it. Nick wondered if she'd actually finished with Carl. Or had she just told him that?

'Nick and I go back a long way,' Nancy said.

'This is Nick? The one who's just got out of prison? Nick from the nick?' Carl laughed. 'The grass is always greener, eh, Nick?'

Nick tried for a tolerant smile. He'd heard them all.

Carl pulled off the panel behind the right speaker and reached into it. 'Where's my tin?'

'Kitchen table.'

'I hope you haven't given this shit any of my coke.'

Nancy didn't reply.

'Isn't he a bit old for you? What are you, mate, forty?'

Nancy used her matter-of-fact teaching voice. 'If you're taking the tin, leave me a bit of hash, Carl. You know I can't sleep without it.'

Carl opened the green Golden Virginia tin and pulled out a half-ounce lump of hash. He broke off a small piece and tossed it to Nancy.

'That's the last you're getting from me.' He disappeared into the bedroom. Ignoring Nick, Nancy followed him.

'You're the one who said you didn't want to be exclusive.'

'You knew I was coming round. That's why you had him here. That's why you're wearing that underwear I bought you, to rub it in my face. Fuck it, Nance, we're really through this time.'

'You're not through until I say you are.'

Nick wished he hadn't had the coke. His brain was rushing. Last time he'd had coke was five and a half years ago and he'd been arrested while high. He ought to get out of here.

In the bedroom, the row raged on. Nancy was detailing all the women Carl had fucked, groupies who followed his band.

'I wasn't there but Mel was and she said you went home with the little slapper after the gig. Then there was . . .'

Nick's bike was still locked to the railings outside the flat. He was so high that, in no time at all, he had cycled home.

12

Sarah accepted Eric's dinner invitation because she had nothing better to do. Parliament didn't restart until the twelfth. She had made two visits to prisons in the break between Christmas and New Year, even though both governors had told her it was beyond the call of duty. She'd even eaten Christmas dinner at Wormwood Scrubs, which was about to appoint a new governor, to demonstrate that New Labour took problem prisons seriously. Her Tory predecessor had visited every single prison in the country during her term. Sarah didn't know how she'd managed it. When parliament was sitting, her days were so full that she barely had time to visit the loo.

When Eric called her to say that he'd got a table at a new restaurant not far from her flat, she'd hesitated. He added that there was something he needed to tell her in person.

'What's so sensitive that you can only tell me face to face?' she asked, as soon as they were seated.

'I wish you'd talked to me before you agreed to join the board of the Power Project,' Eric said.

They were in a restored building on the edge of the old City General hospital site, overlooking the Park. Hart's had only opened the month before. It was already near-impossible to get a table. The decor was smart, cool. The tables weren't packed together. Best of all were the smart leather booths that seated four. Eric had managed to secure one of these for just the two of them. A chief constable must have more clout than an MP. Eric introduced her to the maître d', who assured Sarah that, in future, she would always be found a table at short notice. They took their menus, then resumed the conversation.

'Why do you say that?' she asked, chewing on a freshly baked breadstick. 'You were at the meeting in which we all agreed to support it.'

'There's support and support. Let's talk about it later, when we've relaxed properly into the evening. I do recommend the calf's liver.'

'I like the look of this place,' Sarah said. Hart's felt like a New Labour restaurant. Wooden floors, airy, with geometric, multicoloured paintings. It used to be the reception wing of the General and it had retained a temple-like, healing air. Eric began to show off.

'The chef used to be at Le Manoir aux Quat'Saisons, Raymond Blanc's place. Have you ever eaten there?'

Sarah had to confess that she hadn't.

'Maybe I can take you some time.'

She ordered a crab starter, followed by duck. Eric went for the pâté and calf's liver. Sarah had a glass of Sauvignon Blanc with her first course while Eric ordered a bottle of Gevrey-Chambertin and started it with his.

'You didn't really bring me here to talk about the Power Project,' she said. 'Why such short notice?'

Eric gave what was nearly a blush.

'Someone let you down?'

'My wife, to be honest. This was meant to be a conciliatory family dinner before I went skiing. After which I have the new flat to move into . . . as I think I told you. When it became clear that my moving plans were definite, she . . . what do they say, these days, *threw a wobbler?*'

'I think it's *throw a wobbly.*'

'One of those, anyway. Doubtless I deserved it.'

'Doubtless. Now, since you brought up the subject, stop fooling around and tell me why you wanted to warn me against the Power Project. You got me into it.'

'I can't go into operational detail about ongoing investigations. All I will tell you is that the corruption generated by the project's predecessor goes very deep. The council, my own force, even. It's too early to set up a new project that has any chance of keeping clear of such systemic, far-reaching corruption.'

'Drugs are a huge economy,' Sarah said. 'Corruption seems to be inevitable. That doesn't mean you shouldn't try to protect vulnerable people. Unless you're saying that Kingston Bell is as bad as Frank Davis was.'

'I don't have anything against Bell as yet. He's out of his depth, perhaps, but he's well-meaning. None of our investigations link him with the previous regime.' Eric's explanation, as it went on, was prosaic and a tad patronizing. Kingston Bell was employing people who were too immersed in drug culture. He himself was lucky to have escaped a custodial sentence for cannabis possession in his teens.

'Come on,' Sarah said. 'Nearly everybody I know dabbled with drugs in their youth. First-hand experience is almost a qualification for the kind of job that Kingston's taken on.'

'And you know he's just hired a convicted drug dealer?'

'Nick Cane? Yes. In fact, I wrote a reference for him.'

'I remember your connection with Cane and I think it's unwise of you – especially now that you're a Home Office minister – to retain it. Yes, in principle, a drugs agency like the Power Project has a lot of potential benefits, but you should let other, less ambitious MPs soil their hands with this one.'

'I am ambitious and I hope Kingston's ambitious, too. For that matter, I hope Nick Cane's still ambitious. He was, back when I knew him well. Rehabilitation's not a dirty word, is it?'

'Not a dirty word, but a precarious one. I wanted to warn you about the company you keep. Now I've done it. You're a bit of an idealist, Sarah.'

'Only a bit?'

'Tell me how an idealist deals with prisons.'

This time his smile was more generous than patronizing, and Sarah remembered what a useful ally he could be.

'It's hardly the most fashionable of subjects, is it? Not many prize-winning novels or zeitgeist movies about the state of the prison system. I visited two last week. God, it's depressing . . .'

Ninety minutes later, Eric took her home. Despite the half-bottle of wine and large vodka and tonic he'd drunk, he drove, saving her a seven-minute walk. Maybe, when he offered her the lift, he'd hoped she'd tell him to leave the car at Hart's, pick it up in the morning. But she wasn't tempted. He got out to open the passenger door. She couldn't remember the last time anyone had done that for her. She gave him a peck on the cheek.

'Happy new year,' she said.

'Don't forget what I've told you about the Power Project,' he reminded her. 'Extricate yourself.'

'I'll think it over.'

In bed, not long afterwards, she found herself thinking, not about Eric, or Nick, but about Paul Morris. Eric had given her a good excuse to call him the next day. Was it okay to phone a family man at this time of year?

Nick was immersed in a video of *Hill Street Blues*, which he'd salvaged from the stuff he had stowed in Joe and Caroline's attic. He'd religiously taped the show, editing out the ads, because he knew he'd want to watch it all again one day. Now he had the time. The phone rang. He looked at his watch. Not far off midnight.

'I've dumped him properly this time,' Nancy said. 'Come round.'

Nick carted his bike down the iron steps and was at hers in ten minutes. Nancy looked distracted, but happy that he was there. They hardly talked. She took him straight to bed, where Nick took his time making love with her. He couldn't get her to come, but she didn't seem to mind.

'Here, I have something for you.' She opened the drawer of her bedside table. 'I made Carl give this back. Now you're the only man with my key. Use it any time.'

Nick didn't know how to react. He hadn't asked for a key, nor whatever commitment came with it. Were they in a relationship? Okay, fine, they were.

'Is this you keeping your new year's resolution?' he asked, kissing her on the forehead.

'I guess so. Do you want to get up and have a drink, or a smoke?'

'I'm happy just to lie here and hold you until we fall asleep.'

'Okay, I guess,' Nancy murmured.

They spooned, though Nick had the sense that Nancy would have preferred it if they'd got dressed, got smashed, maybe made love again later. But it was too late to suggest that, for she had fallen asleep. Nick stared at the ceiling. The room was partially illuminated by light seeping through from a street lamp. Nancy dressed well, but she was a slob. Piles of clothes littered the floor. Polly, despite a houseful of kids, had kept her place meticulously clean. Nancy began to snore. Nick thought how he should have brought the video with him. He wanted to know how the episode ended.

The morning after her evening with Eric, Sarah thought, Sod it, and called Paul Morris on his mobile.

'I have one or two concerns that I need to go over with you before the next Power Project board meeting.'

'Sure,' he said in his warmest voice. 'It'd be great to catch up. How about this evening?'

He suggested a small trattoria in an alley a stone's throw from the Old Market Square. They drank good Chianti and ate mediocre cannelloni. He certainly hadn't brought her here for the quality of the food. They discussed Labour's continuing popularity and the conspiracy theories that were going round about the death of Princess Di. Paul's knee kept brushing hers. She thought about him in her bedroom at Hambleton Hall, wondered what would have happened if Eric hadn't shown up too.

'You had some concerns about the Power Project?' Paul said, while they waited for their main course.

Sarah had forgotten the pretext for tonight's dinner. But, once reminded, she got straight to the point. 'Paul, when you asked me to take this on, you didn't tell me that Kingston Bell had a drugs conviction.'

'One minor count of possession, when he was nineteen. If we want people working for us who know the scene, they'll have been involved in the past. They have a white guy working there who has a much more recent conviction for a much more serious offence. But he's rehabilitating himself.'

'I'm aware of that.'

'Who told you about Kingston? The police?'

Sarah didn't reply.

Paul took her silence for a 'yes' and carried on talking. 'Nottinghamshire has one of the most racist police forces in the country, we both know that.'

'We do, and we've both done a lot to try and change the situation, but I'm not convinced that racism is what we're talking about in this instance. You got me into this, Paul. Would you personally vouch for Bell's integrity?'

Paul's eyes met hers for a moment, then she watched him go into himself, looking for another answer. He was the sort of person whose first answer was usually taken as gospel. As was she.

'He's a religious man. We go to the same church.'

'As I recall, the head of the Crack Action Team claimed to have seen the light in prison. Once bitten.'

'You can never be one hundred per cent sure of anything,' Paul conceded, 'but I wouldn't have asked you to join the project's management committee unless I was convinced of Kingston's probity.'

'If there's the slightest doubt about that, I'll have the place closed down. His speaking at a legalize cannabis conference recently didn't help.'

'Understood. That was naive. I know that, in a sense, King's continuing the philosophy that's associated with the old regime. But we both know that the philosophy was spot on. It's the implementation that stank.'

His smile was reassuring, but she noticed a flicker of doubt around the edge of his lips. She moved the conversation on. Both tried to resume the flirtatiousness of the earlier part of the evening, but they had run out of safe topics. After a cursory discussion of their respective Christmases, neither of them felt like ordering dessert.

In the shadows at the brow of St James Street, they shook hands, then walked off in opposite directions.

13

On Friday afternoon, Kingston Bell flicked through Nick's timesheets and glanced at his evaluation form. They both knew the timesheets were an elaborate fiction. There still wasn't enough work to occupy Nick. If he hung around the office waiting for clients as much as he'd claimed on the form, he'd go crazy. King didn't seem bothered.

'The paperwork is the pits but you have to do it,' he told Nick. 'I'll get Chantelle to fill in my part later.'

Nick nodded. Chantelle gave the impression of holding the place together. Only thing was, the evaluation form was meant to lead to an interview that set objectives for Nick's future development. Without it, he couldn't pass his probation period.

'Did you want to say something about targets?' Nick asked.

'Don't be telling me what I want to say.'

King had a temper that leaped out when you least expected it. Nick wasn't sure if it was genuine, or merely a means of maintaining control.

'Sorry. I only meant . . .'

King shook his head as if to negate his previous outburst.

'Are we done?' Nick asked.

'Yeah. Take it easy. Always quiet this time of year. Be grateful you don't have to go to the Release conference in Manchester with me, waste your weekend.'

Nick knew that King relished his conference appearances. He liked to dress up in a suit and present himself as a God-fearing friend of the oppressed. It was a big difference to how he appeared at work, dressed down in sweatshirts and trainers. He made Nick, in his button-down shirt, blue jeans and bomber jacket, feel smart.

'He give you the form for me?' Chantelle asked Nick on his way out.

'Nope, sorry.'

Chantelle gave one of her expansive shrugs then returned to her book of crossword puzzles. She wore thick glasses for reading that, combined with the shorter afro she had come back with in the new year, made her look academic. Nick would like it if she was sweeter to him, so he made an effort.

'How was your Christmas?' he asked, as his boss breezed by, dropping Nick's evaluation form onto Chantelle's desk. Chantelle did not attempt to hide the crossword book, but picked up the form, ignoring Nick's question. Then, when he was at the door, she called him back.

'There was a message for you. Client, I think.' Chantelle wrote down a number. The 0797 code told him it was a mobile. Without asking, he used Chantelle's phone. The call went straight to answerphone, no personal message. He hated leaving messages on mobiles. Clients often didn't check their messages because it cost them credit, so you never knew if they'd got the message anyway. He hung up without leaving one.

Sunday was the last day before the parliamentary recess ended. Sarah had made a loose arrangement to visit Chesterfield on Boxing Day, but Mum had cancelled, for vague reasons. Sarah suspected that she had a new man friend. There had been various male friends over the years since Dad left, but no official boy-friend, no hint of remarriage. Last year, Mum had retired from the council, where she'd had a job in housing. Sarah had asked if she planned to move elsewhere.

'What, and leave all my friends?' Mum replied. But there was precious little evidence of friends when Sarah visited. Sarah had joined the Labour party here, as soon as she was old enough to, twenty years ago. She still had friends in Chesterfield, friends she only saw when she had to come over and give a speech. Comrades, perhaps, rather than friends, although 'comrade' was a loaded term these days. Nobody used it at the Commons.

This was her last chance to visit Mum before the new session started and Sarah's free time became even more precious. She had left it late. Sundays were often given over to the contents of the red boxes she brought home in a locked briefcase. This dark afternoon, there was no such excuse. Driving into Chesterfield, a Derbyshire town dominated by the crooked spire of an old church, it occurred to Sarah that she had wanted to get away from her mother since Felicity was thirty-six, the same age that Sarah was now.

Felicity Bone was sixty-one. Sarah's father, Kevin, were he still alive, would have turned seventy last year. Mum had been Grandad's constituency secretary when she met his only son. Dad was a bright, bohemian Cambridge graduate. He had gone to the same college, Caius, as his father had before him. Dad would have liked Sarah to go there too, but, in a minor act of rebellion, she chose Nottingham instead. Not that, by then, Dad was around for her to rebel against.

Sarah was an only child. Felicity didn't have strong maternal instincts, but she did have a strong sense of pride. She liked going out with a successful (or so it seemed, for a while) Cambridge graduate with a rich, famous father. She was seven months preg-nant when they married. It pleased Kevin to have a daughter, and he was a good father, at first. He was less good as a provider, but there was always Grandad to fall back on.

Mum went back to work at the council before Sarah was one. Dad had sometimes stayed at home to look after her. He had a job with his father in the early days of the marriage, as some kind of parliamentary adviser. He wasn't in Chesterfield much. Sarah remembered being impressed by parliament the one time Dad had taken her to visit. Being in London suited Dad, for he had a whole other life there. In the late sixties and early seventies, he worked as a book reviewer, a travel journalist, the editor of a trade journal. But work never took up much of his time.

When homosexuality was legalized, in 1967, Dad had little reason to hide the most important aspect of his London life. He left for good in 1970, when Sarah was eight. Her dad never paid maintenance but occasionally bought her extravagant presents. His dad, Sir Hugh, regularly sent money to Felicity and, doubtless, to Kevin too. When Grandad died, Dad got most of his money. After that, he stopped any pretence of work.

Grandad had been a shrewd investor, so there was plenty of money. Sarah's share had paid for her small flat in London. Her dad inherited enough for a three-bedroom place in Spain, with a pool. Sarah visited twice. Dad, in his fifties, toned down his behaviour while she was around, but there was still enough going on for her to see the kind of life he led. He had a bottle open and a joint on the go from lunchtime onwards. Both were shared with handsome young men nearer Sarah's age than his own. Sarah, having joined the police, had become – to Dad's eyes – uncomfortably straight. Her second visit was nearly five years later. By then, she was taking her first steps in a political career while Dad, unknown to him, had contracted HIV.

'I had a great time,' he'd told her the last time they met, in hospital. 'I don't regret any of it, except spending so little time with you. I'm sorry I couldn't live with your mother and see more of you. I thought we had for ever to figure things out between us. But there's no such thing as for ever. There's just time.'

She'd meant to visit again before he died, but he'd declined rapidly. When she went back, three weeks later, it was to bury him. At the time, she thought that the wrong parent had died. She and Mum had fallen out when Sarah left the police and moved into politics. Mum realized what her ex-husband had died of, said that he had it coming, that if anyone was going to catch the gay plague, it was Kevin Bone.

Lost in memories, Sarah had driven the last part of the journey on autopilot. She turned off the Chatsworth Road and parked outside Mum's terraced house, with its tidy, narrow front yard. Her mobile rang. Sarah answered at once, relieved to delay the inevitable.

'Andrew! How are you?' It was a voice from the more recent past, Nick's oldest friend.

'Very well indeed. I wanted to wish you a happy new year and remind you that I owe you a meal, restaurant of your choice. Be great to catch up.'

'Restaurant of my choice?'

'In Nottingham or London. Entirely up to you. I have a little business to do in Nottingham. In fact, I'll be there later.'

'I'm in Chesterfield just now, I'm afraid. But how about Alastair Little's?'

'Consider it booked. When?'

'You'll have to talk to Hugh, my diary secretary, about that. You don't mind eating late, do you?'

'Not at all. I'm still a night owl.'

'Great. How are you getting on with Gill Temperley?'

'Swimmingly. She takes my money. I use her name. Not a lot else for her to do.'

'Really? You offered me a full-time job doing whatever it is she does for you.'

'I'd have invented more work for you, if only for the pleasure of your company.'

The net curtains in Felicity's front bay windows parted. Sarah saw her mother's hawk-like profile, filled with the mean expression that – in her mind's eye – Mum always wore.

'I've got to go, Andy.' She used the old name affectionately. It was funny how you could feel affectionate about some people from the past, when you had no particular reason to like or trust them still, just because they knew you when you were young and yet to be fully formed. But with other people – particularly, perhaps, family, although Sarah had never had enough family to make a firm study of this – the past kept looming up like a shipwreck, one that had been long since abandoned and which only a fool would return to. For the wreck was bound to have deteriorated further over the years. To swim back into it was stupid and dangerous.

He shouldn't be in Nottingham this weekend, he tells you. He's skiving off a conference for you. You weren't expecting him. You were hanging out down the Broadmarsh when the moby rang. You told him where you were. Fifteen minutes later, he's parked on a side road near Meadow Lane. He takes a good look at your pupils.

'You been smoking?'

'I was with Shaz. She had some weed.'

'Don't smoke in the daytime. You can lose weeks that way. Months. You could be reading, doing something useful.'

He sounds like a dad, but you've never had a dad, and you quite like that. It's cool he cares enough to tell you off. Still, you have to fight back.

'I work hard Monday to Friday. I have an extra class on Sunday and do my homework then, too. But I take Saturdays off and the day's so long, you know? If I'd known that you were going to call . . .' You realize that you sound like a fifteen-year-old, which is what you are. 'Anyway,' you whisper in his ear, 'smoking makes me really, really horny. How long have we got?'

'Long enough.'

This afternoon, he moves the car to the back of the antique markets, which are all closed by mid-afternoon. The road's full of cars parked for the football, but the game is still going on. He likes the risk that someone will come along. The two of you move into the back of the four-by-four, fold down the long seat, and spread out the blanket he keeps beneath. You go down on him, giving head just the way he taught you to. Then he goes down on you, until you let him know you're ready. Then you fuck each other for a long, long time, until you come again and again.

'You're a god,' you tell him. 'I love you, God. Oh, God!'

'I love you too,' he says, coming at last. 'I'll always love you. We're always going to be together.'

Afterwards, driving you back to the hostel, he isn't so soppy.

'How are the lessons going?' he asks.

'Fine. I'm just doing English now. At school, they say I'm bound to get a good maths grade, but I need help with English. The teacher's good.'

'I'll give you some more money to pay him, but don't go spending it all on weed.'

'I never pay for weed.' You risk a question. 'Do you still smoke?'

'Still?'

'Don't tell me you didn't smoke weed when you were young.'

'When I was a teenager, everybody smoked. But after that, only now and then, to be polite. I like to keep a straight head.'

'It's great when you're straight, yeah?' you say.

'What is that, a song title?'

He gets it. 'You're pretty cool for an old guy,' you tell him.

He pulls up at the end of the road that backs onto the hostel. You look around to make sure there's nobody who will spot you.

'When will I see you again?'

'Soon as I can make it, babe, but I've got a lot on my plate.'

You kiss him tenderly on the lips. 'Make it really soon. I love you.'

He doesn't say it back again, but he smiles and you know he's yours. You can't believe you ever doubted him, offered your body to somebody else. Dunt matter. Didn't happen. This is for always. Now and for ever.

14

'You didn't go home last night, did you?' Nick's sister-in-law said, making gravy to go with the pork tenderloin. 'I phoned you this morning and you weren't there.'

'Maybe I'd gone out to buy a paper.'

'I phoned three times to ask you to ask you to pick up some mustard powder when you were cycling over here. In the end, I had to send Joe out for it.'

'Okay,' Nick said. 'You got me. I stayed the night at a friend's.'

'It would have been fine for you to bring her over. We can always stretch to one extra at the table.'

'Thanks, but it's early days.'

'Someone you met at work?'

'No, she's a teacher.'

'Primary or secondary?'

'Secondary. English.' That seemed to please Caroline, a teacher herself. He told her how Nancy had written to him in prison, but he had only started seeing her recently, when she split up with her boyfriend.

'She sounds nice,' Caroline said. 'You must bring her round.'

'I'll see how it goes.'

After dinner, Nick and Joe shared a spliff in Joe's snug. Since

Phoebe was born, this was the one room in the house where he was allowed to smoke. He'd sorted the room out recently, put a few photos and other football memorabilia from his County days on the walls and added a CD ghetto-blaster. There was enough space for two old armchairs.

'This is sweet,' Nick said, referring to the room.

'Won't last for long. Caroline wants this to be the baby's room when she moves out of our bedroom in a few months.'

'I thought she was going to have the room I used to have,' Nick said, referring to the few weeks that he'd stayed here when he got out of prison.

'Eventually, but this room's nearer ours and by the time she moves . . .'

'You're not trying again already, are you?'

Joe gave a bashful grin. 'Not yet, but we don't want too big a gap between kids. Better if . . .' He let the sentence drain away.

'You're probably right,' Nick said. There were six years between him and Joe, too many for them to have been friends growing up. He took another toke of the African grass and added, 'This is good stuff.'

'I'll bet you're making some connections where you're working.' He put on a stoner voice. 'When are you going to hook us up with some really high-quality weed?'

Nick shook his head. 'People don't get problems with stuff like this. I had a parent come round the other day. Her kid's getting through nearly a hundred quid's worth of killer skunk every week. Can you believe that?'

'How old is he?'

'Seventeen, just dropped out of college. All he wants to do is stay in his room and smoke. Him and his mates listen to sounds, watch videos. They're too stoned to get off with girls. Only other thing they do is play computer games.'

'I can't imagine wanting to get that high all the time.'

'Lots of 'em do, though. They don't know any different.'

'What do you tell him?'

'Nothing. He won't come in, doesn't see it as a problem.'

'Well skunk's not like smack . . . you know, addictive.'

'I dunno about that. High, the world's an easier place.'

The grass was stronger than the Moroccan hash Nick usually had. Both men fell into silence. Perhaps Joe, like Nick, was thinking about what they had just been saying. Dope always helped Nick to think. There was a time when he thought it made him more perceptive, more intelligent in a way. In certain tribes, he'd read, cannabis was revered and used only on special, religious occasions. Stoned, Nick could hear his thoughts, follow a trail to the end and, sometimes, locate solutions to complex problems, such as how far and how fast to take his relationship with Nancy.

Next day, however, he could rarely remember where his thoughts had taken him. He usually drank too much when he smoked. Nothing cerebral about his reasoning processes then.

'Do you really think that?' Joe asked, replying to something that Nick had said a short while ago, but had no recollection of.

'Sure,' Nick told him. 'I always say what I think. What else is there?'

Joe nodded, as though Nick had said something profound, and stubbed out the joint. Then, without needing to discuss their next move, the two men went downstairs to watch the Sunday game on Sky Sports. At half-time, Caroline came down from her post-dinner nap.

'How's work?' Nick asked. His sister-in-law had just gone back to school after maternity leave.

'A slog. I wish I'd negotiated to go back part-time. Next year I'm going to see about a job share. Actually,' she went on, 'there was something I meant to mention. I've got a year eleven tutor group and I overheard something the other day, might interest you. One of the girls was talking about her boyfriend, said he worked for a guy called the King.'

'Worked as what?'

'I'm not sure. I thought I heard them use the word "power" but when I went over in her direction, she clammed up, which made me suspicious. Isn't your place called the Power . . .?'

'*Project*, yes.'

'What's the philosophy behind the name? Let me guess: *Just saying no gives you the power*?'

'Something like that. What did you hear?'

'The gist of it was that he had the best drugs in town. But perhaps I misheard the *power* bit.'

The second half of the match started. Nick didn't waste time reflecting on what Caroline had just told him. He used to teach teenagers. They liked to bullshit. Also, he had something else on his mind. Last night, he'd gone to Nancy's, used his key to let himself into her maisonette. They didn't have a date. She'd mentioned something about a drink with people from work, meeting him after. He'd figured on catching her when she got home, but she hadn't been there. And she hadn't come back, either. He didn't have her mobile number. It was written down in his flat and it hadn't occurred to him that he might need it.

He'd waited until one, then slept – badly – in her double bed. He'd expected to be woken by her, but she hadn't appeared, although he'd stayed there until midday. This was when he'd decided to walk over to his brother's for Sunday dinner. He'd not left a note. It was early in their relationship and he didn't want to screw things up by making her feel guilty. But he'd like to know where she'd been, whether she'd deserted him deliberately or had a screw loose and forgotten she'd given him a key along with an open invitation for a late-night visit.

*

'I've been thinking about Grandad a lot lately,' Sarah told Mum. 'I wish he'd lived to see me in the Commons.'

'I don't. Your grandad would never have voted to cut money for single mothers.'

Sarah was surprised that her mum had been following the news, and knew how she had voted. She went on.

'I'm not for scroungers. I was a single parent, but I always worked. Not everyone has the choice.'

Sarah had never thought of Mum as a single parent when she was growing up. Only recently had she begun to imagine what it must have felt like from her side, with a husband who was only ever half there, relying on her father-in-law for financial support.

'Have you seen any more of that Nick fellow?' Mum said, changing the subject. She never liked talking about Dad or Grandad, whereas she had always liked Nick. Last year, Sarah had made the mistake of telling her that he had been back in touch.

'Only briefly. I've talked to him about work a couple of times.'

'Work? I thought he was a teacher.'

'No, he's a drugs worker these days, trying to get young people off crack cocaine. I'm on the board of the place where he's based.'

'That can't pay as well as teaching.'

'No.'

'Does he have much experience in that field, drugs?'

Fuck it, Sarah thought. I am a grown woman and a government minister, there is no need for me to lie to my mother about men any more.

'Yes, he just served five years in prison for growing cannabis on a large scale and for possession of four hundred pounds' worth of cocaine.'

'I see.' That shut Mum up. She went to get the Lancashire hotpot out of the oven. It was worth the drive for the meal, if not the company. Proper hotpot, with mutton and lambs' kidneys and red cabbage baked with apple on the side – a meal that took Sarah back to childhood. She poured another glass of the very good Côtes du Rhône she'd brought with her, giving Mum a larger glass. Sarah needed to be able to drive home later. She had not stayed the night here since the eighties.

'Your father was fond of that stuff,' Mum said, putting a steaming plate in front of Sarah. 'Oh, I don't know about the cocaine, but I expect so. He tried everything else, or so he told me.'

'He smoked dope when I visited him in Spain in the eighties,' Sarah said. 'It made him – well, mellow, I suppose. More content.'

'Did he offer it to you?'

'No,' Sarah lied, then tasted a bit of crumbling potato. It was still too hot. 'And if he had, I would have refused. I did that stuff at university, a bit, but I'd long since stopped by then. I was in the police, for Christ's sake. When I first saw him with it, I thought he was trying to shock me.'

'He'd have had stronger ways than that to shock you.'

Sarah wasn't sure what Mum meant. She wasn't sure that she wanted to know.

'Anyway,' Mum went on. 'There's something I've put off telling you. Now, I don't want you to worry about this . . .'

'So this is where you live.' Nancy was waiting outside Nick's flat when he cycled home after watching the game at his brother's. He hadn't given her his address.

'How did you find me?'

'Directory enquiries. Why didn't you ring me last night?'

The truth was usually the best option. 'I didn't have your mobile number with me. But I went to yours. Where were you?'

'You don't want to know.'

'Don't I?'

'No. I'm here now.'

'You'd better come in, then.'

Once they were inside, Nancy took off her Afghan to reveal a short skirt and sheer blouse, through which he could make out every aspect of her Wonderbra. She had either dressed up for him or, more likely, she was still wearing what she went out in last night.

'Did you get any more dope?'

Nick patted the back pocket of his jeans. 'Picked some up this aft.'

'Maybe you could sort me out. Now that I've given Carl the push.'

'Maybe I can.'

'Skin up and I'll make you happy.'

Nick was still feeling vague from his pre-match smoke with Joe, but sat at the table and did as she asked. Next thing he knew, Nancy was on the floor, beneath the table, pushing his legs apart. It was a long while before they got round to smoking the joint.

Nancy had to teach the next day, so at half ten Nick walked her to the bus stop, both of them very stoned on Joe's grass.

'When can I see you again?' he asked.

'Whenever you want,' she said.

'Maybe we should do a normal date thing, like go to a movie.'

'I like going to movies,' she said. 'By about Wednesday, I've adjusted to the teaching week and can stay awake through a whole film.'

'Wednesday it is then. I'll give you a ring.'

The bus was coming. 'Okay, lover,' she said, kissing him once more.

She waved from the bus, giving him a warm buzz. This was real. He had a good job and a girlfriend most men would envy him for. If anyone had told him this a year ago, when he was still banged up and suffering from the inevitable accompanying depression, he'd have said 'dream on'. There was a TV series called *Dream On* that he used to watch before he was sent down. He hadn't thought about it for years: a surreal comedy, full of old film clips.

Nick knew that he would always have this five-year hole in his life. Prison didn't count. He hadn't grown or developed there, however much he'd read or worked out. He had closed down. Those missing years counted for nothing. In a sense, he had not long since turned thirty. Which made Nancy just the right age for him.

When he got back to the flat, the phone was ringing.

'Nick. Sorry, did I wake you?'

'Andrew! No, I just came in. It's been a while. What can I do for you?'

'I'm in Nottingham this week, thought we might have a pint. How's Wednesday?'

Not a good idea to stand up Nancy, Nick thought. 'Wednesday evening's no good. Tuesday or Thursday?'

'No, I'm just there for one night. Do you get a lunch hour? Why don't I come and see where you work, Thursday lunchtime?'

Nick gave him the address. He wasn't sure about bringing a figure from his old world into the new. But this was Andrew. He had never been able to say no to his oldest friend.

15

You seem to be losing focus, your maths teacher says. You suck at science. Your form teacher asks if anybody from social services will be coming to the parents' evening. You swear at her. Social services haven't got staff to cover parents' evenings. One time, the form teacher made the mistake of asking about your parents: like you know, or care, what happened to them. All you know is that your mother was your age, sixteen, when you were born, and twenty-three when she pissed off and you were taken into care.

Your lover wants to do it without condoms. That's how much he loves and trusts you. He knows you don't do it with dirty lads, no risk there. He doesn't want to give you a baby. He wants to give you an education.

You go to see the school nurse. She tells you where to go to get put on the pill. The safe sex clinic is on the next street to the Power Project. You're early, so you stand outside the place King runs, where Teach works. You're tempted to pretend to have a drug problem, see how they treat you. There's a lad you see sometimes says you should try acid, says it'll blow your mind. But you want to keep your mind straight so that you can pass exams. You want your lover to be proud of you so that when you can get together properly he'll want to make babies with you, to bring up a family.

You're not stupid. You know he probably has kids already. You don't want to know how many, or whether he's married to the baby mother. It doesn't matter. Nothing matters when you're with him. The doctor tells you to keep using protection for at least two weeks. He says that, after that, it might be okay to forget one day, but never two, or you'll have to use protection for the rest of your cycle. He asks you a bunch of personal questions that you answer truthfully. Sex doesn't embarrass you. Sex is something you're good at. Sex, you enjoy. Sex and study are the two things in life that you want to get right.

On the street, you see Teach. He must be leaving work.

'What are you doing round here?' he asks.

'I was looking for you,' you lie.

He offers to buy you a coffee, takes you into a place called George's where nobody gives a toss about him being with a girl in school uniform. You talk to him about school. He gives you some advice. Then you tell him about the parents' evening. You don't tell him that you've already rung him once, bottled out of leaving a message.

'Ask Alice to go,' he says. 'I'll bet she would.'

'Alice doesn't know the right questions to ask,' you tell him. 'Would you come with me?'

He gives you a funny look. Not nastily, though. Like he's confused, or moved, even. Maybe he's remembering that time you came onto him. Still, he must get that a lot. Nick might be pushing forty, but he's still got it. Today, you're trying to treat him like a dad, but you don't really know how that works.

'I know it's a lot to ask. If there was anybody else . . .'

'Tell you what,' he says. 'I'll have a word with Alice, see if she'll go. I'm not being mean. Thing is, if I go, people might get the wrong idea. But I'll brief Alice, make sure she asks the right questions.'

You try not to give him too big a smile, for you know that he doesn't want to flirt and neither do you, you're in love with someone else. Instead you thank him, hoping you sound like you mean it, because you think you do.

'You're all right.'

'I still take your money off you.'

'But you don't like doing it. And you never ask where it comes from.'

'Should I ask?'

Your eyes meet. You have a couple of lies ready, but this is not a guy you want to lie to.

'Probably not,' you say.

A light drizzle fell on the city's Lace Market. Nick was heading towards the Old Market Square when he remembered something and hurried back to the Power Project. He had left his Walkman in the drawer. Over the last couple of nights, he'd made a mix tape for Nancy. He wanted to give it her tonight. This was the first mix tape he'd made since leaving prison. Making it was, he told himself, another sign that he was getting back to his old self.

It wasn't six yet. The office was still open and Chantelle was there, flicking through the contents of a filing cabinet. When Nick breezed past, she gave him a flustered look. Nick unlocked his office. There had, inevitably given their client base, been a few thefts. Kingston had had locks fitted on all the office doors during the Christmas break.

Nick's phone rang. He had no need to answer it, but he did.

'Hi, I'm Roger Curtis from . . .' Nick didn't catch what paper the guy was from. 'Been trying to get you. I'm doing a piece on allegations about the Power Project, want to get your side of the story.'

'I'm not the . . .'

'We've had reports that workers have allowed crack cocaine to be consumed on the premises. Any comment?'

'No. I . . . uh . . .' Nick had heard similar stories. Far as he could tell, they all related to the disbanded Crack Action Team.

'You yourself have a conviction for possessing cocaine, Mr Cane. Quite a lot of the stuff. Are you clean these days?'

'Listen. I think . . .'

'I've done an interview with an underage girl, a working prostitute, who insists that she has been offered cannabis by her drugs worker, who told her that if she replaced her crack habit with a cannabis one she'd be much safer and happier. Is that official Power Project policy, Mr Cane? Do you have any comment about the quality of that advice?'

'What paper did you say you were from?'

'Perhaps we can meet and I can talk this through with you?'

Nick put on his most formal voice. 'The person you need to talk to is Kingston Bell. I'm not an official spokesperson for the Power Project, so I am not in a position to answer any of your questions.'

'Mr Bell refused to talk to me. What do you think he's trying to hide?'

'I've finished work for the day,' Nick said. 'I'm going to hang up now.'

On the way out, he told Chantelle. 'Just had some journalist on the phone, didn't say where from, sounded like he wanted to stir the shit.'

'He's been calling everyone. Hope you hung up on him.'

'Of course,' Nick said. 'Almost at once.'

She smiled in a curious way. 'See ya. Wouldn't want to be ya.'

This was a catch phrase that Nick's clients used from time to time. Must be from a song, but Nick didn't know which one. He was out of touch. He put his headphones on and left the building, tried to forget about work.

There were two things about mix tapes. The first was that the person who most enjoyed listening to them was almost always the guy who made them. The second was that by the time he gave the tape to the recipient, he would be sick of half the songs on it. Nick had tried to second guess Nancy's reaction to the songs, not get too self-indulgent. For instance, he'd chosen the Verve's 'Lucky Man' rather than 'The Drugs Don't Work', even though he liked the latter song more. He wanted a song that reminded her of the first time they slept together, but one that gave a positive message, too. 'The Drugs Don't Work' was mournful. Even the title was a downer. The single came out the day after Princess Diana died, and was all over the radio for weeks, during which time he'd tried to puzzle out its meaning.

Often, you could bend the lyrics of a song to fit your own preoccupations, but these were oblique. The words might be about watching somebody die. The drugs that didn't work were painkillers. But most illegal drugs were used to kill pain, too. Nick didn't want the mix tape to give Nancy morbid thoughts. He wanted to tell her that he was lucky to know her. Walking home, he sang along with the next track on the tape; 'The Man Who Loved Life' by the Jayhawks. He checked each lyric carefully for irony and unintended messages. A mix tape was like a love letter. Every line might be pored over for significance and sincerity. You'd better say what you meant.

Sarah was surprised when Paul Morris invited her to dinner again, so soon after their awkward Italian meal. Doubly surprised when he offered to cook for her.

'I got the feeling,' he said, as he poured tonic over her vodka, added several ice cubes and a slice of lime, 'that you don't get out much in London. You're all work, work, work.'

Was he saying that she didn't have friends here? If so, it was true.

'I do eat out in nice places when I can, but often there's some work agenda. And I don't cook, not really. Plus my kitchen in London is crap.'

'Mine's not exactly great.' Paul's place was in what, technically, might be described as lower King's Cross but would soon, she suspected, be rechristened Clerkenwell. 'I'd better just check the starter.'

Sarah wasn't sure what kind of food to expect. He returned with a tray. Four kebabs on wooden skewers. Monkfish with peppers and courgettes. A spicy dressing. A yoghurt dip. Pitta bread on the side.

'Nothing too fancy, I'm afraid, but it should go rather well with the Petit Chablis you brought.'

It did. By the time they had finished the beef stroganoff he'd made for a main course, they had got through both the Chablis and a bottle of Pinot Noir. He couldn't be trying to seduce her, Sarah thought. She was decidedly drunk and far too full. But then Paul began talking about his wife and children.

'We were only kids when we met and we had our own kids too early. It's an old story. The guy gets an education, broadens his horizons. The wife works hard, looks after the kids, doesn't change, doesn't want him to change. What would you do?'

Paul was younger than Sarah, yet he had been with Annette since before Sarah met Nick. His wife, like Paul, had a Guyanese background.

'I can't imagine,' said Sarah. 'Kids complicate things. How old are yours?'

'Youngest is ten. Oldest does GCSEs this year.'

'It sounds like you know what you have to do. Hang in there until the youngest leaves home.'

'Another eight years? That's asking a lot.'

'You've got a separate life in London now. Doesn't that make things easier? I'm guessing that you haven't been entirely faithful to Annette.'

'Why would you think that?' he murmured.

'That's a stupid question from a man who turned up in my hotel bedroom at midnight with a bottle of champagne,' she pointed out.

Paul laughed. Then his expression became serious. 'I don't mess around in Nottingham. I've seen a couple of women since I moved here in the week but nothing . . . significant happened. I took a silly risk when I came to your room that night. I'm sorry if I embarrassed you.'

'You embarrassed yourself.'

'I don't mind that. You're the sort of woman who's worth making a fool of yourself over.'

His hand squeezed hers, hard. Sarah tried to work out what signals she was sending. She wanted to come over as kind but serious, yet suspected that she was semaphoring 'randy'. 'I'm really flattered,' she said, 'and I'm not turning you down flat. But, for now, I think I'd better phone for a taxi.'

When she'd made the call, he stroked her hand.

'Are you saying that you'll only see me if I leave her?' he asked.

'I don't want to be the cause of you leaving your wife and kids.' She decided to be open with him. 'Thing is, I haven't got time for a real relationship, and I'm not sure about a fling.'

'Because you don't do flings, or because I'm married?'

'Because . . .' Sarah stood up. 'I don't know. I had a thing with a married man once. It was nice. It was useful to my career. But, afterwards, I felt dirty. I felt guilty. I don't want to feel like that again.'

'I understand.' He stood too. She let him hug her. The hug became a kiss. A lovely, long kiss. The more it went on, the more their hands roamed. Sarah wasn't feeling so full now. She could go to bed with him. It had been the best part of a year since she'd been to bed with anyone.

Outside, a taxi sounded its horn.

'Saved by the bell,' he said, and they both laughed.

He saw her to the front door. 'Next time, you won't get away so easily,' he told her.

16

Nick and Andrew met for a lunchtime drink in town.
    'I can't stand all that *what if* crap,' Nick said, describing
the romantic movie he and Nancy had seen the night before. 'It's
infantile. For people who can't face up to what's really happened.'

'"Mankind can stand only so much reality,"' Andrew quoted.
'Where's that from, *Hamlet*?'

'I think it's John Donne.'

'Odd. The ones I remember are usually Shakespeare. You sure?'

'No. Anyway, I've told you about my love life. What about
yours?'

'I continue to like them young and impressionable or older and
experienced, but discreet.'

'You mean you're still fucking married women and waitresses.'

Andrew smiled enigmatically. 'Let's talk about the place where
you're working. You said you wanted advice.'

Nick told him the background. 'I need to make a success of this
job. I'm on three months' probation with just over a month to go
and I have trouble filling my hours. It's not for want of trying.'

'Shouldn't your boss be telling you what to do?'

'He says that if users don't come in I'm meant to go and find
them.'

'Sounds like a shit job.'

'It's the best one I'm likely to get.'

'Why don't you show me the place?' Andrew asked. They were in the bar of the luxurious Lace Market Hotel, which was where Andrew was staying. He hadn't told Nick what business he had in Nottingham.

'I'd need to think of a story about who you are.'

'A potential donor.'

'I don't do fund-raising.'

'Introduce me to the boss. I'll impress him. I might kick some money his way. Or to the charity that funds the place. Long as it's tax deductible.'

The Power Project was a five-minute walk away, past St Mary's Church, through the old Lace Market, across Hockley. There was, as usual, no sign of King. Nick introduced Andrew to Chantelle and Leonard. Then they sat in Nick's small office.

'I can't see you doing this for the rest of your working life,' Andrew said, looking at the unimaginative advice posters blu-tacked to the wall. 'You want my advice, work out the real chain of command. Not the city council side of things, the drugs charity. Go to London. I can't employ you, but if you need a place to stay, there's always a room at mine.'

Nick briefly imagined himself working for a charity, living in Notting Hill instead of Nottingham.

'Drugs work's got a big future, but you want to be at the policy end, not the sharp end. How many other people in your line of work have got a good degree, a teaching qualification?'

'Nobody round here.'

'Exactly.'

'I've only been out nine months. I'm lucky to have a job.'

'Think positively. What you did wasn't wrong, just illegal. You've already turned it into a positive. You're an intelligent guy with expertise in both drugs and prisons. If you're going to stay in Nottingham, you ought to figure out how to take your boss's job. What's he like?'

'Articulate. Not particularly charismatic, but he gives off an air of authority. Borderline sanctimonious. Bit of a control freak. Doesn't like discussion or argument much, especially from me.'

'You probably make him feel insecure. I've met people like that.'

'Have you now?' The door opened. How long had King been stood outside, listening? Andrew held out his hand.

'I'm Andrew Saint, of Saint International Solutions. Nick has been showing me round. I'm considering . . .'

King ignored him. 'Did you give an interview to the *Daily Mail* on Monday?' he asked Nick, his voice frighteningly neutral.

'No. A newspaper called me, but I referred them to you.'

'And I refused to talk to them, but they sent me a copy of their article anyway, asked me to comment on it before they go to press tonight. Look!'

Nick saw exactly why his boss was so pissed off. LABOUR COUNCIL RUNS JOB SCHEME FOR DRUG DEALERS was the headline. He scanned the story. Sordid rumours, dressed up as investigative reporting, with spurious interview quotes, half of them from him: 'Cane refused to comment on his own drug use but did not deny that teenage prostitutes had been counselled to switch from crack cocaine to cannabis as it was "safer".'

'I've been stitched up,' Nick told King. 'Can we get a lawyer onto it?' As soon as the words were out of his mouth, he knew how weak they were.

'Got the money to pay a lawyer? Think you can take out an injunction to get every single copy of the paper off the streets?'

'Most of what they've written is really about the Crack Action Team, not us.'

'Why would they care about that? These guys know what they're doing. They tried to bounce me into giving them a quote or two. I'm going to spend the next two hours talking to board members when I should be with my kids at football training. Thank you for that. Oh, and you're suspended.'

Thursday night, late, he phones, tells you where to meet him. He's been drinking, you can tell when you get to the hotel. That's why he couldn't drive to pick you up. He doesn't break the law, except for one law, and you're almost legal. Will he still want you then? You've grown a cup size in the last six months. Most girls would be happy about that, but you're not. Sometimes, when you use a bed, he inspects you like he's appraising you.

After you've done it, he falls asleep. He's never fallen asleep before. Does that mean he's got more relaxed with you? Or is he just tired and drunk?

It's midnight. You have to go to school in the morning. You don't know whether to wake him or just go. Trouble is, you spent all your cash paying for the taxi here. You try to wake him, but he swears and turns over. You're in a shabby hotel on the Mansfield Road. You could walk home from here but it's dark and cold and uphill all the way. Once you get close to the hostel you'll get hassle from punters or pimps. You can't face that. So you phone a cab and reach into his wallet. The taxi will only cost a fiver. You take a tenner. If he was awake, he would give you a lot more, but you're not a thief.

You can't help looking at the contents of the wallet. Two hundred quid or so. A condom, extra strong. No photos of wife and kids, but there is a driving licence. You memorize the address, in case you ever need it.

'What are you doing?'

He's sitting up, wide awake, and suddenly you're scared of him.

'I tried to wake you. My taxi'll be here any minute. I don't have any money left.'

He gets out of bed. 'You spent all the money I gave you last time?'

'I put some in my savings account. If you keep money in the hostel, people nick it. I only need a fiver, but you haven't got anything smaller than ten. See?' You open your purse and pull out the ten you just took, show him that there's nothing else in it.

'You should have woken me.' He's not angry, just sleepy. 'Wait a mo.'

Outside, the taxi pulls up.

'I'm coming with you,' he says, and before he puts his wallet away he gives you half of the contents. 'Still taking English lessons?'

'Yeah. They're good.'

Five minutes later, you're back in Alexandra Park, sneaking into the hostel long after curfew. All the girls do it. If the wardens kicked up a fuss about dirty stop-outs, half of you would be turfed out. You could do with a shower, but it'll have to wait until morning. Doesn't matter, you feel good about yourself. He wanted you enough to see you on a weekday, to wait for you in a rented room. And now you know where he lives.

17

At least the story didn't mention Sarah. The news about her being part of the Power Project board had only been on local media. She wasn't yet on any of the project's stationery or publicity material. Kingston had left a message at her parliamentary office to warn her, but she was already on the train home so had missed it. Today, she'd had several messages from the *Nottingham Evening Post* on her machine. She returned the call from Brian Hicks, the local journalist she was most friendly with. He wanted to interview her. Today.

'We don't want to turn against the project. But it is front page news.'

'If I were you,' Sarah insisted, 'I'd have a different lead story ready.' Reluctantly, she agreed to see him later. Then, even more reluctantly, she called Nick, at work. A brisk female voice informed her that he wasn't in today.

'Is he ill, or working in the field?'

'You might find him at home,' the young woman said, coldly.

Sarah dialled his home number and let it ring a dozen times. She was about to hang up when he answered.

'I wondered if you'd call.' Nick sounded hungover.

'I tried you at work first. Why aren't you there?'

'King suspended me last night.'

'On what grounds?'

'He didn't put it on paper, but if he had "talking to the press without permission" just about covers it. Not that I actually talked to them for more than a minute. You know how the tabloids distort things.'

'I do.' Sarah was furious at Nick for letting himself be played, but chose her words carefully. 'You should have hung up rather than say anything.'

'I know, I know. I've been an idiot.'

'I'll see if I can get the suspension lifted when I talk to King. But there's a few things I need to get straight with you first.'

She ran through the *Mail* article, establishing what had been said and not said. They had nothing but gossip and hearsay, nothing dirtier than the allegations Sarah and the drugs charity's chief executive had discussed in their meetings at parliament, and found to be unsubstantiated. The demonstrable truths in the article were the drug-using backgrounds of some of the drugs workers. But that was easy to spin. This wasn't a line of work for total abstainers.

She ended the call and the phone immediately rang. Her assistant, Hugh. The *Guardian* wanted Sarah to do five hundred words for tomorrow's opinion pages about drugs policy. This was their way of both showing support and getting a news story out of her. Better there than the *Indy*, which was soft on cannabis.

'Find out what the deadline is and I'll run it by the party and the Home Office. If I can, I will. And tell them I want the standard NUJ fee donated to the Howard League for Penal Reform.'

She rang the Power Project again, got the same woman. This time, she told her who she was. 'Tell Kingston I'm on my way over. I want to meet him in fifteen minutes.'

'He's not here at the moment.'

'Then you'd better find him.'

*

By dinner time it was sorted. The *Evening Post* would run a sympathetic story the next day. A complaint had been made to the Press Council, which would clip the *Mail*'s wings should they be tempted to run more scurrilous nonsense. Kingston Bell had agreed that his instinctive suspension of Nick Cane was not in the project's best interests. Luckily, the suspension had not been leaked to the media. The punishment had been withdrawn and would not appear on Nick's employment record. All staff would receive immediate training on media liaison issues. The next board meeting would take place three weeks early, at a date on which Sarah was able to attend.

Sarah had had to cancel several of her planned meetings for the day. Rescheduling them would cut into her red box time on Sunday. She'd hoped to find time to drive to Chesterfield, visit Mum, who was about to go into the Royal Infirmary for her exploratory operation. She'd have to ring her instead. Mum said she wasn't worried. She didn't like it when Sarah tried to play the dutiful daughter. So Sarah rarely did. But she mustn't forget to ring.

She took one more look at the tabloid before she threw it in the bin. The photo they had of Nick was an old one, probably from his trial. His eyes looked shifty. At least her relationship with him hadn't come out. If the *Mail* had got on to that, they would have had a field day.

Sarah wondered whether she should tell the Home Secretary about having given a former lover a reference for a sensitive job. It hadn't occurred to her at the time that it *was* a sensitive job. Naive, naive, naive. Too late to bring it up now without making herself look weak or, worse, stupid and unprofessional. Almost as stupid as letting Paul Morris talk her into joining the board at a time when she was too busy being a minister to give the project enough focused attention.

Paul. He would be in Nottingham. She could legitimately call him for advice about how to deal with the media situation. She would like to see him again. Perhaps she could invite him round. She'd told him that her cooking wasn't up to much, so he'd understand that she only had one thing on her mind. That, too, would look weak. But sometimes you had to give in to your weaknesses.

Jerry phoned Nick to ask if he could fit in an extra lesson. She must be flush, he thought, glad to have something to take his mind off yesterday's train wreck, to cycle to Alexandra Park on a cold but clear Saturday afternoon. He chose his route carefully to avoid the steepest part of Woodborough Road. This involved turning off Alfreton Road, where his flat was, onto Forest Road, which he followed for its full length, past the recreation ground and cemetery on his left. He cycled through the red-light zone, which was quiet at this time of day. The women he saw were seasoned, in their twenties and older, not the young crack addicts who tended to appear after dark.

There had been a purge on kerb crawlers recently, their names listed in the *Evening Post*. A Crown Court judge, two university lecturers, the manager of one of the city's most popular department stores. It didn't seem to have had an effect on business, though. The girls stood on Forest Road, at the end of side streets they could disappear down if they saw someone they wanted to avoid. Nick couldn't imagine paying for sex but, in prison, he'd met plenty of men who did. For them, sex had to be dirty and anonymous. The more sordid, the better.

For Nick, sex was something to celebrate, at the heart of a life lived well. Inside, that first year, he'd often fantasized about Nancy. Now that he was sleeping with her, he ought to be happy, even if his past life was all over some scummy tabloid. Nancy didn't care. She'd rung him last night to tell him as much, drunk after 'a night out with the girls'. He'd been the subject of discussion in the staff room all day, she told him.

'Did you mention that you were going out with me?'

'Are you kidding? I never let anyone there know anything about my private life. Whatever you say leaks like a sieve, ends up reaching the kids.'

'Were the kids talking about it?'

'No. The story didn't mention the school. You're ancient history. The only ones you and I taught when we job-shared are in the upper sixth now. I'll tell you one funny thing, though. Remember Eve Shipton?'

'Of course.' Eve was the head of English when Nick taught there. 'How is she?'

'She seems okay. Don't see her as much as I used to since she was promoted to deputy head. She remarried while you were away, a nice guy. Anyway, she confided in me when it was just the two of us. Said she always liked you, hoped that this story in the paper wasn't going to set you back.'

'Did you tell her you'd seen me?'

'I told her you'd asked for some help with the syllabus for your private tuition. She asked me to give you her best if you got in touch again. I got the feeling that she used to have a thing for you. I thought you'd like to know that you're still a hit with the middle-aged mums.'

Eve would be about fifty now, her kids starting university. Seven years ago, as his boss, she'd allowed him to negotiate a job-share. That was after he'd found the caves beneath his flat in the Park, was working all hours setting up a cannabis factory. He'd had to make up some crap about wanting the extra time to write. He wasn't sure that Eve had believed him.

Eve was a handsome woman who had lost confidence in her allure. After her husband left, she was lonely, and Nick had escorted her to the pictures a couple of times, foreign flicks at Broadway. One night, seeing her back to her car, he'd tried to give her a peck on the cheek good night. The kiss hit her mouth instead of just to the side, and he was surprised to find she'd left her lips more than a little open.

They kept the affair secret at school. Eve was another reason why Nick made no move on Nancy when they worked together. His lover would have known. Eve used to tease Nick about Nancy's crush on him.

It was she who brought an end to the affair. Possibly she sensed that Nick was getting out of control. He was doing too much coke at the time, though never around her. Officially her rationale was that she had begun to date a guy her own age and might decide to sleep with him. Of all the break-ups that Nick had had, this was the most civilized. He wondered what Eve looked like now.

Perhaps because of the kerb-crawler crackdown, some working girls had moved further down Mapperley Road, near to Alexandra Park. Nick cycled past a girl Jerry's age or younger, wearing fishnet stockings and crudely applied bright red lipstick. Something occurred to Nick, something so blindingly obvious that he should have thought of it weeks ago, when he first got the Power Project job. An opportunity.

At the hostel, Alice was pleased to see him. They talked a bit about Jerry's parents' evening, which she had been to at his request.

'What day are you at the drop-in centre this week?' she asked.

'I'm not. Keeping my head down.'

'Why?' Alice asked.

He was relieved that not everybody had read the story about him. 'You don't want to know. But can I ask you something? Would it be okay for me to talk to some of the girls here about drug issues? I'm not saying you've got a huge problem or anything, just for my work.'

Alice gave a wry smile. 'Glad to hear we only have a normal-sized problem.'

'I'm having trouble getting young people to come into the Power Project, and it's them we're most meant to help. If I could talk to some of the girls here, it would really help me meet my targets.'

'You're just offering advice, right? Counselling, like you do with me at the drop-in centre?'

'Yeah.' Nick began to think aloud. 'But more informally. I could just say that I'll be available at certain times and anything said will be in complete confidence. How does that sound?'

'I don't have a problem with it. I'll mention it to the other wardens at the weekly meeting on Monday if you like.'

'That'd be terrific. Want me to come to the meeting?'

'Couldn't hurt.'

That would give Nick more time to work out his ideas. Until now, he had kept his work with private pupils separate from his drugs job. But there was no reason why they couldn't connect.

Nick and Jerry spent an hour talking about Shakespeare, then she told him about what the teachers had said at parents' evening.

'Alice played a blinder. She asked some good questions. They reckon I might get seven GCSEs at C or above.'

'That's great.' Nick told her about his new scheme. 'Do you think you could mention it to some of the other girls, tell them I'm all right?'

'S'pose. But you know most of the others think I'm super straight cos I only smoke a bit of weed. Half of them will take anything going.'

'Tell them I'm not there to make them stop taking anything, just to offer advice on how to tell if their drug use is turning into a problem.'

'They might be cool with that.'

Nick realized he was doing exactly what the *Daily Mail* had accused the Power Project of doing. Because it was the right thing to do.

18

Sunday night and he's back. You meet him late on, get into his four-by-four. Seats down, side lane; he hasn't got long before he has to get back to his wife and kids.

'Missed you, babe.'

'I missed you, too,' you tell him. 'Let me show you how much.'

'Wait.' His phone is ringing. You listen to him do business. He doesn't try to hide stuff from you any more. It's all about weights, transport, distribution. When he's done, he talks while you suck him, says that when you finish university you can work for him if you want.

'One day the government will get wise, legalize drugs and tax the fuck out of them. Until then, there are fortunes to be had. Make sure you get a language or two. Dutch would be good. Most of them speak English, but it's useful to know what they're up to when they talk among themselves.'

You say you will.

'How are the English lessons going?'

'Good. Teach came round yesterday after I rang him. He said I was doing really well with Shakespeare.'

'You like him a lot, this guy?'

'He treats me like an equal.' Your lover frowns, so you add, 'But there's no funny stuff. He's never made a move . . . that way.' You don't say that he once turned you down. 'He's nice, is all.'

'Men are only nice to you if they want something. Remember that.'

On Sunday afternoons and evenings, Nancy did preparation and marking for the teaching week ahead. She didn't want to eat with Nick's brother and sister-in-law, who kept inviting her. She didn't want Nick at hers, either.

After dinner at Joe and Caroline's, then the football, Nick cycled to the drop-in centre near the train station. He wasn't due to do a shift. Since starting at the Power Project he'd cut down the number of nights he volunteered. Tonight, though, he was at a loose end, and an extra body was always welcome.

Sundays were interesting. Less underclass, more of the amorphous middle class looking to work out how to get through the long week ahead. Alice was among them. She had been clean of hard drugs for several weeks: no relapses this year.

'Completely clean or are you using other substances?' he asked her, after the usual small talk.

'A bit of spliff. A lot of vodka and fags.'

'You're doing great.'

'Keep telling me that. We're short staffed. I've got to do four twelve-hour shifts this week. Even one five-pound bag would make them a lot easier to get through. And I ask myself, where's the harm? Lots of people manage a habit their whole lives.'

'They manage it until they don't manage any more, or they get a batch that's way stronger than they're used to and they OD.'

Alice gave him a dismissive look, as if to say, *this is me you're talking to.*

'Okay, let's say you're right, and some people manage a smack habit their whole lives. They enhance their lives with a weekend fix or three. But you're not like that. You keep shooting up until it's gone and then you want more. It's called an addictive personality.'

'Have you got one of those too?' Alice asked.

'I managed okay without the booze in prison. Giving up weed was harder but I did it, rather than lose remission.'

Alice pointed at the cigarette in Nick's hand.

'One day, cigarettes will have to go, too, but I've cut down. Ten a day.' And a half-ounce of tobacco for his spliffs, but he didn't mention that.

She stood up to go. 'When are you next at the hostel?'

'Seeing Jerry on Saturday.'

'I'm on shift then, drop in and have a brew with me.'

'I'll walk you out,' Nick said. He let the co-ordinator know he was going, then saw Alice to her bus stop. On the way, he made a small confession. 'I mentioned that I might be doing those drug advice sessions to Jerry, so she could prime some of the other girls. I hope that was all right.'

Alice didn't seem to think he'd gone behind her back. 'I hadn't forgotten,' she half apologized. 'Tomorrow I'll check with the others. But if some of them are away, it becomes my decision, and I'll say yes.'

He thanked her, then asked something that had been on his mind. 'Where do they get the stuff, your girls? Dealers, boyfriends, pimps?'

'All three are the same people,' Alice told him. 'For someone who spent five years inside, you can be quite naive sometimes.'

Nick stopped off at the Peacock on his way home. The pub used to be his regular haunt, back when he was a young teacher with a Labour party membership card. He'd only been back once since getting out. That night he'd been snubbed by a couple of people he used to know well and felt out of place. But that was on a weekday night. This evening he was unlikely to know anyone, and fancied a decent pint before he went back to his cold flat.

Nick took a quick look in the public bar. It was nearly deserted. He headed into the lounge and ordered himself a pint of Home's bitter.

'Nick! Haven't seen you for a while. Won't you join me?'

It was Tony Bax, who used to be – maybe still was – chair of the Nottingham West Labour party. They had only met briefly since Nick's release and Tony, too, was on his own. This was a chance to catch up.

'What brings you this way?'

'I do a bit of volunteering at this drop-in centre down by the station.'

'I know where you mean. Good for you.'

Tony was twenty years older than Nick, but they had always got on well. Nick discovered that Tony's wife had died a couple of years ago. Breast cancer. He offered his condolences. He told Tony about his job, being turned over by the *Daily Mail*, and a little about his time in prison. By their third pint, Nick was getting the older man's frank assessment of Sarah's performance as an MP.

'She's a fast learner, but she's also a workaholic. She'll have spent all day doing her Home Office boxes. I doubt the woman has a social life. You used to be friendly with her, yes?'

'At university.' This was the line that he stuck to. Apart from his brother and Andrew, there weren't any people left in Nick's life who knew that he and Sarah had lived together for the best part of two years. Nick meant to keep it that way.

'What side of the party was she on then?'

'No side. It was student politics. We weren't Marxists or in a faction like Socialist Organizer. I suppose you'd say we were on the Bennite left.'

'Most of us were. Did she have a lot of friends at uni?'

'There were always people around because of the campaign, and then with her being president. I didn't know her before. Why do you ask?'

'You know what they say: it's useful for politicians to have a hinterland.'

That's right, Nick thought. I used to be her hinterland.

Pubs closed early on Sundays, at half ten. The two men walked up Mansfield Road until they got to the top of the hill, where they went in different directions.

'I'm glad to hear you're at the Power Project,' Tony said, in parting. 'There are quite a few people talking the place down. They think Bell's lightweight. Good to know that there's someone we trust there.'

Nick walked along Forest Road with a pleasant buzz of belonging. He knew how King would hear Tony's use of the word 'we'. White people had one of their own inside. But the 'we' that Nick heard was different. It was an Old Labour, socially committed 'we'. The 'we' that thought it understood the way the world worked and wanted to make it work more fairly.

This weekend, Nick had made a start at turning his job into something that made sense. Tonight, his only regret was that he didn't have Nancy to go home to. A taxi approached and he considered flagging it down, showing up at hers as a late-night surprise. But he didn't want to push things. It was nearly eleven. She might already be asleep. He turned left onto Alfreton Road and into the unlit side passage beneath his flat. Getting out his keys, he anticipated the joint he would have when he got in, accompanied perhaps by a whisky. Just a small one: he didn't want to be hungover tomorrow.

The first blow, to the back of his head, caught him by surprise. The second left him on the hard dirty ground. Then the kicking began. He managed to cover his head. His attacker didn't speak, but went about his job thoroughly, until every part of Nick's body cried out with pain. He was left spread crooked across the concrete, barely conscious and desperately cold.

19

Sarah decided to visit the Power Project before she caught her Monday train to London. The receptionist, an attractive woman with cheap clothes but designer glasses, seemed to recognize her.

'King isn't in yet. Shall I give him a ring on his mobile?'

'No need. I'd like to see Nick Cane first. Is he here?'

She wanted to make sure that Nick's suspension had been lifted, as promised.

'I'm not sure.' She rang his office. Sarah could hear his phone ringing from the reception area. No reply.

'Sorry,' the receptionist said.

'Is there anyone in, apart from you?' Sarah asked.

Her silence said it all. Sarah looked at her watch. If she walked briskly, she could make the ten twenty-eight to St Pancras. She left without another word.

At the Home Office, Sarah checked her diary for the week. In addition to her usual round of ministerial meetings, paperwork and briefings, she had to answer questions in the House, a monthly task that required careful preparation. On Wednesday, before Prime Minister's Question Time, she was to meet the Prison

Governors Association. On Thursday it was Stonewall, the gay rights organization. They would want to know when she was going to act on her campaign to allow condoms in prison, to reduce the spread of HIV.

Sarah had undertaken that campaign in the last parliament, when she was in opposition, before she became a junior minister. The issue featured nowhere in Labour's manifesto. Stonewall would have to accept that, while Sarah remained committed, the time wasn't right to implement a move that would be too much of a challenge to people's prejudices. She might mention President Clinton's gaffe in legalizing homosexuality in the army too early on in his presidency. The resultant furore had cost him a lot of his political capital. Their time would come, Sarah intended to argue. She was in the right job to make it happen.

A knock on her door.

'Come in.'

Paul Morris stood there, grinning.

'What are you doing here?'

'I had a meeting.'

She knew that Paul had a special adviser role at the Home Office, but he was always cagey about which department he was advising. Assuming he'd had to sign the Official Secrets Act, she'd never pressed him about it.

'I left a message inviting you to dinner the other day.'

'I was confused by it. I thought you couldn't cook.'

'More likely I told you that I *don't* cook. As a rule. But I can cook, as you would have found out, if you'd returned my message.'

'I'm sorry. I've been really backed up. I still am, for a week or two. But I've got my diary on me. Why don't we fix a date?'

They arranged for him to come round on the first Wednesday of February. There was a sparkle in his eyes that told her he knew this really was a date. Despite her scruples, he was on a promise. Sarah returned to her paperwork pile. At least, now, she had something to look forward to.

The police decided to treat the assault on Nick as the random mugging of a drunk on his way home. Not just a drunk, but an ex-con. They discounted Nick's being relatively sober and not having been robbed. The Queen's Medical Centre wanted to keep him in for a day, then sign him off work for a couple of weeks. He had a cracked rib, and bruises all over his body, but it was the effects of exposure that the doctors were most worried about. He had not been found until three in the morning, when a passing student heard him moaning and dialled 999.

The hospital, at Nick's request, phoned his girlfriend and his brother, but it was his sister-in-law, Caroline, who came first, baby in arms.

'Joe's on an airport run,' she explained, 'but he sends his best. We've agreed you must come and stay with us until you're feeling well.'

Nick thanked her without actually accepting the offer. He asked her to ring work, let them know he'd be off for a fortnight.

'Who did it?' Caroline asked, after he had told her the full story. 'Don't tell me it was a jealous husband.'

'No.' Not surprising she should ask that, given Joe's record, but Nick had never knowingly cuckolded anyone. 'The guy didn't say anything, but he was waiting for me. I suspect it had something to do with my job.'

'How come?'

Nick didn't know the answer to this. What had changed in the last week that might have resulted in somebody attacking him? He'd been pilloried in the *Daily Mail*. He'd arranged to see teenage drug users, some of whom, doubtless, had pimps.

'I wish I knew,' was all he said.

'You must have an idea.'

'Another visitor for you,' a nurse interrupted, and they were joined by Nancy. Nick watched the two women sizing each other up. Nancy had been home after work and changed. She wore a short pleated skirt and black boots with heels that made her taller than Caroline. Beneath her expensive black leather jacket was a figure-hugging cashmere sweater. Caroline was still in her teaching get-up: practical trousers and a sweater over a prim, dark blouse. Her long hair was tied back.

'Nick's coming to stay with us for a few days when he gets out tomorrow,' Caroline announced. Nick hoped that Nancy would challenge this, make her own offer. But all she said was, 'That's very good of you.'

'It's what family do,' Caroline said. 'I'll go and make that phone call to your work, Nick.'

When she was gone, Nancy leaned into the bed and gave him a full-on kiss. 'At least he didn't damage your face,' she said.

'He tried.' Nick gave an abridged version of the account he had given Caroline, and the police. Already he was tired of the story. He would get over it.

Caroline returned. 'I spoke to someone called Chantelle. I didn't much like the sound of her. She gave me a *this is probably bullshit but I don't give a damn* attitude. Then she remembered to tell me that Sarah Bone came looking for you this morning. Evidently your boss wasn't best pleased that you weren't there to greet her.'

'I'll bet he wasn't in either.'

'That was the impression she gave me.'

'Nice to see you boys all jump for a powerful woman,' Nancy commented.

'Sarah certainly used to make Nick jump,' Caroline said, and Nancy gave one of her funny little frowns. Nick knew that frown well, from his earliest mentor sessions with her. It meant that she was connecting dots.

Phoebe began to cry. 'Better go,' Caroline said. 'Joe will give the hospital a ring in the morning, find out when it's okay to bring you home.'

'Appreciate it,' Nick told her. 'If you're sure it's . . .'

'I'm sure.' Caroline hugged him, then nodded at Nancy. 'Nice to meet you.'

'So,' Nancy said, when Caroline was gone. 'You and Sarah Bone. How long ago was that?'

'Fifteen years. We were friends at uni.' He faked a chuckle. 'Good friends.'

Nancy smiled and slid a hand beneath the covers to stroke him. 'Fifteen years ago I can cope with,' she said. 'Though, now I think about it, I was just about ready for you when I was fourteen. I was an early starter.'

'And I was a late starter,' Nick said. 'You'd have probably scared the life out of me.'

She laughed and kissed him. Crisis averted. Then he had to push her away. His ribs were beginning to ache again and he needed more morphine.

20

'No, I don't support the bombing of Iraq!' Sarah told Paul Morris over dinner. 'But I'm a member of the government. I have to vote for things I don't agree with. Anyway, I didn't vote in that division. I was visiting prisons in Scotland.'

'Very convenient,' Paul said, pouring her a second glass.

'It saved me a lot of bother in the constituency. We've been bombing the relatives of some of my constituents. I mean, I accept that Saddam is an evil man, but we can't go round the world invading regimes that mistreat their own people. Where would it end?'

'And who decides who is evil?' Paul asked.

In the case of the Iraqi dictator, Sarah thought the issues were fairly clear-cut, but she had decided to go to bed with Paul tonight and wanted to agree with him as much as she could. She murmured, 'Exactly.'

Paul asked after her mum, who was in hospital. Sarah had visited her at the weekend.

'They found something and they're waiting for the biopsy results. It looks like it's cancer, but they've caught it early. It should be operable. I wish the NHS worked more quickly. She puts on a brave face, but . . .'

Paul squeezed her hand. 'You must be worried sick.'

'Yeah, well . . .' She changed the subject. 'How's your new job?'

'I thought you might have invited me round to discuss the Power Project,' Paul said, pushing aside the last of his Harrods chicken kiev.

Sarah had a meeting about the project later that week. She had scheduled half an hour with Suraj Hanspal, the head of the charity that provided its main funding. She sensed trouble, but didn't want to involve Paul.

'I invited you round because I owed you dinner and I fancied your company. There is one thing I wanted to know about the Power Project, though. Who came up with the absurd name?'

'I did,' Paul admitted, with a wry laugh.

'What were you trying to ape, the Manhattan Project?'

'The Crack Action Team was a million times worse. It sounded like the SAS. By the way, there was something I wanted to tell you.'

What now? Sarah regretted joining the project board. It was one piece of bad news after another.

'I'm not going to be in Nottingham much from now on, except to visit the kids. I wanted to hang in there, but things have got too strained for Annette. We've agreed to go for a legal separation.'

Sarah had been sort of hoping to hear this, but was careful to make light of the announcement. 'I'm sorry you and Annette have decided to call it a day. I know it's been a long time coming.'

'I'm not sure Annette realized until recently,' Paul confessed, and she felt sorry for him. She reached across the table and held his hand. He lifted her hand to his lips and kissed her fingers softly, near the nails.

'You've been very patient with me,' he said.

'You've been patient, too,' she told him. 'But you don't have to be patient any longer.'

*

The doorbell rang around four on Thursday, just as it was getting dark. Nick, still in his dressing gown, struggled to the door. He'd been back in the flat for a couple of days, but hadn't returned to work. A call from Kingston had indicated that it would be in everybody's interest if he kept his head down for a while.

Nick thought it would be Nancy. She hadn't visited him during the week he was at Joe and Caroline's. He had left a message saying he was back home and he knew that her school day finished twenty minutes ago.

It wasn't Nancy, but Jerry. She was still in school uniform.

'How did you find me?' he asked.

'Your address is next to your number in the phone book.'

'Oh. Right.'

'You don't mind me coming, do you? Only I checked at the Power Project and they said you were off sick. I've been round a couple of times. This is the first time I've found you home.'

'I was staying at my brother's before,' Nick explained.

'Some of the girls were asking when you were going to talk to them,' Jerry said, after making them both a brew. 'I told them what a cool guy you are, how you'd done time for growing dope, got them interested.'

'Sorry I couldn't come when I said.' Nick and Jerry had never discussed his time in prison. He'd hinted at having been in trouble to explain why he was no longer a school teacher. 'You saw the story in the newspaper?'

''Fraid so.'

'I should start work again next week. How about I come round Sunday?'

'Not a good day. A lot of them are busy. Monday's better.'

Busy turning tricks? Nick didn't ask. 'What book have you brought with you?'

'*Great Expectations*. Have you read it? I'll bet you have.'

'I've taught it a couple of times, but I don't have my notes here. We could have a general chat, then arrange a proper session?'

'Sounds like a plan.' She handed him the book and Nick opened it at the first page.

'Why don't I read a bit to you? Get us both into the story.'

There was always something that caught him unawares when rereading Dickens. The second paragraph contained a line he'd forgotten: the 'five little stone lozenges, each about a foot and a half long' that marked the graves of Pip's five brothers, who had died in infancy. This matter-of-factness moved him, but Jerry did not seem to react to it. When he'd finished the chapter, they talked for a while about the way that it was written, and the things that fear could make people do. Then there was a light, familiar knock on the door.

While Teach is answering the door, your phone vibrates.

You check the message. It's him. He wants to see you. Now. You think about it for a moment then text back, saying where you are. You'll wait on the corner, just down the road. He replies that that's okay. Ten minutes. Teach returns with a woman in tow.

She's thirty or so. Tarty, but not in too obvious a way. Plenty of make-up, push-up bra, skirt shorter than yours, despite it being frozen outside. She stares daggers for a second, but softens when he introduces you, makes fake conversation, says a couple of smart things about Dickens.

'I'll bet you're a teacher too,' you say.

'For my sins,' she tells you. 'Nick and I used to work together.'

'Is that right?' You take an instant dislike to her. There's something phoney about her voice, strained. 'How long have you two been together?'

This kind of direct question throws her. You are good at throwing teachers, keeping them on their toes.

'Not long,' she says, with a sigh that suggests they're in the first flush of love and she can't wait to get rid of you so she can take Teach to bed.

'Gotta go.'

'There's no need,' Teach says. 'We still have a chapter to talk through.'

'I got a text while you were at the door,' you explain, holding up the phone. 'I have to meet someone. It's okay, I'll pay for the full lesson.'

'It was hardly a lesson.'

'I've been here half an hour.' You compromise on giving him a tenner and arrange to meet on Monday, before he sees the other girls at the hostel. When you reach the bottom of the steps, you see that your lover is already there, illegally parked outside the locksmith's, instead of the pub where you told him to wait.

'How did you know where I'd be?' you ask him.

'I know everything,' he says.

You believe him.

'Come to bed,' Nancy said.

'Wait.' Nick looked down at the street. Jerry was below, getting into a four-by-four. It might be the one that Kingston drove. Nick couldn't make out the driver, or the licence plates. A lot of people drove cars like that. Andrew Saint had one. Nancy pulled him away from the window.

'It's a trick, isn't it?'

'I suspect so.'

'The way she put that money on the table, I could tell. She's used to getting paid for services rendered.'

'I guess.' Nick remembered what Alice had told him about Jerry. A boyfriend, maybe, not a pimp.

'You're not fucking her, are you? Taking payment in kind?'

'I . . .'

Nancy put a finger to his lips and unzipped his fly. 'Nobody said you had to be exclusive. She's a very pretty girl. But don't get caught. And, remember, there are things that only an experienced woman can do well.'

He'd assumed that Nancy expected him to be faithful. He should know by now that, where sex was concerned, few people were consistent. Nick wasn't like his brother. He'd never cheated on a woman who he'd been in a serious relationship with, not unless you counted the overlap when it was nearly over. But maybe that was cowardly. Men weren't made to be monogamous, he told himself, as they undressed. And neither, Nancy was implying, were some women.

'In retrospect,' Suraj Hanspal told Sarah in her parliamentary office, 'we made a mistake in opening the Power Project so quickly. We thought that a clean replacement organization would minimize the fallout from the CAT fiasco, but people are confusing the two, tarring both with the same brush.'

'We can hardly close the place down because of tabloid lies,' Sarah said.

Suraj didn't reply at once. This was exactly what he was suggesting. 'Failure to renew funding is not the same as closing something down.'

'It's exactly the same,' Sarah said. Would she be so concerned if the project's closure didn't mean putting Nick out of a job? The bad publicity was tarnishing the charity's image. No wonder they wanted rid. 'What about the drug users that the project supports?'

'We don't have reliable evidence that the project is helping a significant number of users,' Suraj said. 'It takes a supposedly enlightened approach, but perhaps it's too enlightened. Ultimately the message has to be based on a condemnation of all drugs use.'

'Legal drugs included?'

'Well . . .' Suraj hesitated and Sarah seized on his moment of weakness.

'Tobacco, alcohol, painkillers, pick-me-ups . . . people are addicted to all kinds to get them through the day. We can't make them all illegal. Or. Wait. Maybe we can. But the government will lose an awful lot of tax revenue if we do.'

Suraj spread his hands in a gesture of defeat. 'Surely you, more than anyone else on the board, recognize the political realities we face.'

'You're right. I'm sorry.' Sarah paused. 'Why don't we compromise? Ask the city to hold back a decision on the next funding stream, see how it goes for a few weeks. Then, after the budget next month, if we decide to let the project run down, we can bury the decision underneath all the good news that the Chancellor of the Exchequer will have for local councils.'

'I'm glad we're agreed.' Suraj stood and shook her hand. 'Most of the workers are on six-month contracts so, on that timescale, we won't need to give notice. Kingston, of course, is on secondment from his council job.'

At a huge bump in pay, as Sarah recalled. 'Yes,' she said. 'It was very good of him to help us out.'

Suraj, happy with their agreement, couldn't get out of the office quickly enough. Sarah had effectively co-signed the death warrant for the Power Project. Nick, having been featured across the *Daily Mail*, would take much of the blame. Unless she could find a way to help him, to change the operation's reputation. Only one person she knew could help with that. Luckily for Nick, she had just started sleeping with him.

21

Nick sat in a circle with five teenage girls, all of them smoking. *Neighbours* was on TV, with the sound muted. Shaz, a scrawny kid who had already boasted about how much she made for her pimp, shared her theory about Nick.

'You're the guy who's screwing Jerry, aren't you? We've been trying to work it out for months.'

Nick had told them that the discussion was no holds barred. Nothing they said would leave the room. He smiled patiently. It was a few years since he'd had a bunch of teenagers interested in his private life.

'Not me, sorry.'

'She talks about you,' said Shaz. 'You're the prime suspect.'

'I used to watch that on TV. Helen Mirren, she's my kind of woman.'

'She's rough as!' Pamela interjected. 'And she's an alky.'

'Is she?' Nick had seen the first two series at the start of the decade, but the story must have moved on while he was away. At least the comment gave him room to open a discussion. 'What makes someone an alky, then? How much do they have to drink?'

'It's not how much, is it?' Kim said. 'It's how often.'

'At least half a bottle a day,' Shaz said.

'Half a bottle of what?' Nick asked.

The girls mostly drank cider, which they said was better value than lager and got you drunk quicker. They all knew lads who overdid the Special Brew or vodka. Pamela reckoned the biggest problems came when you combined booze with other drugs. Speed and booze made lads mental, they agreed. If you were doing crack, you weren't bothered about drinking, you just wanted another rock.

'Except for the comedown,' Kim proffered, lighting another JPS. 'My dad didn't have a booze problem until he started smoking crack. But then he couldn't sleep unless he'd had half a bottle of Scotch in him.'

'Everyone knows you need smack to come down off crack,' Shaz said.

'How old's your dad, Kim?'

'He were thirty-two when he died. Cirrhosis of the liver.'

Gradually, he got them to discuss their own drug use. None of them had a problem, that much they were very clear on. Pamela did 'favours' for her boyfriend, Jem, but he wasn't a pimp, not like Shaz's Beany, who ran three girls. Still, Shaz was the youngest, and his favourite. She was cool with that.

The girls didn't buy dope or crack directly themselves; their blokes did it for them. If they bought, they might get ripped off. None of them admitted to trying heroin, but Nick suspected that, if he got a couple of them on their own, he would find out that they'd chased the dragon.

'What about you?' Teri wanted to know. She had been the quietest up to now. 'I heard you were in the paper. Said you're a cokehead.'

Nick tried to divert the question. 'Do you girls ever take coke?'

'Powder costs a fortune,' Shaz said. 'It's for rich people.'

'Are you rich?' Teri asked him.

'I was loaded for a while,' Nick said. 'Can't say I spent it wisely.'

'So you were a cokehead!' Shaz said, with a cackle. 'Jerry might be straight but she's going out with a cokehead!'

'I'm not . . .' Nick was going to say 'going out with Jerry', but teachers didn't dignify rumours by discussing them and he still felt like a teacher among these girls. He wasn't sure where to take the conversation. It was too early to get any of them to tell him that their drug use was causing them problems. That area was better addressed in a one-on-one anyway. 'Shit,' he said. 'Look at the time. Listen, did you guys find this afternoon interesting? Want to do it again?'

They agreed to continue in a week's time. Nick said he'd be there half an hour earlier, in case any of them wanted to talk to him in private.

'How did it go?' Alice asked afterwards.

'Okay, I think. You've got some real characters in there.'

'Tell me about it.'

'Thanks for your help, setting it up. Can I buy you a drink?'

'No pubs round here,' Alice pointed out. 'We could join the girls, buy a two-litre bottle of Bulmers and sit on a wall up the road.'

'Bit cold this time of year.'

'Jerry told me she met your girlfriend.'

'She did, yes.'

'Go on home to her, then,' Alice told him, her voice more plaintive than bitter. 'You've done your duty with the druggies today.'

Nick headed out into the cold winter rain, cycling against the wind. He could go to Nancy's but he always ended up getting hammered with her, and he had a big meeting with Kingston in the morning. He would see if his brother fancied a quiet couple of pints instead.

Paul brought Sarah coffee in bed. They were at his King's Cross flat. It was the morning after the first time that Sarah had spent the night there. Paul did not make any moves to suggest an encore of last night's love-making. Sarah's mind, inevitably on a day when she had to be at the Home Office soon, drifted to work issues that they had in common.

'About the Power Project . . .'

'Let it go,' Paul told Sarah. 'We did our duty by the place, but it was too soon.'

'That's all very well for you to say,' Sarah told him. 'You're not on the board any more.'

Now was not the time to tell a new lover that she couldn't let it go because she wanted to protect a former lover. This was an affair, not a fully fledged relationship. Secrets were allowed. He stroked her hair.

'There won't be a board for much longer. Look, I'm sorry I talked you into joining it. Truth is, that night, I wanted an excuse to see you. When I showed up in your room and Eric was there, you can't begin to imagine what went through my mind . . .'

'I'm sure I can.'

They both laughed. Paul kissed her, then went for a shower. She was not going to fall in love with Paul, she told herself. She was going to have fun. They had been together for a week and had already, casually but definitively, agreed the terms of their relationship. They would spend one or two nights a week together, but not in public. As far as possible, they would steer clear of each other in Nottingham.

Paul assured her that, he and Annette having separated, there was nobody else in his life. He was almost as busy with work as she was, so the arrangement suited him as well as it did her. Sarah thought she had found the perfect relationship for a junior Home Office minister. Paul was the best-looking man she'd been out with since Nick. One day, maybe, after he was divorced, she'd be happy to have him seen on her arm. But that day was a long way off.

They caught separate taxis to the Home Office. Paul ran an unpublicized policy unit on updating drugs laws. He reported directly to the Home Secretary. As did Sarah. Today she had to formulate the government's response to an EC recommendation that prisoners should be paid real wages for the work they did inside. It was an issue that enraged the kind of voters Labour needed to keep onside if they were to win a second term.

Sarah didn't think prisons should be work camps. That said, only idiots believed that governments profited by having men sew mail bags or assemble cheap radios. Each prison place cost more than several new nurses. Any money paid to prisoners came out of some other budget. The point about work in prison was that it kept dissent down and aided rehabilitation. Occasionally it qualified prisoners to do certain jobs when they got out. Pay for work was an important part of the rehabilitation process but she didn't believe in equal rights for prisoners. There were murmurs from human rights groups that prisoners ought to be allowed the vote. In some countries, that was already happening. Over her dead body.

Sarah wasn't at her best in the Commons that afternoon. Mum had phoned to say that she had a date for her operation. It was still weeks away and she sounded scared. Sarah wasn't used to hearing her that way. At Home Office questions, she had trouble concentrating, gave only an anodyne response to a question about wages in prisons.

'We are committed to fairness and rehabilitation, but we have vowed to stay within the spending limits set by the previous administration and I will not be making any new commitments in the immediate future.'

Then came the question that she had been expecting, one that she had already answered twice, in different forms, when it was asked by opposition MPs anxious to trip her up. This time, however, it came from one of her own, Ali Blythe. In her preamble, Ali reminded the minister that her constituency included one of the biggest prisons in the Midlands.

'Which I hope she will visit at her earliest convenience to see at first-hand some of the problems created by overcrowding, by underfunding, by the medieval slopping-out system and by desperately low morale among both staff and inmates.'

'I would be happy to arrange a visit at the earliest opportunity and hope that the right honourable member will be able to accompany me.'

The convention was that the opening question was uncontroversial with the tricky one coming in the follow-up. This, however, was a friendly question, or so Sarah thought. She sat down. Ali bobbed up again.

'One of the reasons for the demoralization in our prisons is the prevalence of drug use and the unfettered spread of diseases connected with the sharing of needles, including such fatal diseases as HIV and hepatitis. Surely it is now time for the government to take decisive action to prevent the spread of such diseases. I'm sure that the honourable member agrees that a custodial sentence ought not to be a death sentence.'

'I do,' Sarah said. The Home Secretary was at her side, glowering, but she was unable to deny what she had said in the House, more than once. Ali was taking over her issue, knowing well that Sarah could not speak her full mind. In the House, she couldn't even indicate that she was working on these issues behind the scenes, as she was about to assure Stonewall and other organizations. Sarah had to get her head together, but, when she started to speak again, wasn't sure what words would come out.

'I do share the honourable member's concerns and, while there are practical and moral problems associated with needle exchanges that make an early move in that direction unlikely, I look forward to hearing her suggestions in more detail when we undertake the visit discussed in my previous answer.'

Having got through that, it was a relief to be grilled about escapes from open prisons. At least her boss was pleased. Afterwards, he congratulated Sarah on her performance.

'You're clearly on top of your brief. Actually, there's a little something extra you might be interested in taking on. Let's talk next week.'

Sarah had a sneaking suspicion she knew what the something extra was.

22

'He wants to see you,' Chantelle said. 'Soon as you get in.'
'Fine,' Nick said. This was the first time that King had already been in the office when he arrived at work. Wasn't he meant to be in Manchester today? Perhaps he wanted to give Nick his long-overdue assessment interview. It was only a formality, but would mark the end of Nick's probation period.

King didn't ask Nick to sit down.

'What were you doing at the hostel in Alexandra Park last night?' he wanted to know.

Caught on the back foot, Nick tried to explain. 'I was being proactive,' he said. 'Those girls might not have serious drug problems yet, but will have soon. The earlier we get them reconsidering that behaviour, the better.'

'You know I'm on their management board?'

'I wasn't aware of that.'

'So I got a call last night from one of the wardens, said there'd been a fight outside and it all connected back to a visit you'd made that evening.'

'I did clear it with the warden first.'

'You cleared it with *a* warden, one I'm told you're either sleeping with or counselling or both. She's going to get a written warning.

I'm told you've been visiting the hostel for months, seeing a fifteen-year-old girl.'

'That's right, I –' *Never apologize, never explain*, John Wayne once said, but Nick didn't need to stop speaking, because Kingston interrupted him.

'Are you aware of the problems the previous organization got into with underage girls? Exchanging drugs for sex? Prostitution! And you sully my work here with your dirty –'

Nick knew that he had to reply definitively, at once.

'I am not having sex with that girl!' he interrupted. 'I'm teaching her, and have been since before I began work here. If you spoke to the warden –'

'Who is a junkie herself! A troubled woman employed out of charity, who should never have allowed you into the place. I'm not going to ask about your relationship with her. I don't want to know. But I'm issuing you a warning, a written one, and this time it won't be rescinded, no matter how important your friends are. Get out of my sight.'

Humiliated, Nick couldn't face returning to his office. He had nothing to do there. He left the building, ignored by Chantelle, who was busy typing a letter. Probably his written warning. The moment he was outside, Nick got out his fags and sucked on a Marlboro Red. Unless he found a way to turn this situation around, he'd be back on roll-ups soon.

Nick might have fucked up by not getting proper clearance but, in the big picture, he was sure he'd got it right. There was nothing to stop him being in that hostel except, perhaps, the possibility of embarrassment to his boss, whose connection with it he had been unaware of. He was too proud to ask Sarah to intervene again. And the situation wasn't as clear cut as when she had helped him before. Then, he had been ambushed. This time, he had walked into trouble with his eyes open. Anyway, it was the wrong end of the week to find

Sarah in Nottingham. She would not be here until Thursday evening at the earliest.

He needed an exit strategy. The ideal time to get a new job was when you still have the old one. He walked down to WH Smith's by the Broadmarsh Centre and picked up a copy of *Time Out*, with its jobs section. Nick wasn't going to sign on the dole again, not if he could help it. He could stay with Andy in London. The papers said the country was enjoying a New Labour boom. There ought to be a place in it for him.

He's supposed to be working away, but you see him in town when you're coming out of the safe sex centre. He doesn't see you, so you follow him. You think he's going to the Power Project, but he isn't. He turns the other way, towards the Victoria Centre. You used to shoplift there when you were younger. You nearly got caught once. Then you started seeing him and he spotted a silk scarf you'd taken, asked how you could afford it. You told him and he made you promise never to do it again, said it was too easy to fuck up your future.

You watch him turn into Jessops, the big department store. He walks purposefully, like he knows where he's going, over to the left-hand side. The toys section. And then there's a girl, no more than ten, running to him.

'Daddy, Daddy!'

He lifts her up and hugs her. You hear him say, 'Happy birthday!'

So that's why he's here.

The little girl is not alone, of course. There's a boy, a couple of years older, wearing the same uniform, one that belongs to a private school up the hill. You pass the kids coming out of there some days when you skive off early. Then there's the wife. You try not to look at her. She's nothing like you. A little overweight, but that's what comes of having two kids and living on your own during the week. Comfort eating. That's if she is living alone.

Why would he lie to you about being away during the week? But if he's lying to her, he can just as easily lie to you.

You watch them play happy families. Then he glances in your direction. You turn sharply without making eye contact, hurry away. Outside the hostel, you smoke some weed with Shaz and have a few slurps of her cider. Beany comes round and asks you to go back to his. Right in front of Shaz, who he's screwing, he tells you that you're the best-looking lass in Alexandra Park and, if you go with him, he'll treat you like a film star. He'll get you higher than the moon. You tell him to dream on. Your mobile rings.

'Did you see me earlier?'

He might be lying to you, but you can't lie to him.

'I was in town for the clinic. I just happened to see you in Jessops. I wasn't following you.'

'I didn't say you were. Listen, honey, it's you I love. You I want to be with. When you're old enough, I'll leave them for you. I mean it. But you have to be patient. I've got a position in the world. I can't be with you in public, not until you're older.'

'I am patient. I can wait. But can't I see you tonight? Just for a while.'

'I don't know. It's my daughter's birthday. I'd be lucky to get out of the house for half an hour. That's not enough time.'

You know where he lives. You know that he is telling the truth. It would take him half an hour to drive to you and back home again.

'I don't mind if it's only for five minutes. Text me if you can make it and I'll meet you up the road, okay?'

'I'll try. If I do come, it'll be late.'

'I love you.'

'I love you too.'

He hangs up. You try to work out how you feel. He is married, with two kids. You suspected all of that before. It's no surprise, still less a betrayal. Now that you've seen his wife, you know she's no competition. She's twice your age and twice your size, blacker than him. The good thing is he's told you about her, about his kids. Honesty's important. So is family. You could be a big sister to his daughter, you'd like that, not having any brothers or sisters yourself. You could be a kind of aunty to his son. The kids'd resent you at first, of course they would, for stealing their dad from their mum, for being white. But they'd soon see how much you love him, how much you need each other.

There are worse things than growing up without two parents. There's never knowing who your dad is, being taken into care when you're six years old and having a mother who last visited you when you were ten. There's being sat down by a social worker you've only met once before and being told that your mum has done herself in and no, you can't go to the funeral because it's already happened and there probably wasn't much of a funeral anyway because it doesn't sound like she had any family or friends.

There's going back to your third foster home in as many years and finding out that you're bleeding between the legs and not understanding what's going on and not wanting to talk to the foster carer who you can't stand and having a row with her in the morning because there's blood on the sheets and don't you know how to use a Tampax, then being told that you're not wanted and you're old enough to live in a hostel now, with other forgotten girls like you, until you're old enough to fuck things up on your own. That was when you thought about doing yourself in, too, now that suicide had become a family tradition. But you didn't. You kept your head down. You worked at school. You plotted. You saved your virginity for someone worth giving it to. And one day, at long last, he turned up.

He doesn't call tonight. You sleep badly. Then he's there, next day, in his four-by-four with the shaded windows, on your walk to school. The other girls tease you after he slides the door open, just a little way, so they can't see who's waiting for you inside. You're an hour late when you get into maths and a couple of the girls clap. The teacher is mad with you. But you don't care, because he took his time and made you come. Then he made you promises, promises that you know he'll keep, if you will only wait for him.

You will wait as long as it takes.

23

Caroline invited Nancy round for Sunday lunch. Nick wanted to take her, but Nancy wasn't keen. On Sundays, she tended to be hungover. Also, she had marking to do, lessons to prepare. Caroline, used to getting her way, switched the invitation to dinner on a Saturday night.

Family mattered. Joe, Caroline and Phoebe were the only family Nick had. He pressed Nancy to accept, even though he figured the two women were unlikely to hit it off. Why did relatives insist on meeting girlfriends? If a couple were engaged or living together, okay. But Nick and Nancy were having a good time, was all.

'You'll like Joe,' Nick insisted the evening before the meal. 'And Caroline's fine, when you get to know her.'

'I'll be on show all evening. I don't do dinner parties. Nobody does, any more.'

'It's not a dinner party, just family supper, with lots to drink.'

'Why can't we eat out?'

'They've got a new baby and they're not comfortable with sitters yet. It'll be all right, I promise.'

They were sharing a bath, lit by candles on the window ledge. Nick cradled Nancy from behind and gave her a back rub. The doorbell rang. She shot out of the bath like it was about to explode, crushing Nick's thighs.

'Hey! I'm still recovering from the last time I got knocked about.'

'Sorry.' She grabbed a towel and hurried downstairs, leaving the bathroom door half open. Nick heard somebody come in, followed by muffled conversation. He could almost hear what was being said. A bloke. The voice was familiar. Somebody who hung around the hostel where Jerry lived. A young black guy he'd nodded at when locking up his bike. Or not. Lots of people had similar voices. Was there a takeout service that delivered near by?

Two minutes later, Nancy returned.

'What was all that about?' he asked.

'A little treat. You'll find out later on.'

She had brought the bottle of wine back to the bath and refilled their glasses.

'I've told you about my week. What about yours? How was work?'

Nick had yet to decide whether to go back to the hostel on Monday. Alice had probably told the girls that the session was cancelled. Nevertheless, he felt like he owed it to them to turn up, tell them what was going on. If Kingston was embarrassed by that, tough. Nick was already on his way out. He explained all this to Nancy.

'If you don't get through your probation period, what will you do? Can you afford to keep on the flat?'

Was she going to offer to let him move in with her? Nick wondered.

'I'll get by,' he said. He wasn't going to tell her about the money he had stashed – the rainy day money from Andy, given out of guilt that he wasn't around when Nick was arrested. Some secrets were best kept secret. He and Nancy weren't at the stage in their relationship where they told each other everything. Maybe they never would be. She washed his hair. Then she started hassling him again about Saturday evening.

'Tell them I'm not well. I really am stressed, Nick. I get head-aches all the time and I'm not good with new people. They'll understand.'

'They won't. And Caroline has probably already prepared lots of the food. I'd still have to go round. You'll enjoy yourself, I promise.'

Nancy did not look in the least convinced.

They spent Saturday together, shopping and eating lunch in town. At Boxer, on Bridlesmith Walk, Nancy bought him a new shirt to wear that night. Then she asked what he wanted her to wear. Always a difficult call, when a woman asked about clothes. Nick suggested that she not show too much cleavage. Caroline hadn't got her figure back after the baby, he said. What he meant was that he didn't want to spend the evening with Joe staring down his girlfriend's top. Nor would Caroline.

But when she came out of the bathroom that evening, an expanse of breast bursting out of her top, he saw that she'd ignored him.

'These days,' she told Nick, 'if you've got it, you flaunt it.'

'It's only my brother and sister-in-law.'

'This should make the evening more interesting.' She lifted her bag from the table to reveal two neat lines of coke laid out on a mirror beneath.

'I dunno . . .'

'Confidence booster,' she said. 'Always works.'

She had her head down and hoovered up the line in one go. Nick hesitated before following suit. Joe wasn't stupid. He would spot that Nick was coked up, probably be pissed off if there wasn't any for him. And Nick was trying to stay off the class A drugs. Their taxi sounded its horn.

'You've got some more to take with us?' he asked Nancy.

'What do you think that delivery was, yesterday night?'

Ping! It was the first line he'd had this year and it sent his mind into overdrive. It was odd, how much one could enjoy the taste of bitter mucus sliding down one's throat. It was odder still, to him, how much Nancy loved the stuff. Other women he'd known had only dabbled. Probably Nick ought to feel guilty, snorting a line before going out to dinner. He wondered how many people across the city were doing the same.

24

He needn't have worried about inappropriate cleavage. Caroline, in a flattering red dress, showed off just as much bosom as Nancy did. Nick's sister-in-law hugged him tight, reminding him how close they had once been. He guessed she'd had a couple of glasses already.

'I can let go a bit tonight,' Caroline said. 'We've moved Phoebe onto the bottle, so I don't have to worry about getting her drunk on breast milk.'

Nancy, Nick noticed, didn't even pretend to be interested in Phoebe and her development. The two women talked school in the kitchen, while the brothers chose music and talked about bands. Pulp had a new album coming out at the end of the month. *This Is Hardcore*.

'Think they'll play Nottingham?' Nick asked his brother.

'Not likely. They're an arena band now and we don't have an arena.'

'I hate gigs in arenas.'

'If you want to see major bands, you're going to have to get used to it.' Joe lowered his voice. 'You keep sniffing. Have you done some charlie?'

'Nancy had a line waiting for me when I showed up,' Nick confided.

'She's a find, int she? What's she doing with a loser like you?'

Nick laughed. 'If you're interested, I expect she'll sort you out later.'

'Just don't let Caroline twig. She'd freak.'

When he was a footballer, Joe stuck to pints and not too many of them, but he'd been retired six years, grown a bit of a beer belly and was up for most of the things that he'd missed while pursuing a football career. Fatherhood didn't appear to be slowing him down.

Nancy joined the men.

'Tell me what Nick was like when he was young,' she asked Joe.

'Give me a line of coke and I'll tell you anything you want to know,' Joe said, with a wink.

'Naughty boy.'

An understanding was reached that this was not for Caroline's ears. She tolerated Nick and Joe smoking dope but class A drugs were another matter. Joe took Nancy upstairs, ostensibly to see the photos from his footballing days. Nick joined Caroline in the kitchen.

'Anything I can do to help?' Nick felt bad that everyone but her was about to destroy their appetite.

'You're as bad as Joe, timing your arrival for when everything's done. Need your drink freshening up? Dinner's only ten minutes away.'

'Mind if I stand in the doorway and have a quick smoke?'

'Be my guest.'

This could have been his home, Nick reflected, as he watched Caroline dress the salad. Phoebe could have been their baby asleep upstairs. He and Caroline had been lovers for a few weeks, seven years ago. Joe had finished with Caroline, but came to his senses, asked her back out. Caroline, who had kept her relationship with Nick secret, kicked the elder brother into touch. She got Nick to promise that he would never tell Joe about the two of them.

An unexploded bomb lay waiting for his brother, but it had been buried so deep that it was no longer a threat. Since Nick got out of prison, Caroline had only referred to it once.

'How are the injuries?' Caroline asked when Joe had poured the wine and the four of them were dipping wedges of French stick into home-made dips. Nick noted that she'd waited until Nancy was around to ask this question. Nancy, who had not visited once while he was staying here, convalescing.

'Okay,' he told her. 'The odd ache and pain, but I take a couple of paracetemols and I get by. Solpadeine are the best. You get a shot of caffeine and a taste of codeine as well.'

'Codeine's a lovely drug,' Joe said. 'I had it neat when I broke my leg.'

That injury had ended his footballing career.

'Doesn't it give you constipation?' Nancy asked.

'Only if you take large doses, regularly,' Joe told her. 'Which, of course, I did.'

Everyone laughed.

'They gave me morphine, in hospital,' Nick said. 'God, it was lovely. Nothing mattered. Pain was something that was happening off in the distance. You could float around on your thoughts, drift off into dreams. Helped me empathize with the heroin users that I counsel.'

'Don't be tempted,' Caroline said. 'How's the job going?'

'You don't want to know,' Nancy said.

Caroline gave her a sharp glance that said *I do want to know, thank you very much*.

'Nancy's right,' Nick said. 'My boss is nervous about me doing anything that might get us in the papers again. I'm not sure I'll even have a job in a fortnight. Any work going in the taxi business, Joe?'

'I'm always short on the night-time switch,' Joe said. He began to talk about the shortcomings of his switchboard operators.

They were costing him money and they were costing his drivers money. He'd had to let the best operator, Nasreen, go.

'Why did she leave?' Nancy asked.

'She went to work for Yellow Cars,' Caroline said.

Nick knew that the real reason Nas had left and wouldn't be coming back was that Joe had been having an affair with her while Caroline was pregnant. When he missed Phoebe's birth, Caroline put her foot down. Nick wasn't sure if she'd worked out who the other woman was. He hoped not, because now Joe was going on about how wonderful Nas was and how he should have talked her out of leaving.

'Couldn't you get her back, offer a bit more money?'

'Perhaps we should wait, see if Nick needs the job.'

Joe topped up everybody's wine glass. Caroline asked about the film *Sliding Doors*, which Nancy and Nick had seen. Was it was worth hiring a babysitter so that she and Joe could go and see it together? Nancy slagged it off, giving away the entire plot. Nick helped Caroline clear the plates.

'Is she always this hyper?' she asked him in the kitchen.

'I think she's a bit nervous.'

'What's there to be nervous about? It's not like she's your fiancée and we're your parents!'

Nick kept conversation going over the main course, a fish stew. There was a period when the coke and alcohol balanced perfectly, making him both lucid and amusing. They talked about New Labour, the minimum wage and what school Phoebe would go to when she was old enough.

'I expect we'll have moved by then,' Caroline said.

'News to me,' Joe told her and they began on the ins and outs of moving to snooty, middle-class West Bridgford on the other side of the river.

'I'm just going to powder my nose,' Nancy said, getting up.

'Literally?' Caroline asked.

The younger woman didn't look back. Joe and Nick exchanged a glance, agreeing that it was wisest not to acknowledge the knowing comment. When she came back, Nancy had clearly been thinking up a subject that she could talk comfortably about. She broke into the schools and property conversation to ask where Joe and Caroline were going on their holidays that year.

'Nowhere,' Joe said. 'Sounds like we'll be saving up for a new house.'

Nick was divided between annoyance that Nancy had left half of her dinner and the temptation to do another line himself. Nancy apologized for not finishing.

'I seem to have lost my appetite,' she said. 'I never eat much.'

If she was fishing for a compliment about her figure, she had come to the wrong house. There was still cheese and chocolate mousse to come.

By ten, they'd got through dinner and were onto the fourth bottle of wine. They were all drinking at roughly the same pace, but coke raised your tolerance and Joe had returned from his snug with a little rubbing-the-nose gesture aimed at Nick. He put on a CD by the Lemonheads, a group who had evidently been big while he was away. Nick liked it until Nancy, showing a complete lack of tact, began singing along with a track called 'My Drug Buddy'.

'I'm just going outside for a cigarette,' Nick said.

'Not a joint?' Caroline asked.

Nick ignored her. Resisting the lure of the line waiting for him upstairs, he stood in the doorway of the kitchen sucking on a Marlboro Red, listening to Caroline steer the conversation to Joe's drug habits.

'What's got into you tonight?'

'In truth . . .' Joe said, then seemed not to know what to say next.

'Truth, truth, truth,' Caroline repeated, starting to sound seriously drunk. Nick had never heard her like this before. 'Let's have nothing but the truth, shall we?'

Nick went into high-alert mode. Caroline wasn't used to the wine. She wasn't going to tell Joe and Nancy about them, was she? It would do none of them any good to dig that body out of the ground tonight.

'You know what I wish?' Caroline said. 'I wish that I could snort every last line of coke, blunder through life high on ecstasy, have sex with whomever I fancy whenever I fancy then chill out afterwards with a spliff and a Scotch and a sleeping pill or two if I need one to come down. It looks like a fantastic life, and if I didn't have a six-month-old baby upstairs –'

'If *we* didn't have a –' Joe interrupted.

'Let me finish! Now, what was I . . .?'

Nick returned to the room.

'Here he is!' Caroline announced. Nick suspected that she barely knew what she was saying. 'The man who started it all. You know, when I met Joe, he'd never touched dope, never mind anything stronger. But then football finished with him and he started spending time with his big brother.'

'Don't blame Nick,' Joe said.

'Maybe Caroline's right,' Nick said. 'I did start you off.'

'I remember the first spliff we shared,' Joe said, in an attempt to lighten the mood. 'It was Red Leb. What happened to Red Leb? You never get it any more.'

Caroline wasn't finished, but she turned on Joe now rather than Nick. 'I thought when Nick got sent down you'd stop, or slow down anyway. But no.'

'You used to like a joint,' Joe pointed out.

'To keep you company. So as not to look like a prude. I used to like the way it made me horny. But it had the opposite effect on you, didn't it?'

'Maybe,' Nick suggested, 'we should all share a spliff for old times' sake.'

'Maybe you should . . . oh, forget it.' Caroline got up from the table and Joe hurried to the kitchen after her.

'I left you a line chopped out upstairs,' Nancy said.

'I know, but I've had enough for now.' He was having trouble handling Caroline as it was, and Joe wasn't helping.

'Then you don't mind if I do? Your sister-in-law's hard work.'

'She's been pretty tolerant, considering she has to deal with the new baby and everything,' Nick pointed out, but Nancy was already on her way back upstairs.

Within half an hour, Caroline had gone to bed, accepting with tired grace their exaggerated praise for the meal she'd cooked. Nick and Joe shared a spliff in the snug. Nancy, wired on coke, only took a few puffs.

'I don't want to chill out,' she said. 'I want to go dancing. Nick, will you take me dancing?'

'We can dance here,' Joe said. They went back to the living room, where he put on Pulp's 'Common People'. Nancy flicked through Joe's CDs and came up with a single called 'The Key: The Secret'. Nick liked it, at least he did until Nancy insisted on playing it three times in a row. Joe, gamely, danced beside her, but after the second play, Nick collapsed into an armchair. He'd never been much of a dancer. He was relieved when Nancy suggested that he call a cab. They were home by one and in bed by five past.

'That went well in the end, didn't it?' Nancy said. 'I like your brother.'

'He liked you, too.'

Coke made her into a hyper-charged courtesan in bed. Nick's disappointment with the earlier part of the evening soon vanished.

2 5

On Friday evening, Sarah left a message on Nick's machine, asking to meet him. She wanted to know what was happening at the Power Project. He didn't return the call until Sunday lunchtime.

'Sorry about the delay,' he said. 'This is the first time I've been home since you called.'

'You dirty stop-out.' A month since, she would have felt jealous about him spending the weekend with another woman. 'I came to see you at work three weeks ago,' Sarah added. 'I thought you might get back to me.'

'I had . . . a situation. I'll explain when I see you.'

'If the problem's what I think it is, I'm not sure if I can help, but I have a bit of time this afternoon.'

'That'd be great,' Nick said. 'Want me to come to you?'

'Sure.' They agreed on three.

Had Nick got wind of the news about the project being wound down? Sarah doubted it. Kingston Bell hadn't been told yet. She had another meeting with Suraj this week. Budget week. The Tory spending limits had been adhered to, and it was time to start handing out a few sweeties. But not to the Power Project. Nor to the prisons budget, she feared. Not sexy enough.

*

Nick came by an hour later, looking a little the worse for wear.

'Good night last night?' she asked, and he smiled bashfully.

'I'm seeing a woman called Nancy. A teacher I used to work with.'

'That's nice.' A teacher was more Nick's style than his last girlfriend.

'How about you? With anybody?'

'No time. I was asleep by nine last night, utterly exhausted.'

'The rest must do you good. You're looking great these days.'

'Thanks.' She had spent ten minutes making herself up for him – and for Paul, who might call round later, after taking his kids to the ice stadium.

Nick followed her into the flat and she noticed that he was walking awkwardly. 'Started playing football again? You look like you got the worst of a bad tackle.'

'I haven't played since I finished uni.'

'Did I tell you that I've started to play? We have a women MPs team at Westminster, game every Tuesday morning. Not that I have time to play most weeks since I became a minister. What happened?'

'I took a kicking. I had a hairline fracture, a cracked rib, a few other aches and pains.'

'Jesus. Who did it?'

He told her. Random street violence on a Saturday night.

'You don't think it was connected with your job?'

'Why would it be?'

'You work with addicts who have pimps, dealers, people who might want you to stay out of their lives.'

'Nothing comes to mind. The only person who doesn't seem to want me to do my job is Kingston Bell. But I shouldn't be telling you about that.'

'I disagree. I'm on the board and I was your referee. I need to know.'

'I'm glad you said that.' He told Sarah how he had received a written warning. 'My probationary period ends this month. I could be out on my ear with no notice.'

'Lots of the Power Project workers' contracts expire in the next few weeks,' Sarah said, carefully. 'The future funding's not guaranteed.'

'The papers say the budget's going to be a generous one.'

'That doesn't mean it will be generous to the project.' Sarah got a few more details from him, could see the disagreement from both sides. There was no point in sugar-coating the situation. 'Best I can do is see Kingston on Monday morning before I catch the train to London, make it clear I'm still backing you. What you're doing with the girls in the hostel sounds fine, but that story in the *Mail* didn't do you, or the project, any good at all.'

Nick nodded acquiescence. She was sorry to have put a glum expression on his face. The coffee was ready. They talked about family. Nick's baby niece. He asked after her mum and she told him about the operation, which was scheduled for the week after next. A biopsy had confirmed the presence of a cancerous tumour, but it was in the early stages. Nick sympathized.

'So I expect you're seeing more of her.'

'I've been three times this year, which is a record in recent times.'

'You two getting on any better these days?'

'Not really. It was easier when Grandad was alive. We both behaved better when he was around.'

'You know he'd have been very proud of you,' Nick said.

'Thanks for that. I still miss him, you know. I –'

The doorbell rang.

'Expecting somebody?'

Sarah looked out of the window. There was Paul's car. He was very early. Normally, her heart would have leaped, but the prospect of her new lover and her ex-lover sharing the same air made her feel uncomfortable.

'It's a colleague from the Home Office. He's early. I'm sorry, Nick, it's an urgent policy discussion. I'm going to have to throw you out.'

'No problem. Thanks for fitting me in.'

She answered the door, standing back so that Paul would not try to kiss her.

'Paul, this is Nick Cane. Nick, Paul Morris.'

The men nodded at each other rather than shaking hands. Despite what Sarah had told Nick, he gave Paul a suspicious look, as though he suspected a relationship between them. Paul no longer wore a wedding ring. Could Nick read her so well? Paul, also, looked momentarily ill at ease.

'Who was that guy?' Paul asked, when Nick was gone. 'Didn't I see his face in the paper recently?'

'Yes, that was Nick, who works at the Power Project.'

'What was he doing here?'

'We're old friends.' Sarah didn't elaborate on the reason for Nick's visit. 'How long have you got?'

'An hour or two. I promised I'd eat dinner with the family.'

'Then let's go to bed. We can make up your cover story later.'

The sex was hurried, less satisfactory than their love-making in London. Sarah was beginning to wish that she had stuck to the rule about keeping clear of each other in Nottingham. Especially when Paul asked about Nick again.

'You went out with him?'

'At university, yes. It was him who persuaded me to campaign for student union president. But keep that to yourself, would you? I don't think that having had a relationship with a notorious dope dealer would do my reputation any good.'

'My lips are sealed. Now, regarding what I'm supposed to have come round for . . .'

She'd been hoping against hope for some new funding streams for the Power Project, but instead the Home Office was looking to back away from schemes that employed former drug users. No matter what strings Sarah pulled, Nick was unlikely to have a job for much longer.

'Did the Home Secretary have a word with you about my policy unit?' Paul wanted to know.

'No. Should he have done?'

He looked away evasively. Sarah figured she had guessed right.

'I'm meeting him tomorrow. He said there was something he wanted to ask me.'

'Ah. I was premature, sorry.'

Not for the first time today, Sarah thought, but was tactful enough not to say.

26

'Is Kingston in?' Nick asked, when he showed up at work on Monday morning.

'He's with someone at the moment,' Chantelle said.

Nick hoped that it was Sarah. 'Can I make an appointment?'

'You know he don't work that way. I'll tell him you want to see him.'

Five minutes later King came straight into Nick's office without knocking.

'Nicholas. We need to talk.'

'Yes.' Nick couldn't quite figure the expression on King's face, but he didn't like the way he'd used his full name. If King had seen Sarah, he was likely to be pissed off with Nick for getting her to interfere. Yet his face was doing a reasonable impression of kindly.

'Your probation period ends this week,' King pointed out, sitting down in the plastic chair opposite Nick. His close-cropped hair was starting to go white behind the ears. 'I'm not going to fail you.'

'Uh, I see.' Nick was surprised. 'Thanks.'

'Unfortunately, I can't pass you either. Thing is, most of the project's funding is short term, and coming to an end. I'm going to have to let people go. Unless there's some good news in this week's budget, I may be out of a job myself. So, listen, we've had our differences, but this is nothing personal.'

'Of course not,' Nick said, trying not to sound sarcastic.

'I'll be happy to write a reference saying that you made a promising start.'

'Thanks.'

'In the meantime, you've accrued a week's holiday. We can't afford to pay you after this week, so I'm instructing you to take the whole week off.'

'You mean that's it? I'm finished.'

'No hard feelings.'

'Of course not,' Nick said again, then shook Kingston's hand.

It took him two minutes to gather his stuff and get out. He handed his keys to Chantelle at reception.

'I guess you'll put my P45 in the post.'

'Yours and everybody else's,' she said, then gave him a sweet, sympathetic smile that he hadn't realized her face was capable of. 'Good luck.'

'Thanks,' Nick said, trying not to sound gutted. 'Same to you.'

He was on holiday, he reminded himself, walking through the Lace Market. He could do whatever he wanted. But there wasn't much he felt like doing late on a Monday morning. He headed for the Central Library on Angel Row, where he looked through some jobs pages, borrowed an oral history of the New York punk scene and ate a buttered scone.

It was a clear, fresh day, so he walked up Derby Road towards his flat. He considered ringing Andrew Saint, but decided to leave it. He could go and see Nancy tonight, tell her what had happened. But Nancy wasn't big on sympathy and Monday wasn't one of the evenings he spent with her. She preferred to keep work nights and pleasure nights separate. He was the same when he was a teacher.

At three, he decided to cycle over to the hostel, keep his appointment with the girls. Now that this was his own time, King could hardly complain.

Alice, on the other hand, could. She wasn't pleased to see him. 'I was given a written warning for inviting you in.'

'I should have checked that you got permission,' Nick said. 'The wardens' meeting was postponed and I didn't want to let you down.'

'Really sorry I got you in trouble. Did you cancel the girls today?'

'I told Shaz to tell the others, but I don't know if the message got through. Why are you here? Didn't you get told off too?'

Nick explained his situation. 'But I'd better go, don't want to get you into more trouble.'

'Dunt matter. I'm leaving anyway.'

'Why? Nothing to do with this, I hope.'

'Don't laugh,' Alice said, 'but I'm going to train to be a social worker.'

'Good for you.'

'I gave in my notice today. They'd already done my reference, so there's nothing your boss can do to hurt me.'

He and Alice went through to the TV room. Jerry was there, still in school uniform, along with two of the other girls.

'We thought you weren't coming,' Jerry said.

'I wasn't supposed to, but I thought I'd poke my head in.'

'Like a good poke, do you?' Teri teased. 'Jerry does.'

'He's too old for you lot,' Alice told them.

That provoked some hilarity. Alice stayed for the session, which was a replay of the previous week's, but more relaxed, with less self-censorship. Alice, freed by her resignation, talked about her own experience of smack.

'It's great. It's so great that it takes over your life. And it takes over your mates' lives. And you see girls you went to school with selling their bodies so they can fill their system with shit, chasing a thrill that keeps getting further and further away.'

The girls didn't seem shocked that Alice had once been a user, but they didn't think that what happened to her would happen to them.

After half an hour, they were going in circles, and Alice's shift was coming to an end. Nick decided to call it a day. He explained that his job as a drugs worker was over, but told the girls about the drop-in centre near the train station.

'I'll still be here every week or two to tutor Jerry, so if you want a word, you can catch me. It's been good, getting to know you.'

This was a civilized ending, he told himself, better than his sudden non-appearance would have been. He tried to find Jerry to arrange their next teaching session, but she wasn't around. Alice saw him to the door.

'You were good in there,' she said.

'You were better. You demonstrated to them that you can get clean, restart your life.'

'You helped me with that,' she said. 'What will you do next?'

'No idea. Keep volunteering, maybe try for work in London. My brother owns a taxi firm, he might give me a bit of work on the switchboard.'

'Good luck,' she said. 'You deserve some.'

She kissed him on the side of the lips and was back inside before he had unlocked his bike. It was too cold a night to hang around.

'Is this him?'

Nick turned to see Shaz, accompanied by a black youth, who was both taller and broader than him.

'Yeah,' Shaz said.

'You gonna walk with me, Nick Cane?'

Before Nick could decide how to answer, Shaz had hurried inside. The lad, not much more than twenty, had both hands shoved in his pockets. Nick had seen him before, and he'd met plenty like him inside. This was the lad who Nick had thought he'd heard round Nancy's not long ago, making a delivery. Best not to give him any clue that he'd made that connection.

'Happy to walk with you,' Nick said. He held the bike on his right side, making sure to position it between himself and the youth.

'What you want with those girls in there?' he was asked.

'I was talking to them about drugs. It's my job.'

'Shaz said you tried to talk her out of working for me.'

'I suppose that's how she might have heard it.'

'You saying she's thick or something?'

'No, I . . .' Nick could hear himself sounding like a middle-class wanker, getting into territory he didn't understand. 'I was doing my job, right? As it goes, the job's just finished, so you and me, we don't have an issue.'

'That's for me to say. Shaz says you're a dealer.'

'Used to be,' Nick admitted, sensing an imminent threat. He calculated how quickly he could lift the bike to protect himself.

'You into running girls now?'

'No.'

'You'd better not be. I know where you live. See?'

'Seen,' Nick said. He thought this was the cool response, but the lad reacted with an angry, uncertain frown. Did he think Nick was correcting his grammar? 'Look,' Nick went on. 'We don't have a problem. All I was paid to do was keep girls like Shaz from developing bad drug habits. That suits you too. Nobody wants to pay for a girl who looks like a raddled addict.'

Raddled. Ouch. Wrong word, Nick thought. Condescending.

The youth drew his left hand from his pocket, revealing a Stanley knife.

'Don't . . .' he said, then thrust the knife at Nick so quickly that he barely had time to get out of the way, '. . . tell me my business. You go near Shaz again, I'll cut you proper. Understood?'

'Understood,' Nick said. The knife, he realized, had grazed his leather jacket, leaving a scratch.

There was nothing further to say. He must resist the impulse to speak. Nick mounted his bike. They were still on the uphill, rough road out of Alexandra Park. The boy glared at him, but the knife was back in his pocket. Nick pedalled hard until he was safely ahead of his assailant. Then a thought occurred to him and he stopped.

'Was it you,' he called back to the lad, 'who had me beaten up before?'

The guy gave him a blank look. Nick wondered whether he had made himself clear. He put his foot on the kerb to steady himself. The youth had nearly caught up with him.

'You said you know where I live. Does Jerry work for you? Is that why you did me over, to keep me away from her?'

'I don't know what the fuck you're talking about,' the youth said. 'Shaz reckons that Jerry, she's working for you. You pretend to be a drugs counsellor, but you're setting up your own stable. You better stay off my hood or you're going to find yourself back where you just came from. See?'

'I see,' Nick said, 'and, I swear to you, we don't have a problem.'

He pumped his legs as hard as he could and cycled to the brow of Woodborough Road. He could cut across here, have a flat journey all the way home. But he had been spooked and wanted to get away quickly, so he turned left and freewheeled down the long, steep hill into the city.

The Home Secretary had a word with Sarah on the way out of Home Office questions.

'I believe you know Paul Morris.'

Sarah replied cautiously. 'Yes, he used to be one of our county councillors. I worked with him when he was chair of the police committee.'

'You're aware that he came here to work for me?'

The Home Secretary's tone gave no sign that he suspected her relationship with Paul. They had been very careful so far.

'Kind of. He was cagey about what his new job entailed.'

'As he was asked to be. In confidence, then, he's in charge of a small policy unit looking at drugs policy. Reclassification, how we deal with offenders, where we want to be in ten years' time – that kind of thing.'

'Legalization?' Sarah asked, cautiously.

'Partial decriminalization is one of the options on the table.'

'And who does this policy unit report to?' Sarah asked. 'You, directly?'

'Me and an ad hoc committee comprising . . .' He named a senior police officer, two cabinet members and a chief government scientist. 'The other day, Paul happened to mention you, said you were involved in a project in Nottingham. He intimated that you were liberal on policy but hardline on enforcement. Does that accurately reflect your position?'

'To a degree. I meet the chief constable regularly to talk about enforcement issues.'

'I know how frustrating it is to have to keep your true opinions to yourself. It must have been galling when Alison Blythe had a go on issues she knows you have to keep quiet about.'

'That's politics. The pressure groups I used to help haven't got the same access now I'm in government, so they've found a new MP who wants to make a name for herself.'

Sarah hadn't spoken to Alison since Home Office questions. She was still angry with her, but it was best to be philosophical about it with her boss.

'The committee I'm referring to meets once every six weeks. I'd like you to join it. Membership is not conditional on your remaining prisons minister, but is conditional on your being in the government. The committee's workings are to be discussed with absolutely nobody outside the committee. Understood?'

'Understood.' He was taking her acceptance for granted. Even so, Sarah wasn't sure she should say yes. 'Can I have some time to think about it?'

Her boss frowned. 'This is a step up, Sarah. A chance to change the way the country works. Don't you want that?'

'I do. It's just . . .' She couldn't tell him that she was sleeping with his policy adviser. Why should she? But should she mention that she had an ex-lover who was a convicted drug dealer and now worked for the Power Project, thanks to a reference from her? It was a conflict, a potential embarrassment she ought to sidestep. Still, if the committee was secret, where was the risk? 'It's just that I want to do what's best,' she finished, weakly.

The Home Secretary frowned. He didn't like dithering.

'You can have until tomorrow's post-budget meeting to make up your mind. The committee's just met, so it won't convene again for five weeks or so. And, I repeat, discuss this with nobody.'

Sarah returned to her poky office. She couldn't sound out Steve Carter, as she normally would. The person she could most happily discuss the whole issue with was the last person she should talk to. Nick.

Ought she to discuss it with Paul? But she already knew what her lover wanted – her on the committee. Sarah was annoyed that, in this, Paul was manipulating her even more brazenly than when he persuaded her to join the Power Project board. Yet she couldn't help admiring his persistence, his commitment. He was a man who saw what he wanted and didn't rest until he got it. Up close, she was beginning to see that work was Paul's life. He spent time with his kids, but didn't talk about them. He liked sex, but he liked it quick. She had let him think that she shared his view of the act – a physical need to be sated, not lingered over. She didn't.

*

Spring is just round the corner. You're nearly up to date with your coursework. In English, you're on for As in both language and literature. You could probably afford to drop the extra lessons now. Your lover tells you to find someone to tutor you in science instead, that's where you're weak. But you've already given up on science. You can get by without it.

Shaz crashes into your room.

'Got a message for you. That Nick Cane. Steer clear of him.'

You play it cool. 'Why?'

'Beany don't like him.'

'Why do I care what Beany likes?'

'He thinks he's trying to muscle in on his girls.'

'That's crap and you know it.'

Shaz doesn't know it. 'You fucking him or fucking for him?'

'I'm not fucking anyone,' you lie.

'Never?'

'Never never.' You know you've made a mistake as soon as the words have left your mouth. Shaz gets a grin on fast, gets out the room faster. You hear her stamp to the TV room, so you follow her.

'Jerry's a virgin!' she shouts, announcing it to the whole hostel. 'Jerry's saving it for teacher boy until he marries her!'

You go after her. You want to tell her about your lover, but you promised not to tell, no matter how much you're provoked. Break that promise and he might break up with you. So let them think you're a virgin. Let them think you're wet for Nick Cane.

'Is that right?' Pamela asks. You shrug, like the question doesn't deserve an answer. Shaz leans in close.

'He's a fucking user. They're all fucking users. Beany doesn't want him coming here again, or he gets hurt. Understand? He's been warned.'

'Warned by who?'

'Warned by Beany.'

You don't have a class with Nick for another week. Maybe you'd better arrange to go to his. The decision can wait. Nick is built. He can look after himself, could take down Beany no trouble at all.

Except Beany doesn't play fair. Beany carries a knife. You've heard the girls he runs talk about stunts he's pulled. Beany is part of a chain. The guys above him, you don't get in the way of. Shaz, on the other hand, Shaz is nothing.

'Fuck off,' you tell her.

She comes at you, sharp nails digging into your skin. You go at it for ages. The warden has to pull you off her. You've got a few scratches, but she has bruises, bad ones. She won't be earning any money for Beany tonight.

Other girls get into fights all the time. You don't. Least, you never have until now. Winning doesn't make you feel good.

That night, you ring your lover. He came on Saturday but not on Sunday and you missed him. You want reassuring. Your face is a bit messed up and you feel like a kid, caught in a playground scrap. He isn't there, but later he calls you back.

'Everything will be all right, babe. Those other girls, they're getting jealous cos they can see you're going places. When you finish your exams, I'll sort you out with a flat. Then, when you get to uni, I'll be ready to leave home, live with you. Promise me you can wait that long.'

'I can wait as long as you want. I love you.'

'I love you too. We're going to be together for ever.'

You hear his other phone ringing. You wonder if he really is away, in another city, like he says. That day you spotted him in the Victoria Centre, he had an excuse about his daughter's birthday. But he could be lying about that. You could go to his house, watch it, find out. Only you don't want to do that. You want to trust him, about everything. Because if you can't trust him, who can you trust?

27

At the second budget since the election, Gordon Brown kept within his self-imposed spending limit, set by the previous government. Despite the limit, he managed to raise child benefit by £2.50 a week above the rate of inflation, the largest increase ever. He also announced the new working families' tax credit, which would give working parents up to £100 a week for the first child and £150 for two or more children. Whatever the thinking behind the cuts to lone parent benefits back in December, most of the financial damage had now been reversed.

Sarah hadn't seen this coming. Perhaps the rebellion had sharpened the Chancellor's thinking. Or maybe this had always been part of the plan. A loyalty test, followed by hard proof that the government knew best. The announcement, when it came, got a huge cheer. Sarah joined in. Ali Blythe, leaving the chamber after the debate, looked happier than she had in ages.

'Tea?' Sarah suggested. 'We have a prison visit to arrange.'

'Got to talk to my local paper then pick up Petra from the childminder. But I'll get my secretary to talk to yours, yeah?'

'Yeah.' Sarah would have liked to know what Ali thought of the budget, particularly the benefits U-turn. She was sorry that they had fallen out. Sarah could use more friends in the Commons, especially female ones. One day, Ali would learn that she needed friends too.

Sarah had a couple of messages waiting, asking her to comment on the budget. She ignored them and returned to the Home Office. There were three other Nottingham MPs. The *Evening Post* could do without a quote from her.

The Home Secretary was running late and she had to wait ten minutes for her post-budget briefing. She checked the messages on her phone. Mum's operation had been delayed. The surgeon had been taken ill. No wonder, given how over-committed and over-worked surgeons were. Meanwhile, Mum's cancer must be spreading. Sarah could have made a phone call, got her seen quickly, but Mum wouldn't let her. She'd already offered. No favours, Mum said. And as for going private, forget it. Mum might have little time for politics nowadays, but she was old Labour through and through.

Sarah was still getting used to her mobile phone. She noticed an envelope symbol blinking on and off: messages. Most were from the whips' office. Except for one, from Paul. *Conflab later? Can get to your place for 9 p.m.* 'Conflab' was their code for sex. She cursed when she realized that the text had been sent yesterday.

'You should have known I wouldn't read it!' she told Paul on his mobile, two minutes later. 'I barely know how to open my text messages.'

'Then learn to. I was in a meeting and couldn't get out to call you. Set the phone to vibrate when one arrives.'

'I don't think my phone does that.'

'Then I'll buy you a new model. Come round tonight and I'll teach you to vibrate.'

Sarah laughed. 'Maybe. I have to go now. Talk later.'

She was shown into the Home Secretary's office for her budget debrief. There had been no money for building new prisons or restoring old ones. The EC law about paying prisoners a minimum wage for work done inside was not to be implemented. After talking to prisoners and prison officers, Sarah had started to come round to the idea of increasing prison wages, making them more than token. But her boss had told her it was too controversial. God forbid that prisoners might be rehabilitated by getting them to associate honest work with receiving honest pay. Let them sew mail bags and be happy.

When they were done, Sarah's mind was saturated. There was something else they were meant to discuss, but she couldn't, for a moment, think what it was. She played for time.

'I don't suppose we can look again at the issue of making condoms freely available in prisons? It's as important as needle exchanges and . . .'

'You're like a stuck record on that topic. I thought we went over this yesterday.'

'True, but who knows how long I'll be in this job. I'd like to achieve one solid, life-changing policy before I go.'

'Then find something less politically sensitive to campaign for. Government is about collective decisions, not individual campaigns. Licensing prisoners to have gay sex, safe or otherwise, in prisons is not the message we want to send out.'

On her way out, Sarah realized that she'd forgotten to tell her boss her decision about joining his drugs reform committee. And he, annoyed, had forgotten to ask her. So he could bloody well wait.

28

'Is this okay?' he asks, after buying you a coffee.

'I guess.' You'd prefer somewhere more private, but this will do. You're hardly likely to run into Beany and his crew, or anyone from school, here.

'Why did we have to stop meeting at the hostel? And where did you get that scratch?'

Two questions, one answer. 'Shaz.'

He nods like this makes sense. 'I got a warning from her pimp when I was round on Monday.'

'Beany's a prat, but he's connected. You don't fall out with him.'

'We can meet at my place in future if you prefer, after school. It's just that this morning, my girlfriend's there, having a lie-in.'

You talk about the book for fifty minutes, then he looks at his watch. 'Okay, here's what I want you to do before next time.' Your phone rings. A couple of the oldsters at the next table give you a look when you answer it. What's a girl like you doing with an expensive mobile phone?

It's him. 'Finished your lesson yet?'

'I will have in two minutes.'

'Wait for me outside the casino. I'll pick you up in five.'

'Great.'

You arrange to go to Nick's, after school, the Monday after next. 'Unless I get a job,' he says. 'Doesn't seem very likely, but you never know.'

'This is a job,' you remind him. 'You're good at it.'

'Thanks for that,' he tells you and, for a moment, you think he's going to kiss you on the forehead. Then you realize that this is a public place, and you don't want to be late for your lover, so you hurry out of the library, round the corner and across Maid Marian Way. His car pulls up a few seconds later and you get straight in. He squeezes your thigh before setting off.

'Did you fire him like I told you to?' he asks.

'No. I need a couple more sessions on Dickens,' you tell him. 'After that, I can do without him.'

He doesn't argue, just drives. He doesn't tell you where you're going. Which is fine. You're happy for him to take you anywhere he wants.

Nick let himself into the flat. He was carrying eggs, bacon from the market, sausages and a couple of croissants for good measure.

'I'm back.'

No reply.

'Hope you're hungry.'

Still nothing. She must be in the bathroom. He dumped the food by the sink and opened the bathroom door. Condensation on the walls. Nancy had had a shower, using the rubber attachments connected to the bath taps. But she wasn't there. He called her name. Then he looked around. No note. Nothing.

Nancy could be erratic. She wasn't the same woman he knew seven years ago. Then, she was anxious to please, eager to succeed as a teacher. Now, she was anxious only to please herself, eager only to get trashed. Impatient, too, which must be why she hadn't hung around for him. He'd left no food in.

He'd find her at a café down the road. But she might have left a note.

He had her mobile number written down. Nick reached for the pad that he kept beneath the phone. But before he could locate the number, there was a loud banging on the door.

'Police!'

Nick thought quickly. The dope was stashed outside. He should be safe. Nancy hadn't had anything with her, so she couldn't have left stuff lying around. At most they would find a couple of roaches in the bin. But what had brought the police here in the first place?

He opened the door. Two uniforms and two plain clothes, the older one with a narrow, two-inch scar below his left eye. Drug squad, they looked like. And they had a search warrant.

'Go ahead,' he told them. 'You'll find nothing here.'

'They all say that,' Scarface told him.

He stood in a corner of the room, where he could see what they were doing in both the living room and the bedroom. If they wanted to fit him up, however, it would be their word against his. Who was behind this? Maybe Beany or his boss wanted to set Nick up, believing him to be a rival. The dealers were bound to have bent coppers on their payroll. Nick's chest hurt, his heart pounded away. A panic attack, brought on by the fear of going back inside. He was out on licence. Get caught for the smallest thing and he could be sent down for the three years of his sentence he hadn't yet served. Beany knew that when he threatened him on Monday. One roach and a vindictive magistrate could be enough to put Nick back inside.

Nick tried to take short, regular breaths. The police didn't bother with the bathroom. They seemed to be paying most attention to the drawer next to the kitchen sink, where Nick kept screwdrivers, spare plugs and the like. Scarface seemed surprised when the drawer proved drug-free.

If they were going to set him up, Nick told himself, they would have done it by now. He might be all right. But who would go to the trouble of arranging a bust when there was no guarantee that Nick would get caught out?

The cops looked pissed off. Nick began to breathe more easily.

'Want to search me?' Nick offered. Scarface ignored him, but looked at his colleagues. The uniforms shook their heads. So did the other plain clothes. They hadn't had time to search properly, surely? Scarface clapped his hands together.

'Okay, let's call it a day.' His manner to Nick changed sharply. 'Sorry to inconvenience you, sir, but we have to act on information received. I hope we haven't made too much mess.'

Nick shook his head and let them leave. What the hell was all that about? Before he could think it through, the phone rang. Nancy.

'You had an unexpected visitor,' she said.

'How the hell do you know that?' he snapped.

'Because I was there when the plant happened. I'm at mine. Can you get down here, now?'

'Give me ten minutes,' he said.

'And if you bought breakfast, bring it with you. I'm starving.'

29

Sarah usually saved her red Home Office boxes for a Sunday, but tomorrow she was due at her mum's. She might work through this evening. Paul was with his family and she'd had no other offers for Saturday night.

Had Paul really left his wife? Sarah didn't want to press him about that. He said they were separated but hadn't told the kids yet. At weekends, he slept in the spare bedroom. So, in theory, he could come out on a late-night booty call. But it was risky. He might be seen.

She opened the box. Wormwood Scrubs had yet to find a new governor. The man in temporary charge had instituted a purge on illegal drug use in the prison. 'Zero tolerance' was the stupid American phrase he used in the report. Over Christmas dinner, Sarah had listened to prisoners' complaints. One of their biggest gripes was about the quality of the toothpaste – the stuff they got was so rough that many had constantly bleeding gums. She looked through the report again. No mention of toothpaste.

Tempting to write a note. Bu she had to leave decisions, big and small, to the temporary governor.

The phone rang. Eric.

'I was wondering if you had plans for dinner tonight?' the chief constable asked.

'None. You'd be saving me from a very boring evening.'

'Excellent news. Where would you like to eat?'

'Go through it all again.'

'Christ, Nick, you sound like you don't believe me.'

'It's not you I don't believe. It's that I can't take in what happened.'

The sausages in the pan started spitting. Nancy tied an apron over last night's dress. She sliced some mushrooms, then told the story again.

'I'd just got out of the shower when I heard him come in. You'd only been gone a few minutes. I thought you'd forgotten something. I opened the bathroom door and saw his back. He was going through a drawer by the sink. I was naked and I was scared. I didn't know what to do. So I closed the bathroom door, quietly as I could. Then I locked it, hoping he wouldn't hear. And I waited. I heard him go, waited a little longer, then got dressed.'

'How much of him did you see?'

She unwrapped the bacon.

'Just his back. He was wearing jeans and a blue hoody, with the hood down. His hair was quite short, shaved I think.'

'What colour?'

'It matched his skin. Black. My first thought was to get out, in case he came back. Then I tried to work out what he was looking for. I mean, you don't have much, but there was stuff he could have taken. The stereo. I'd left my purse on the table. But he'd hardly had time to look in more than that drawer. I wondered what you kept in there.'

'Just tools, tape measures, stuff like that.'

'That was all I noticed at first. Must have taken me a good . . . oh, two seconds to spot that he hadn't taken anything at all. He'd put something in.'

'What?'

Nancy ignored the question. 'I looked out the window in case the police were already there. Then I got dressed, let myself out of the flat and waited until there was a bunch of people walking by on Alfreton Road, so I could slip in behind them, in case anyone was watching. All the time I was waiting for a bus, I thought I was going to have a heart attack. I was sure someone would know what I had on me.'

'*What?*'

'I put it under the bin, outside.'

There was a small yard at the back of Nancy's house, big enough for the bin and a few potted plants. Nick went out and lifted the bin, saw the plastic bag. This was what the police had been looking for. The bag was full of paper wraps. There must have been a hundred of them. Nick didn't pick it up. He didn't want to get his fingerprints on it. He knew what would be inside. Crack cocaine. Ten pound wraps. Over a grand's worth. Enough to put him back inside and give him a new sentence the same length as the old one.

Somebody wanted him out of the way. And wanted it very badly indeed.

'Did you look inside?' Nick asked when he returned to the kitchen.

'Of course I did. I wanted to be sure. But I wore my kitchen gloves. Why didn't you tell me, Nick?'

'Tell you what?'

'He just walked in. He had a key.'

Nick shook his head. 'No key. The lock on that door's pretty pathetic. A credit card might have done it. A palette knife, used the right way, would slide it open.'

'You don't have to lie to me. He was making a delivery. You're dealing again.'

'If you really think that, why did you take the stuff?'

Nancy hesitated, turned the bacon in the pan over. 'In case I was wrong. In case someone was trying to get you into trouble.'

'You saved my skin.' He told her about the attempted bust.

Nancy sliced two tomatoes in half and threw them into the pan. 'Why would anybody want to set you up like that?'

'That's what I'm asking myself.' He didn't mention Beany, because he reckoned he was the guy she bought her coke from. But wouldn't she have recognized him? 'It might have been the guy who beat me up last month.'

'Planting crack is a lot more serious than beating you up.'

'I suppose.'

She put in the mushrooms, a little too late. He liked them cooked to a crisp. 'You can't stay there,' she said. 'You'd better stay with me for a while.'

'Thanks. I really –'

'You'll soon get fed up of me,' she interrupted. 'Men always do.'

'Not me,' Nick promised, recklessly, for she had just kept him out of prison.

'Do you want fried bread?'

He did. She cut a couple of slices and somehow fitted them into the pan, putting the bacon on top so that it made space and didn't overcook. Nick ran through the list of people who had grudges against him. There weren't many. Beany. Beany's boss, whoever that was – somebody in a long chain that probably ended with Frank Davis, or whoever supplied the former head of the Crack Action Team. Who else? Wayne, who had offered Nick a job a few months ago, wouldn't do something like this. Nick's turning him down wasn't a strong enough motive. It had to be connected to Beany.

Didn't it?

Tonight, Sarah fancied a curry. The best to be had was at the Saagar, on the edge of Sherwood, a mile or two out of the city on the Mansfield Road. Its humble location and purple flock wallpaper belied the outstanding quality of its food.

Her only complaint, if complaint it could be called, was the menu's insistence that every customer order a main course. The portions were enormous and she was trying to watch her figure. It was weeks since she'd been to the gym, which was the only exercise she got. She ate her niwabi lamb and all but a quarter of her Peshwari naan. Then she pushed the plate aside.

'Do you see much of Paul Morris in London?' Eric asked, casually.

'We've had dinner a couple of times,' Sarah replied. She didn't want to sound guarded about this, nor to rub Eric's face in her new relationship. 'He gets lonely, stuck in the smoke all week.'

'Yes. He must miss Annette and the kids. They grow up so quickly at that age. Do you come across him at the Home Office?'

'No.' She needed to shift topic. 'How's the new chair of the police committee shaping up?' Sarah asked, trying to remember who it was.

'Solid enough. It's not an enviable position, for a politician.'

'I suspect Paul was glad to have an excuse to dump it.'

'I suspect he got exactly what he wanted to get out of the post,' Eric said, his eyes not meeting hers. Did he know about her and Paul after all? Time to tackle a sensitive subject, Sarah decided. The restaurant was full and noisy. In their corner table, they would not be overheard.

'Thanks for your advice on the Power Project, by the way. Looks like it's winding down, so there's no need for me to extricate myself. God knows what, if anything, will replace it.'

'In time, other agencies will soak up the funding, fill the gap.'

'Yes, and Kingston Bell will manage to make it look like another achievement on his CV. He was promised an honour if he took it on.'

'I didn't know that,' Eric said. 'Never hurts to have a coloured OBE.'

'Black,' Sarah said sharply. 'Nobody uses "coloured" any more.'

'We're always behind the times in the police force. By the way, are you still in touch with your former friend, who used to work with Kingston?'

'Not for a while. Why do you say *used* to?'

'Some of my lads had reason to visit his home today. He gave them to understand that he was no longer employed at the Power Project.'

Instantly, Sarah went on to high alert. 'Visit Nick. Why?'

'A tip we couldn't ignore. He was accused of dealing crack. The caller told us exactly where to find his supply.'

'Crack? That's absurd,' Sarah said, her anxiety mounting. But was it so preposterous that Nick would return to selling drugs, given his lack of other opportunities? Had she let her feelings for him blind her to his recklessness, his addictions? 'He would never . . . what did you find?'

'Nothing. He's good at squeezing out of trouble, is Nick Cane.'

Sarah felt an immense sense of relief. The waiter came to take away their plates and returned with a basket containing two hot white flannels. She took one and slowly wiped her face, neck and hands with it, calming herself down.

'Who gave you the tip about Nick, if you don't mind me asking?'

'A confidential informant, according to one of my officers. It's a scummy business. The officer himself is under surveillance.'

Sarah knew that there were corrupt officers on the force, hard to know how many. Eric had made it his mission to eradicate them, but it was a slow, difficult process.

'Under surveillance for what?'

'I can't tell you. Let's just say that, when the matter came across my desk for approval, I made sure the suspect officer didn't go on the raid. Possibly that helped your former friend.'

Sarah gave Eric her warmest smile. 'I really appreciate that, Eric. Nick doesn't deserve to go back to jail. But I'd still like to know who tried to set him up. A dealer maybe? Somebody with a grudge against Nick because of his work?' Sarah remembered that Frank Davis was said to have several quite senior officers in his pay. 'Could it have been someone connected with Frank Davis? Can he control things from prison?'

'Prison staff confiscated a mobile phone from Davis early on. Since then, they're meant to have kept a close eye on him, but prison officers are poorly paid and notoriously corruptible. Davis is only on remand, where conditions are less strict. But I can't think why he would have it in for Cane.'

'When does he go to trial?'

'The case has been delayed twice, but it's currently scheduled to start in a week's time.'

'Loads more bad publicity for drugs work in the city.'

'It'll be a good time to bury the closure of the Power Project, if that's what you plan to do.'

'I guess. It feels bad, putting people out of work.'

'And Cane was once a good friend, I know. But while he may be innocent in this case, your continued association with him could end up costing you dearly.'

'I'm aware of the risk. I appreciate your concern, Eric, but I'm not somebody who tends to desert old friends.'

'You're a politician. When needs must, you have to be prepared to drop anyone and everyone. I shouldn't have to tell you that.'

Their eyes met, and the hardness in his evaporated. 'I keep forgetting,' he said. 'You're an idealist, that's why you went into politics in the first place.'

'Sometimes I need reminding of that,' Sarah told him.

They paid the bill and crossed the road to wait for a taxi in the DG cabs office opposite. Sarah should not have been surprised when, in the back of the cab, Eric kissed her. She kissed him back.

'You haven't seen my new flat yet,' he told her.

'I'm sorry,' she told him. 'I'm very tired. And I'm not ready to . . . you know.'

'I do know,' he murmured. 'But I'm not giving up hope. You'd tell me if I ought to give up hope, wouldn't you?'

'I'd tell you,' she agreed, and kissed him back, more enthusiastically this time. Enjoyed it, too.

Which complicated things.

30

Nick was all for dumping the crack, but Nancy wouldn't let him.

'What else am I going to do with the stuff, sell it?'

'Aren't you curious to at least try it once?' Nancy asked.

'No. I'm not going near the stuff for the same reason I won't touch heroin. I might like it too much.'

'Chill out,' Nancy said. 'I'll put it where nobody can find it. Why don't you have a bath? I'll get rid, then join you.'

Nancy's bath was much bigger than the one in his flat. She set it running before she left. Nick read the paper while he soaked. When she returned, half an hour later, he had unwound sufficiently to enjoy sharing the bath, drying each other off, and all that followed.

'What did you do with it?' he asked, later, when they were dressed.

'A friend's looking after the stuff. You don't need to know who. Have you worked out who put it there yet, and why?'

'I think it must have been a guy called Beany.' He told her about Shaz's pimp. He noted that Nancy didn't react to the name, so maybe he wasn't her coke dealer. 'Or, more likely, whoever runs him.'

She listened carefully, then asked a few questions. 'All you did was try and talk some sense into a few teenage girls. Why would anyone waste a grand's worth of crack because of that?'

Nick thought for a moment. 'Maybe the crack was meant to find its way back into the supply chain via a bent copper.'

'A bent copper would have planted the stuff, not sold it on afterwards.'

She was right. Nick came at the problem again. 'To the guys higher up the chain, a grand is a small price to pay to get rid of someone.'

Nancy remained unconvinced. 'You say the girl's got a boyfriend?'

'There must be a guy who gives Jerry the money she uses to pay me.'

'It's more likely to be him. He thinks you're getting too close to her.'

'Jerry doesn't do drugs. I don't think her boyfriend's a dealer either.'

'The successful dealers don't do drugs themselves.'

She had a point. But it didn't bring Nick any nearer to working out who was out to get him. 'Are you sure it's okay if I stay here for a few days while I figure things out?'

'Stay as long as you need.'

That night, she produced a rock that she'd taken from the bag of crack and ground it down so they could snort it. Nick had hardly any. He didn't need coke paranoia: people really were out to get him.

They watched a Tarantino movie called *Jackie Brown.* Nick enjoyed it, but fell asleep before the end. That night, for the first time, they didn't have sex, but made up for it in the morning. Afterwards, Nick offered to cook, but Nancy had marking to do and lessons to prepare.

'Aren't you invited to Joe's for Sunday dinner?' she asked.

Nick took the hint and cycled over to his brother's.

*

After dinner, settled in the snug, Nick filled Joe in on what had been happening.

'At least there's a plus side,' his brother said, when Nick was done. 'You get to live with the gorgeous Nancy.'

Nick wasn't sure how much to confide in Joe. They didn't usually talk about relationships. He tried to explain how the crush he'd had on Nancy, once consummated, hadn't turned into something deeper.

'She *is* gorgeous, and the sex is great, but I'm not sure Nancy's someone I'd want to move in with,' Nick said.

'You're kidding. Why not?'

'She can be . . . neurotic. Our conversations are kind of limited.'

'I forgot, what you want is a mutual self-improvement class. Nancy's a sex, drugs and rock 'n' roll girl. Ideal. What's not to like?'

Nick struggled to answer this. 'I'm not fit to live with anyone, yet.'

'That, I can relate to. When do you think it'll be safe to go home?'

'I have no idea. First, I need to work out who's after me, make peace with them. The only way I can do that is through Jerry.'

'Then go to the hostel, see her.'

'Maybe I will. In the meantime, what's the chance of me getting some work on the switch, like you mentioned the other week?'

Joe frowned. He didn't really want his big brother working for him, that much was clear.

'Managing the board is hard work,' Joe said, 'and the pay's not great, compared to driving. You'd have to come in and shadow for the evening, see if you get on with it. If you do, I can put a few night shifts your way.'

'I'd appreciate it.'

The afternoon's match began, but Nick wasn't in the mood to watch football. He decided to cycle over to Alexandra Park, see if he could talk to Jerry.

*

He shows up unexpectedly, without phoning first. He's just there, at the hostel, talking to Alice, when you come in from sharing a spliff with Shaz and Beany, who's on at you again to treat him nice. You laughed. What's Beany got to offer when you have a man like this? Look at him now, wearing a smart suit, Alice giving him that smile that tells everyone he's the big man and, girls, you'd better treat him like a god.

'I think you've met Jerry before,' Alice suggests. He claims not to remember, asks if you've been to church today. You say you have and Alice gives you a look, as if to say there's no need to lie. Then she says, 'I think you have a visitor.' He glances over your shoulder, stares daggers. Behind you, outside the hostel doors, Nick is locking up his bike. You want to say *I'll get rid*, but Alice shows your lover through to the wardens' office. You don't know what to do. You get out your phone and text. *I dint ask teach to come. Tell me where to wait, i'll be there x*. Then you go and find Nick.

Teach says he wants to talk to you alone.

'Now's not a good time,' you tell him.

'It won't take long.'

You take him to your room. He sits on the edge of your bed. You glance out of the window, hoping your lover doesn't walk by, see Teach making himself at home. He's the jealous type, you know that. So are you.

'Something funny happened yesterday, while I was with you,' Nick says.

'What kind of funny?'

'Someone tried to get me into trouble. Someone who knew that I wouldn't be at home.'

'Ah.'

'The question is, did Shaz or Beany know that you were having a lesson with me?'

You have to think carefully about the answer. Everything's getting a bit tense. Beany didn't know about your lesson. Shaz was still in bed when you went out. Only one person knew where you were, and he's outside right now. You won't tell on him, but you won't lie to Nick either.

'I don't think so,' you say.

'How about your boyfriend? The one who pays for your lessons.'

Nick doesn't mess around. He gets to the point. Normally, you like that. Today, you want to avoid the question.

'What happened to you?'

'Somebody tried to set me up. If it wasn't Beany or somebody he works for, then the only person I can think of is your boyfriend. Might he think there's something going on between us?'

'Why would he think that?'

'You're an attractive girl. Lots of blokes would be tempted.'

You lower your eyes. 'I'm sure it wasn't him.'

'Help me here, Jerry. I'm on parole. If you're dangerous to be around, I'm going to have to pack this in.'

'I understand,' you tell him. You don't, not really. Your phone buzzes. A text. You read it. 'Got to go,' you say. 'Why don't I see what I can find out, call you?'

Teach isn't happy with this, but he leaves. At least he hasn't cancelled your next lesson. Those lessons keep you sane. You change out of your jeans, then wait until Nick's bike has disappeared around the corner before you join your lover in his four-by-four. You take a deep breath before you get in. His hand goes straight up your skirt, his favourite skirt, but you pull away. It's time to get real.

'What did you do to Nick yesterday?'

He scowls and you know you're right.

'Why?' you ask. 'Why did you do it?'

'What I do and why I do it has nothing to do with you. Understand?'

You're not having that. It's not fair.

'No, I don't understand. If you hurt Nick, we're finished. Got that?'

His eyes narrow, then he does something he's never done before in the year and more you've been together.

He hits you.

'This is the fourth time you've visited me this year,' Mum said. 'You must think I'm not long for this world. Don't worry, there's no other bugger in my will.'

'I can't believe how long they've made you wait for this op.'

'I'd've been in quicker if they thought it was serious.'

Sarah wasn't sure if this was true. The government was only just getting to grips with the National Health Service. She'd been in the Commons last week when the secretary of state for health gave a statement about hospital waiting lists, which were still rising. The government had pledged massive amounts of spending, but turning things around would take time. Time that Mum might not have.

'Have you looked into going private?' Sarah asked.

Mum gave Sarah a look of such disdain that Sarah was sorry she'd opened her mouth. It wasn't about money. Mum didn't live extravagantly, but she was comfortably off. It was about betraying your principles. Sarah changed the subject, stumbling into a conversation about neighbours she hardly knew. When her mobile rang, she was relieved. The Home Office.

'I have to answer this,' she apologized to Mum, who shrugged and picked up her *Sunday Mirror*.

'I'm sorry to disturb you at the weekend, Minister, but we thought you'd appreciate a heads-up.'

A prison guard was being held hostage at Wormwood Scrubs. This was an operational matter, over which Sarah had no influence. No say, either, but ultimate responsibility. She listened carefully. This incident wasn't directly attributable to the acting governor's crackdown on illegal drugs, but was likely to be connected. Hash and heroin were thought to dull violent tendencies. Deny them, and you made violent behaviour more likely. Turn a blind eye, and so what?

'Okay,' she said when she was fully appraised of the situation. 'I'll return to London tonight, rather than tomorrow morning. Let's meet at seven forty-five.'

She explained what had happened to her mum. 'I might need to go on the *Today* programme.'

'Don't expect me to find Radio 4 on the dial. I always have it set to Radio 2,' Mum said. 'If you've got to leave early, I'd best get dinner in the oven.'

3 1

Dave Trapp was at least a decade older than Nick, his fair hair silver at the edges, but he acted younger. He spoke to Nick like they were fellow professionals, rather than probation officer and ex-offender.

'Don't get down about your contract being terminated. It's not like you were sacked. You got some work experience out of it. Are you still volunteering at the drop-in centre?'

'Yeah. I'll put my hours up now that I have more time.'

'And the private English coaching?'

'I have three students. I'll look for more. Exams are less than three months away. There are bound to be some desperate parents about. My brother might give me work on the switchboard at his taxi firm, too.'

'Good stuff. Take heart. There's a booming economy out there. You've had a setback, but there are bound to be more opportunities.'

'Sure.' Nick thought about telling Dave about the police raid. But if he did, he would have to tell him about the crack, or the story wouldn't make sense. On the other hand, if Dave heard about the bust later, it would look odd if Nick hadn't mentioned anything. He decided to downplay it.

'By the way,' he said, when Dave got up to show him out. 'I had a visit from Old Bill last Saturday.'

Dave frowned. 'You'd better sit back down.'

Nick gave the bare-bones details. 'They didn't find anything. There wasn't anything to find. But somebody had tipped them off. I think it must be connected with the Power Project, someone with a score to settle.'

Dave nodded. 'Makes sense. I have heard worrying stories about the project and its predecessor. Did you read the thing in the *Guardian*? They did an exposé that embarrassed a lot of people. No wonder the Crack Action Team got closed down.' He hesitated, then added, 'Which reminds me: I saw you quoted in one of the tabloids.'

'They made something of nothing.'

'Be on your guard. All in all, perhaps you're best out of that job. Do you have any idea who called the police on you?'

'No. But I am worried that they'll keep trying to get me sent down again. To be honest with you, I stayed at my girlfriend's this weekend. I'm worried about going back to the flat in case it happens again.'

'You can't live your life that way,' Dave told him. 'I'll make a note in your file. You still have two years of probation, but the first one has gone really well. That will count in your favour if anything comes up that might provoke a recall. If something does happen, don't wait for your next scheduled meeting. Call me at once.'

Monday lunchtime. The hostage situation at Wormwood Scrubs had fizzled out overnight and the media hadn't got hold of it. No radio interview. Sarah needn't have returned last night. But the early start meant she had cleared her desk. Leaving the chamber after immigration questions, she passed Alison Blythe, who looked knackered.

'Ali, hi. How are things going?'

'At home, terrible. Petra's teething. I hardly get any sleep.'

'That must be rough.'

'It is.' She hesitated, then her words came out in a rush. 'Sorry I ambushed you at Home Office questions the other week. I should have warned you first, co-ordinated our approach to the issue. But I'd promised to ask a question and I was so low on sleep . . . still friends?'

'Of course,' Sarah said. 'We have to stick together.' Then she seized on a thought that had been brewing for a few days. 'Actually, I've got a suggestion. Maybe you could run it by a few people. We're not going to get anywhere with prison-issue condoms or needle exchanges, not in the short term.'

'So I'm wasting my time?'

'You're never entirely wasting your time. It's a drip, drip effect. But there is another tack I was going to try with my boss. It'd look better if the idea came through you, though. Bleach. The biggest cause of HIV in prisons is dirty needles. Not just for junkies, but through tattoos, which are a huge factor in spreading infections. If we make bleach available in a controlled fashion, for cleaning needles, it would help. Next Question Time, ask me to investigate it, would you?'

Ali looked thoughtful. 'Couldn't bleach be used as a weapon?'

'I think it's still effective at fairly low dilutions. We don't want people killing themselves by drinking the stuff, either. Why don't you look into it?'

'I will. But shouldn't you get credit for the idea?'

'Happy to share.'

Sarah waited for a car back to the Home Office and ended up getting a lift with her boss.

'The committee I asked you about last week,' he said, when they were ensconsed in the wide, leather-upholstered back seat. 'I take it you're in?'

'Of course,' she told him. 'I meant to ask you for the date of the next meeting. I want to make sure that I keep it clear.'

'I'll email you later. We refer to it as the ABC committee.'

'Very apt,' she replied: the letters referred to the levels of drug classification.

Sarah realized that she hadn't seen Paul for a fortnight, or she could have asked him for the date of the next meeting. Was their fling fading out? Maybe that would be for the best. Chinese walls were hard to maintain in the bedroom. She would be glad to get clear of the Power Project, too. In career terms, it had served a purpose, getting her onto the ABC committee. In personal terms, it had helped Nick, for a while. From now on, it could only get messy.

With luck, the Power Project would wind down naturally. She was meeting Suraj next week to iron out the details. Kingston would return to his job at the city council. The other employees would join the Crack Action Team's former workers on the dole. The project was an easy thing to end. She couldn't say the same for her relationship with Paul. Or, for that matter, Nick.

32

It might be over. He didn't like it when you challenged him. You didn't like it when he hit you. Just the once, and he apologized afterwards, said he was under a lot of stress. You told him to fuck off and got out of the four-by-four. That was a week ago. He hasn't been in touch since.

He only hit you on the shoulder, barely left a bruise. Some girls wear bruises from their boyfriends as a mark of honour, but you don't buy into that. There's stuff in your past, shit you can't remember properly, don't want to remember. You didn't deserve to be hit. You know that violence breeds violence. It's in *Macbeth*. But you're sorry you didn't hit him back.

You ought to be strong. What's to stop you dumping him? You shouldn't be with a guy who's decades older than you. It's not natural. It ought to be possible to stop loving someone. Other girls do it all the time.

But he is your first, your only, and you love him completely. You can't concentrate at school. You could do with one last tutorial with Nick, but don't dare call him, not after what happened. Your lover wouldn't admit anything, but you know he was behind it; you know he moves drugs. You've heard him talk numbers.

Why has he got it in for Nick? Does he think you're screwing him? Is he that jealous? Or could it have something to do with drugs? Maybe Nick isn't all he seems. You don't want to think this, you trust him. You have to trust somebody.

On Friday, at the end of school, your lover texts you. *Am i forgiven yet? cant live without you. see me tmw aft, please.* It takes you all of two minutes to make up your mind, unmake it, then make it again, text back two letters. *OK.*

He doesn't come on Saturday, though. Instead he texts, *Sorry, messy stuff at home, pick you tmw, end of road 4ish xxx.* You could say no, but you don't. You're there the next day, even though it's raining. You have your best underwear on. You get in the front seat and he drives off before you have time to buckle up. Then he starts talking.

'I'm sorry,' he says. 'What I did last week, I'm not that guy. I'll never do it again, I promise.'

'Fine,' you say. 'But if you hurt me again, I'll hurt you back.'

'And I'll deserve it.'

You push your luck. 'I don't want you to hurt Nick either.'

He is silent.

'I know what you did. I don't need to know why.'

'No, you don't. But he can hurt me.'

'Then fix it some other way. It's not fair to get him sent back to prison. Are we cool on that?'

'We're cool.' He sighs. 'I've been under a lot of stress lately, work stuff. It should ease up in the next couple of months. After that, I'll be in Nottingham more. We should think about getting you a place of your own, a place where I can visit you whenever I'm free. What do you say?'

'I say yes.'

'But I don't want you taking other guys there, no matter who they are.'

He doesn't mention Nick's name. He doesn't have to. You go for a short drive. He has the key to two flats, he says. You want to find out when he's leaving his wife, moving in with you, but don't dare ask.

The first flat is at the top end of Mapperley Park, not far from the hostel. It's cold, but you fool around in the biggest bedroom anyway. The place has a 'For Sale' sign, you notice, so you risk the question.

'Is this for you, or for me?'

'Maybe it's neither,' he teases. 'Maybe we're here because I'm too cheap to fork out for a hotel room.' He shakes his head. 'This flat's too modern. Reminds me of the eighties. Let's move on.'

The next place is the top floor of an old house. It's near the city centre and People's College, where you plan to go in the autumn. The bedroom has an old gas fire, which you turn on. Soon, it's cosy. You make love on the mattress. He takes care not to leave stains. After, you stand on the bed, look at the view from the skylight. In front of you, the arboretum. Beyond, the whole city stretches out.

'I like it here,' you say.

'Pass your exams and it's yours. This, or somewhere like it.'

You hug him. 'Are there any more?'

'There's always more. But not today. I have to do stuff with my kids.'

'I'd like to meet your kids.'

He doesn't reply, so you turn to see his reaction. He is staring into space. You said the wrong thing. You will never meet his kids. He will never buy you this flat. The promises men make after sex are bullshit, all the girls say that. Why should this man be any different?

33

Nick stayed in Nancy's maisonette for ten days before taking Dave Trapp's advice. Nancy didn't seem bothered when he told her that he was moving back into his flat. They were cramping each other's style. She got up at seven every day to go to work. At home in his flat, jobless, he could lie in. At Nancy's, he felt cranky and found it hard to get back to sleep once she was gone. Some time after four Nancy got home and started on about her day. Nick feigned interest, but she wasn't fooled. Things were definitely better between them when they didn't see each other Sunday through Wednesday.

This Monday, after his first night back in his own bed, he'd had a lie in. It was gone one and he'd only had a mug of tea and a slice of toast. Nick decided to treat himself to lunch out while he could still afford it. He walked down Derby Road, with its restaurants and antique shops, through Chapel Bar, where the city centre began. He bought the *Post* and took it to the Bell Inn, where he ordered a pint and a ham roll.

The front page headline of the *Post* was CASE AGAINST DRUG DEALER COLLAPSES.

The story spread over two inside pages, reviving all the gossip about the Power Project and its predecessor. It appeared that key witnesses had withdrawn their statements and the Crown Prosecution Service had decided not to proceed. Frank Davis had been released from prison that weekend, after serving nearly five months.

Nick wondered how this news would affect the Power Project. He looked again at the photo of Davis in the paper, tried to recall whether he'd had dealings with him six years ago, when he was growing dope. He didn't think so. He'd kept his criminal contacts to a minimum. Back then, though, Davis was small fry.

Lunch over, he decided to go home. The walk from the pub took less than fifteen minutes and the flat was just as he'd left it. The post had come, a circular. He was waiting for the Power Project to send on his P45, which the benefits people would need to process his claim. The phone rang.

'Nick, it's Sarah.' She sounded formal, like she wasn't alone.

'How are you?' he asked, glad to hear her voice.

'Swamped, as ever. And I've got a situation. Could you meet me at the Power Project office, say at about half three?'

'Sure. But you do know I don't work there any more?'

'I know. Something's happened. I'd rather tell you face to face.'

Sarah put down the phone. Nick would probably assume that she wanted to talk about Frank Davis's release from prison. What an embarrassment that was. She found it hard to believe the latest fiasco. Corrupt police. Lost evidence. Flaky witnesses. Eric had phoned to tell her about it yesterday. He was the angriest she'd ever heard him. The situation was a disaster, he said. The biggest dealer the city's drugs squad had ever caught had just got away with everything – and he, Eric, was ultimately responsible.

Sarah had tried to calm him down, tell him it wasn't his fault. She needed to maintain a sense of perspective. As far as she was concerned, Davis was just another drug dealer.

Suraj, the board chair, had to go to another meeting. Sarah was left with Jed Goodward, the middle-aged vicar, who was deputy chair. Jed had round granny-glasses, giving him the air of a sixties hippy. Sarah had no time for religion, but felt it was useful to have a member of the clergy onside. People tended to trust them more than they did politicians. Chantelle brought in two coffees.

'Nick Cane will be here in a few minutes,' Sarah said. 'Can you call me when he arrives, please?'

Chantelle gave Sarah an intrigued smile. 'Can do.'

'You look troubled,' Jed told her.

'I am.'

'I thought Suraj's arguments about Nick Cane made sense.'

'They do,' Sarah said. 'But they could cost me.'

'If you wanted to be seen as a hardline, anti-drug figurehead, you would hardly have given him a reference in the first place.'

'It's just that I don't want to be accused of personal bias.' If she told Eric what they were planning to do, he would tell her she was being a fool.

'Would I be right in saying that you and Nick Cane used to be lovers?'

Sarah started, and looked up sharply. The expression on Jed's face was a kind one.

'How did you work that out?' she asked.

'Give me some credit for understanding human nature. Kingston told me that you intervened for him once too often. He suspected the same thing, but was far too savvy to hint at it outside our private meetings.'

Sarah smiled. 'Kingston didn't do a bad job here, given the impossible brief that he was handed.'

The clergyman smiled back. 'Don't get me started on impossible briefs. This Nick, do you still have feelings for him?'

Sarah nodded. 'Any kind of romantic involvement is impossible, given my job. We both know that, but we go back a long way.'

'You must still think he's a good man. Otherwise you wouldn't have helped him get this job.'

'No good deed goes unpunished,' Sarah quoted. 'Who said that?'

'A cynic.'

'I try not to be too cynical, but it's an occupational hazard.'

'In my profession, we have the opposite problem.'

3 4

Chantelle told Nick he would have to wait. There was something off about her manner. The usual braggadocio wasn't
there. He tried to make conversation.

'You look nice without your glasses.'

She gave him an odd, distasteful look. 'I'm trying out contact
lenses. They make these disposable ones now.'

'You've got nice eyes.'

She shook her head. 'You're choosing a funny time to come
on to me.'

He didn't know what she meant. 'Perhaps I can collect my P45
while I'm in. I need it.'

'Can't give you that until somebody in charge tells me to,' she
said, in a quiet voice.

Nick didn't hide his confusion. 'Is Kingston in the board meeting?'

Her sour expression disappeared. 'You haven't heard, have you?'

'Heard what?'

'Kingston's dead.'

'You're kidding.'

She wasn't. 'He got in from his badminton game yesterday
evening, dropped dead at the dinner table right in front of his
wife and kids. Stroke.'

Nick swore. 'He looked –'

'He had hypertension. Running this place didn't help.'

'Was it . . .?' Nick wanted to ask if the stroke was connected with the release of Frank Davis. But the question might seem like a slur against a religious man who had just died, so Nick didn't form it aloud.

'What?'

'Never mind. Who's the new boss?'

'You tell me.'

The door to Kingston's office opened. Jed Goodward came out. Nick knew his face from photographs. Fifty-something, almost bald at the front but with long, wispy grey hair at the back, and a benign smile. He held out his hand.

'Nick Cane? Good to meet you at last. Come in, please.'

The only other person in the room was Sarah. She gave him a nod, a forced smile. Jed sat down and put on a let's-get-down-to-business voice.

'Have you heard about Kingston?'

'Chantelle just told me.'

'A great loss. But let's move on to why you're here. We're sorry that your position at the Power Project didn't work out as you might have hoped. I believe that Mr Bell terminated your contract.'

Nick chose his words carefully. 'I was led to believe that it was no reflection upon my performance, that it was simply because funding had been withdrawn.'

'Indeed. The project is to be brought to a premature end. All staff members are being put on notice. Final reports have to be written. There's a lot of tedious administration to be done.'

'I see.'

'What we want to know,' Sarah said, taking over, 'is whether you'd be willing to be the person who does that administration. Come back on the same salary. We'd pay you for last week, of course. In fact, as far as I can tell from Kingston's desk, the paperwork on your termination never went through.'

'I've still got a job here?'

'Yes,' Jed said. 'In fact, we want you to take charge.'

'Me?' Nick was staggered.

'There's nobody else who's qualified,' Jed told him. 'I've looked through the records and the other board members are unanimous. You're the only person with a degree. You have good communication skills. Sarah tells me you have administrative experience.'

Presumably she was referring to his voluntary work with the Labour party. Nick wasn't going to argue. 'How long would the job last, exactly?'

'We could give you three months,' Sarah said.

'And a very solid reference,' Jed offered. 'We would, of course, expect you to be looking for other work while you finished up here.'

'It probably won't take the full three months,' Sarah pointed out.

'And what about the others? Will they all do three months, too?'

'Some. Their contracts vary slightly, so that's one thing you'd have to look into at once. You'd have access to legal advice, obviously.'

'I expect that Chantelle can help me go through the paperwork. She's efficient, you know. I'd like to keep her on for the full term, if possible.'

'Ah,' Sarah said. 'I'm afraid that won't be possible.'

'Chantelle already has a new post,' Jed told him. 'She'll be leaving at the end of the week.'

'Then I'd better get on with things as quickly as possible,' Nick said.

'So you'll take the job?' Sarah said, her face relaxing into a familiar half-smile. 'That's a relief.'

'I'll leave you to it,' Jed told them. 'Thanks for your cooperation, Nick. And, again, sorry you've been messed around.'

He shook Nick's hand again, then left Sarah and Nick alone.

'Are you sure you want me in charge?' Nick asked. 'With my record? There was a police raid on my flat, did you hear that?'

'I hear most things. As for the rest of it, keeping you on shows we're sticking by our guns. Giving ex-offenders a chance. But all we really want is a safe pair of hands to shut the thing down. Put all the staff on gardening leave if that's easiest. You'll have a lot of paperwork to go through.'

'I will.' He paused, looked around at Kingston's old office. 'I'd better get on with sorting this place out if Chantelle is leaving at the end of the week.'

'Today, actually. Sorry, Nick. She has some holiday left.'

Nick felt like he was missing something, but it seemed safest not to ask. Instead he said, 'Sarah, how's your mum? Has she had her operation yet?'

'It's just been delayed again. It's driving me crackers. She's waiting for a new date, but we're probably talking about July. She keeps insisting it's not serious, but she's got a cancerous tumour in her bowel and they shouldn't delay cutting it out.'

'Tell her I was asking after her.' He squeezed Sarah's hand, looked at her. 'Is there anything I can do for you, to help?'

'I don't know.' Sarah seemed distracted. Her shoulders were hunched and the lines under her eyes had doubled since he saw her last. 'I don't think so. There is something on my mind but . . .'

'But what?' Nick asked, when she didn't finish the sentence. At another time he would have pressed her further but, in this context, she was his boss. She was doing him a favour.

'It can wait. Maybe we could have a drink soon, catch up. You can let me know the score here.'

'Great,' Nick said.

'I'll let you catch Chantelle before she finishes.'

Nick walked Sarah to the door.

'Do you want to lock up then come through to the office?' he asked Chantelle.

'Which office?'

'Kingston's office. That is, my new office.'

There was a flicker of surprise, then she stood up. 'I'm all yours,' she said.

35

Paul turned up unannounced at Sarah's flat the evening before the second ABC committee meeting. It wasn't convenient. Sarah had to stay in London until Friday afternoon, which would mean she had no time off at the weekend. And she had a date already. Dinner with Andrew Saint. She had cancelled on him twice since he phoned at Christmas. She couldn't do it a third time. Andrew was the sort of bloke she might need one day. Anyway, she was fond of him. She wasn't good at maintaining friendships, yet he had made the effort to stay friends with her. He had an annoying side, as did most people, but a long shared history overrode minor irritations. Andrew would have known that she preferred French wine to the Australian bottle Paul had brought with him tonight.

'Should I be jealous?' her lover asked when she explained that she couldn't spend the evening with him.

'It's an old friend.'

'The one I met in Nottingham? Have you seen him again?'

'Only at the Power Project.' Sarah didn't want to go into how Nick had been rehired. Earlier Eric had told her it was a mistake. 'This is another guy I was at university with. No romantic history, but we stay in touch.'

'I've missed you.'

'Is that why you've been neglecting me?'

'I've been busy. But I also get the sense that you're cooling off.'

Maybe Sarah should just come right out and say it. *Yes, I am. I'm not convinced you've really left your wife. If I was after an affair with a married man, I could do better.* But her feelings for Paul were more complicated than that.

'We've both cooled off,' she said. 'That's what happens after you've been seeing someone for three months. Let's not have any recriminations.' She looked at her watch. 'I really do have to go.'

'Let me drive you there.'

He'd brought his Shogun into town. Maybe he was telling the truth about living here full time. He couldn't park outside Alastair Little, but dropped her near by, and gave her a lingering kiss.

'I'm sorry I've been such a stranger. But I have been working hard, as you'll find out tomorrow. Can I come and see you in Nottingham, soon?'

'I guess,' Sarah said.

Andrew arrived at the restaurant a minute after she did. They were given a table next to one occupied by a famous actor.

'Did I see you getting out of a Shogun just now, driven by a rather handsome young man?' Andrew asked.

'That was me,' Sarah said.

'The young man looked like Paul Morris, the guy who runs the government's drugs advisory policy unit,' Andrew observed.

Fuck, Andrew was well connected. 'I'm not sure that such a unit officially exists,' Sarah said. 'And, anyway, you're confusing him with someone else.'

Andrew gave her a wicked smile and they began to talk about other things.

Your exams are coming up, only a couple of weeks away. All your coursework is completed, which at least means you have some high grades in the bag. English, for sure. You've had no excuse to see Nick and he no longer visits the hostel. You miss his company.

Your lover hasn't been round for weeks, hasn't even texted. The less you see him, the more you think about him. That last Sunday, in the flat, he told you your only priority should be your exams. He promised you a flat. You must try to keep that in mind.

Shaz is pregnant. So far, she's only told you and Beany. For once, Shaz has power over Beany because he wants her to keep the baby. Baby fathers get more respect. Shaz isn't sure whether to keep it or not. She talks about it with you.

'If I can't stay off the pipe is it okay to have a kid?'

You tell her to talk to her social worker, but you know she won't. You feel sorry for Shaz, so you have a word with Alice. You and her have a proper talk sometimes, when nobody else is around. Alice is off to uni. She's worked her notice and it's her last day.

'You've got the right idea, Jerry,' she says. 'Study hard, stay off anything stronger than weed. It's the only way to get a life.'

'Have you noticed anything about Shaz?' you ask.

'You mean apart from her working as a prossie?'

'She's up the spout.'

You explain what Beany wants and how Shaz isn't sure whether to go along with it. Alice surprises you with her response.

'She shouldn't give a shit what Beany wants. Anyway, he won't be interested when the baby's born addicted to crack and doesn't look like him.'

'Why wouldn't it look like him?'

'Do you know how many blokes she's been with?'

'She always makes them use a condom, she says.'

'Condoms break. You on the pill?'

You nod.

'Good girl. But if you go with anyone new, always make them wear a rubber too. You don't know what they've got. Leave Shaz to me. I'll have a word, make it sound like I worked it out for myself. Fag?'

You shake your head. You can take tobacco in a spliff, but not on its own.

'Seen Nick lately?' you ask.

'Not for a while,' Alice says. 'He started working at the Power Project again, did you know that?'

'No, I didn't. How come?'

'Bloke that used to run it dropped dead.'

'Kingston Bell?'

'That's right. He was on the board here. You must have met him.'

'I guess. What did he die of?'

'Who cares? He was a creepy bastard, tried to get me sacked once. Good riddance, if you ask me.'

36

Running down the Power Project didn't turn out to be as straightforward as Sarah had suggested it would be. Nick unravelled complex financial arrangements, attended committee meetings, consultation forums. It didn't help that Chantelle, who was familiar with this stuff, had finished the day he started. She'd tried to tell him what he needed to know, but he'd had to ring her a couple of times since, only to find that her mobile was never on and she was slow to return calls.

The more Nick looked into how the project had been run, the more respect he had for Kingston Bell. Despite the complex funding and disparate workforce, some good work had been done. But that work had barely begun.

The project's other workers drifted in and out of the office. Nick handed out redundancy notices, asked them to fill in timesheets, delegated what tasks he could. Already, reference requests were coming in, for the workers had little to do but look for new jobs. The only person who didn't have a lot of time on his hands was Nick.

He didn't mind. It felt good to be busy for a change, to have responsibilities. Having been the first to lose his job gave Nick cover from criticism when explaining redundancy terms to his co-workers. Unsurprisingly, none of the others volunteered to take on more than the minimum and Nick, meanwhile, had to do Chantelle's job as well as his own. Working late every night, he saw little of Nancy. She didn't complain. Until recently, she'd had a life that didn't involve him, a life she had returned to. He missed her company. Kind of. He missed the sex.

On Friday nights, Nancy liked to go clubbing. Gone seven, his second week back, still at the office, he called her to suggest that they meet at the Bomb, a small place on Bridlesmith Gate. When Sarah and Nick were students, it had been a cheap-as-chips club called the Hippo. Now it was a bit more hip, with name DJs and a cool, thirty-something crowd. Nick felt comfortable there. But Nancy preferred the scuzzier dives on the edge of town. Tonight she'd suggested Hatch in Sneinton, not far from the open-air market. After a brief negotiation, he'd agreed to meet her there. After eleven. Nancy had somewhere else to be first, it seemed, so he walked over to the hostel. He'd get a bus into town just before the pubs closed.

Alice wasn't on duty. Whoever was didn't answer the door, but a girl on her way out let him in. A new face. He knocked on Jerry's door.

'C'min.'

She was lying on her bed, wearing only knickers and a T-shirt, reading. Her hair, normally straight and immaculate, was tangled and she had a couple of zits on her nose. She sat up, embarrassed to see him.

'Want me to go out and come in again?' he asked.

'It's okay,' she told him. 'Nothing you haven't seen before.'

She got off the bed and put on some jeans.

'I was looking for Alice,' he said.

'She's finished. Left this week. She starts uni in the autumn. First, she's gone travelling.'

'Good for her.'

'Played your cards right, you could have gone with her.'

The timing would have been right, Nick thought. Finish the job with a few quid saved, take a nice young woman on holiday. Alice was a reformed smack addict, but so what? He was a reformed cokehead. And she hadn't spent five years in prison.

'I came to see how you're doing in your exams,' he told Jerry.

They talked. Jerry had English in the bag thanks to coursework already done. It sounded like maths had gone well, which was crucial. You needed maths and English for most things. They discussed what A levels she would do and Jerry seemed to have that sorted out, too.

'Where will you live? Can you hang on here?'

'Would you want to?'

'Not really,' he admitted.

'Social services will help me get a place to stay. There's benefits. School said that the government are promising something called education maintenance allowance. I'll get by.'

She would, he thought. She was determined enough. Intelligence and determination would get her through. Unless . . .

'What about your bloke? The one who paid for your lessons with me? Is he still on the scene?'

'He works away a lot.' Jerry looked at her watch. 'The new warden goes round all the rooms at half ten, checks up on us.'

'Ah.' It wouldn't do to be found here. 'I'd better get going.' He paused. 'What were you reading, by the way, revision?'

She held up a novel that he had suggested to her. *A Gun for Sale*, the one novel that Greene had set in Nottingham, where he'd once lived. 'It's cool,' she said, 'reading about the city all that time ago. Prefer Dickens, though.'

'You've got plenty of time to read both.'

'I like reading old books. It takes me out of myself.'

'Me too,' Nick said, though he hadn't read anything other than a newspaper lately. 'By the way, I'll be back on the dole in a couple of weeks. You can come and see me, if you want. Just for a talk.'

'Thanks.' Suddenly, she threw her arms around him and squeezed, hard. It was a nice hug, the nicest he'd had in a long while. 'You're a mate. You smell good. Taking your girlfriend somewhere good?'

'Meeting her at a place called Hatch.'

'It's a dive. She must be the sort of girl who likes slumming it.'

'Why else would she go out with me?' Nick quipped, then took his leave. He managed to get out of the building without being noticed.

Hatch was one of those clubs with no sign outside. The door policy was obscure. Nick saw people turned away, but the crusty on the door merely nodded at him and took his fiver. Inside, beer was sold in coldish cans and dope was smoked openly. The music was loud house, which Nick was okay with, but he felt less comfortable with the crowd. They reminded him too much of his clients, both at the Power Project and at Victor House.

Sure enough, there was Shug, whom he used to counsel, wearing sunglasses inside, probably thinking they made him look like a rapper. He didn't acknowledge Nick. No sign of Nancy. The place was filling up. The beats getting louder, though the small dance floor still had room to move. Was there another dance floor? If there was, Nick couldn't find it. But you never knew. The place used to be a furniture showroom cum warehouse. It had obscure corners.

He needed to relax. He bought a beer, then got out a single-skin spliff, one of four that he'd rolled earlier. He stood at the edge of the dance floor and smoked it, nicotine and hash easing into the cramped corners of his brain, until the music made more sense and he began to sway with the sounds. Then Nancy was there, in a red skirt and white top, beneath which her black bra was very visible.

'I've been looking for you,' he said.

'I was in the loo,' she told him.

For how long? He stopped himself looking at his watch and they danced for a while, Nancy sharing his drink. Then they took a break. He tried to start a conversation, but Nancy told him she was knackered.

'Long working week.'

'Your exam groups must have finished by now.'

'Don't want to talk about work,' she said. 'I need another pee.'

While she was gone, Nick bought a couple more cans. She didn't come back, so he lit another spliff. Dope helped him to lose himself in the music. Even so, he hoped that Nancy would get bored soon, take him home with her. Somebody tapped him on the shoulder.

'Can I have some of that?' It was Chantelle, wearing leather hot pants.

'Uh, sure,' Nick said.

She took the joint, gave it a couple of deep sucks, then passed it back to him. 'Here for work or pleasure?' she shouted.

'Entirely pleasure. How's your new job?'

'It's Friday night. I don't want to talk about work. Going to give me one of those beers?'

'Why not?' He handed it over. He could get Nancy another one later. Where was she? He passed the joint back to Chantelle, but she shook her head.

'I'm a lightweight. My head's spinning already.'

'That's more likely the nicotine than the dope. Who are you with?'

'Just people.'

Looking over her shoulder, he thought he saw Nancy return, quite enjoyed the idea of her finding him with this tall, good-looking woman.

'Looking for that woman I saw you dancing with?'

'Uh huh.'

'You know she's gone to the back where they smoke crack, right?'

Nick frowned. Was Chantelle winding him up? 'No, she's gone to the –'

'Want me to show you?'

Spliff in hand, he followed Chantelle past the Ladies, through a fire door, across an outside courtyard to a metal door. There was a guy on the door, but Chantelle only had to nod at him. They went inside. It was dark. The air acrid. Nancy was the first person that Nick saw. She had a home-made pipe in her hand, a plastic bottle with a metal stem that she sucked until her face filled with strange satisfaction. Then she saw Nick and her expression hardened. Her eyes darted to Chantelle.

'I'll leave you to it,' Chantelle told him. 'Sorry.'

Nick muttered his thanks and joined Nancy. The music in here was quieter than in the main club, more trancey, with traces of early Pink Floyd. It wouldn't be difficult to have a conversation, but none of the dozen or so people in the room were talking. All were concentrated on their pipes or on waiting for a pipe.

'What do you think you're doing?' he asked her.

Nancy rolled her eyes. 'It's a weekend thing. Want some?'

'No. I think we should go.'

'I'll come back and dance in a minute.' She pointed to the spliff in his hand. 'You do your thing. I'll do mine.'

He returned to the main club, looked for Chantelle. The place was much fuller, so it was hard to spot her. Minutes passed. He stubbed out his spliff and necked his beer. Still no Nancy. Her invitation for him to join her tonight had been half-hearted, he remembered. Now he knew why. He felt partly responsible. She'd probably been using since she took the bag from his. But he had no right to tell her what to do, and certainly couldn't help her when she was off her face.

He decided to call it a night.

Outside, the streets were deserted. It was nearly two. Shouldn't be hard to get a taxi. Or he could walk. A police car drove by and Nick was conscious that he still had two more spliffs in his pocket. But the car didn't slow down. Then a green Ford Escort pulled out from a side road and stopped right in front of him. Chantelle, on her own.

'Need a lift?'

'Thanks.'

He got into the front passenger seat. 'Not giving your friends a lift?'

'They wanted to stay later. Me, I'm not much good after midnight on a working day. I don't take the right stimulants.'

'Me neither,' he said. These days, it was true.

'Give up on your girlfriend?'

'She's not really . . . I can't afford to get mixed up in that stuff, not with my record. She should know that.'

'There's a difference between knowing something and bearing it in mind,' Chantelle said, keeping her eyes on the road.

'I guess it's time to finish the thing we have.' He decided to change the subject. 'You did right, anyway, moving on to a different job when you did.'

'Drugs work, it's like being King Canute, trying to turn back the tide.'

'The thing about Canute was that he was demonstrating to his subjects that his powers were limited. Even he, the king, couldn't turn back the tide.'

'I'd forgotten, you're the teacher. That why you were smoking a spliff in there, going with the tide?'

'Something like that.'

She laughed. They turned off Mansfield Road onto Forest Road, a minute's drive from his flat.

'Where do you live?' he asked her.

'Wouldn't you like to know.'

She was flirting with him a little, but he didn't know whether to pursue it. They were at the Alfreton Road lights.

'Can I invite you in for a drink?' he asked her.

'One more and I'd be over the limit,' she said. 'Anyway, like I told you, I'm done in. But thanks for the offer.'

'Can I call you?'

'You've got my number,' she said.

The lights changed. She turned the corner and pulled up outside his flat. She knew exactly where he lived.

'Goodnight, Nick Cane,' she said.

He took a risk and kissed her on the lips. She let her lips meet his for more than a moment, but her mouth didn't open.

'I will call you,' he said. 'Thanks for the lift.'

37

Rumours of a reshuffle began to build. The government was over a year old. The prime minister was bound to make some changes before the summer recess began next month. Sarah didn't dare hope for promotion. She wasn't strongly enough connected. She hated the way the parliamentary party had already divided into two factions – three, if you included the left-wingers, who had no influence. You were either with Tony or Gordon, no middle ground.

Ideologically, she was closer to Gordon, but, personally, she felt a stronger connection with Tony. Fighting for equality, for fairness, was what had drawn her to politics. Tony had no ideology that she could discern, but he was all for fairness, and he was a winner.

Neither Gordon nor the prime minister was on the ABC committee, so her presence on that wouldn't help her with either man. The committee, in fact, wasn't terribly interesting. For the moment it consisted of Paul and his team presenting information then being quizzed about it and tasked with gathering still more information. Discussion of actual policy seemed a long way off. Still, drugs policy made a change from the relentless misery that was attached to every aspect of her work as prisons minister.

Sarah hadn't rebelled, had kept her nose clean. There had been no major screw-ups on her watch. Had she done enough to justify the prime minister keeping her in her current job? She had pushed for things that her boss didn't want. Been listened to, then ignored. Voters liked to keep prisons far from their minds, and homes. They considered rehabilitation a meaningless word. The UK might have a representative democracy, but that didn't mean its politicians were there to represent the public's views. If they were, hanging would never have been abolished. They were there to exercise their judgement on the voters' behalf. One in three men had a criminal record of some sort, Nick among them. He was often in Sarah's thoughts when she deliberated over policy.

After Prime Minister's Question Time, she grabbed a ciabatta for lunch then went to get some air on the terrace outside the Strangers' Bar overlooking the Thames. The panorama of the city beyond the river was one of the best views in London.

'Sarah!' It was Gill Temperley, in a linen, flower-patterned dress, looking five years younger than when she left government a year ago. 'I'm entertaining a friend of yours.'

There was Andrew Saint, having a conversation with the barman. Non-MPs weren't allowed to buy drinks, but the rule was sometimes relaxed when a guest was with a member.

'Are you two getting on well?' Sarah asked.

'Yes. Andrew's very generous . . . and talented,' Gill said. Then she lowered her voice. 'And rich. Though how he makes his money is a source of speculation. Is he one of those men who manipulates currencies, do you think?'

'Anything's possible.' Sarah said. When they'd had dinner he'd mentioned currency dealing. 'Why don't you ask him?'

'I've tried. Andrew has the politician's trick of giving you a full and frank answer that leaves you no better informed than before you asked the question.'

Sarah smiled. She remembered that trait in Andrew, too. He joined them, carrying a pint for himself and a white wine for Gill.

'Sarah!' He kissed her on the cheek. 'If I'd known you were here I'd . . . what are you having?'

'It's okay, I need to go in a minute,' Sarah assured him. 'Good to see you two getting on so well.' Andrew's eyes darted to the side for a moment and Gill gave him a calming look. My God, Sarah thought, she's sleeping with him. Or, at the very least, thinking about it. There had always been rumours about Gill and her frequently rotated 'research assistants', generally pretty young men with plenty of blond hair. Yet there must come a time when you valued a loyal guard dog higher than a cute puppy. Maybe now that she was out of power and her husband was practically retirement age, Gill felt the need of a rich protector like Andy. Sarah looked at her watch. 'Actually, I'm late already. I came out for a breath of fresh air, to wake myself up.'

'I'm in Nottingham tomorrow,' Andrew said. 'Maybe we could meet up for a drink, if you have time.'

'Sorry. I won't be in the constituency until Friday,' Sarah told him. 'Got to rush.'

She generally caught the train back on Thursday evenings, but this week she was going to the theatre with Paul. It would be only her fourth theatre visit since becoming an MP. She'd wanted to see Marber's *Closer* at the National Theatre for ages. Now it was in the West End, which made a visit easier, but still problematic. You couldn't get back to the Commons in time if your pager went off for a vote, that was the trouble. And staying over on a Thursday cut into constituency time. This week, however, she had nothing on in Nottingham until Friday afternoon. When Paul suggested an outing, their first in weeks, she had agreed at once.

Afterwards, if she could manipulate things that way, they would go back to his, not hers. Because, in the morning, before she caught the train home, she intended to end it. Paul had given her one evasive answer too many and she was convinced that he hadn't really separated from his wife.

Sarah had met Annette twice. The first time was at a county council social function last year. They had hardly spoken. The second time was at Sainsbury's on the Castle Marina, last weekend. When Annette said hello, Sarah didn't recognize her. She'd put on weight. Then, when Paul's wife reintroduced herself, she'd felt awful. Her face must have gone red, through a combination of guilt and fear that the other woman was about to call her over it. That hadn't happened, but it wasn't a feeling that Sarah wanted to repeat. Ever.

Sarah wasn't in love with Paul, had never come close to feeling that way. She didn't want to be the one who broke up a marriage. It was time for both of them to move on.

The exams are over and you can't believe he isn't returning your calls. He's usually in Nottingham by Thursday afternoon, so you text him, repeatedly. No response. Fuck this, you think, and take a taxi to the address you got from his wallet, months ago. You tell the cab to wait, then march straight up to the door. You're wearing a black anorak, have your hair tied back and are holding a large brown envelope.

A kid answers the door. A boy of eleven or so. You say his name.

'Daddy's not here.'

The wife comes to the door. Up close, she's tired, could stand to lose a stone or two. She looks at you suspiciously, but you hold your nerve.

'This needs to be signed for.'

'I can sign for it.'

'In person, sorry.'

'My husband's in London at the moment.'

'When will he be back?'

'Tomorrow, Saturday, I'm not sure. He lives away a lot of the time.'

You see it in her eyes. He isn't just working away. He's gone.

'Perhaps you'd give me his London address. I'll get this redirected.'

She writes it down for you.

'Is that a first-floor flat?'

She shrugs. 'I wouldn't know.'

You thank her for her time. You stop yourself from skipping up the driveway. For you have just seen a deserted woman. Everything he said was true. He has left her. For you.

You take the taxi back to the hostel and tell it to wait again, then you shove a few things in a bag. You're getting on the next train to London.

38

Nick's job had a week and a day to run. There was no prospect of extending his contract. By the end of this week, he would be the only worker left.

When he got in from work, there was a note in the door.

Time you got a mobile, old son. I'll be waiting in the Red Lion. Andrew.

Nick hadn't seen his oldest friend in four months. What was he doing in Nottingham? You didn't come all this way on the off-chance of catching up with a mate.

Andrew wore new, narrower glasses. Every time Nick saw him, he looked a little classier. His beard had shrunk, trimmed around his chin so that it performed only the essential task, detracting from his emerging jowls and wobbling jawline. Andrew bought Nick a pint and a malt whisky chaser.

'What brings you here?' Nick asked.

'A property possibility. Safest place to put your money. Another boom on the way, mark my words.'

They talked about Nick's housing situation. Andrew thought he ought to get somewhere better.

'Or maybe you're waiting for an invite to move in with someone. Who are you seeing at the moment?'

No need for Andrew to ask *if* Nick was seeing anyone. Prison hadn't cured him of his need to always have a girlfriend: little matter whether they were suited or not.

'There was this teacher I used to work with. Bit younger. The sex was great at first, but soon we had nothing to talk about apart from getting wasted. And, after a while, you get tired of getting wasted all the time. You?'

Andrew gave a smile with a trace of smugness. He leaned in, confidentially, although the pub was quiet and nobody sat near them.

'You know me, don't like being tied down. I've been chasing this married woman. Husband works away. Ever been with an older woman?'

'Just the once,' Nick said. 'We had a good time until she realized that she needed someone more mature.'

Andrew gave a sardonic smile.

'How did you meet her?' Nick asked.

'Work.'

'What does she do? No, let me guess. An estate agent.'

Andrew shook his head. 'An MP. You've heard of her.'

For a terrible moment, Nick thought that Andrew was seeing Sarah. But no, he'd said that this was an older woman.

'Go on, then,' he said. 'Tell.'

'Gill Temperley. She was a Home Office minister in the last government, like Sarah is now.'

The name rang no bells for Nick. 'So she's a . . .'

'Tory, yes.'

Andrew had never been political, not really. Even so, Nick was surprised that he had no qualms about pursuing a woman who belonged to, what was for him, the enemy. Thinking about it, he could picture Temperley, vaguely, from before he was sent down: pretty, in a posh way, a shrill voice on the BBC's *Question Time*.

The conversation moved on. Andy repeated his offer of a place to stay in London while Nick looked for work. He didn't reveal anything more about his property deal. Nick asked about his other businesses.

'I've got into a bit of currency dealing,' was all Andrew added to what he had already said. 'Small margins, but lucrative rewards if you have a high turnover and manage it right.'

Andy had to leave before last orders to catch the London train. Nick hadn't told him about the failed bust. He wasn't stupid enough to discuss that in a pub. They went outside, so Andrew could hail a taxi to take him to the station.

'Seen Sarah lately?' Andrew asked.

'Not for months. You?'

'Had lunch with her a while back. I think she's got a new boyfriend.'

'Black guy?'

'Yeah. Have you met him?'

'I went round her flat to talk about some work stuff and this guy came round. She said it was Home Office work and I was hungover, took her word for it. Come to think of it, he looked familiar. Have you met him?'

Andrew hesitated. 'Remember Tall Paul?'

'Vaguely,' Nick said. Andrew had introduced them about seven years ago. 'Never knew his surname.'

'Paul Morris. Big afro? He's cut his hair since then, which is probably why you didn't recognize him. Went into law, then politics. Did quite well for himself, by all accounts. You see, there's hope for all of us.' He held out his arm and a taxi pulled up. 'Stay in touch.'

'I will.' They shook hands, for want of a better gesture, and Andrew got into the taxi.

Nick was tempted to go round to Nancy's, try to sort things out between them. He hadn't been to hers for a couple of weeks.

Since the police raid, things had been strained between them. Then there was that night at Hatch. He'd asked her about it the next time they'd met. She'd said she could handle crack and it was none of his business. She'd hinted that she'd tried it long before he got out of prison. With Carl, presumably.

At least she'd been straight when he saw her last. He'd taken a bottle of wine round. On the third glass, he'd made a tentative enquiry about how she was spending her weekends. Nancy didn't answer directly.

'You're jealous because I'm on the pipe when I could be with you.'

'I didn't say that. I worry about you doing too much. Of course I do.'

'I decide how much *too* much is, not you. Doing that job's changed you. You've forgotten how good drugs can be.'

She was right. Something had changed him. Nick wasn't sure if it was the job, the years he'd spent inside, or just time catching up with him.

'Drugs are good until they aren't,' Nick told her. 'Until you need to take ten times as much and it still doesn't get you as high as it used to.'

'Listen to the guy who got his sentence doubled because the police found four and a half grams of coke on top of all those cannabis plants. The guy who swore he wasn't dealing blow, that he needed that much for personal use. I went to your trial, Nick. Remember?'

That shut him up. They finished their drinks and went to bed. The sex was perfunctory. He hadn't stayed the night. Come to think of it, she hadn't asked him to.

Since he'd told Andrew, he could acknowledge it to himself. He and Nancy were on the way out. She'd always said she expected him to get bored with her, and now he was fulfilling her prophecy. Yet, why? Back when she was twenty-two, they had talked about books, drama, art, music, the lot. Since becoming lovers, they hardly talked about anything. They watched trash on TV and used music as a soundtrack to get smashed to.

But if they were going to finish, he didn't want his last memory of Nancy to be the way it had been the other week, with her grinding her thighs to make him come more quickly.

He'd had three pints and two whiskies, but he wasn't slaughtered. Nancy was only five minutes' bus ride away and she might be pleased to see him. Best, he decided, to phone first. She picked up on the second ring. Nick started on his smarmy apology before she could say a word.

'Nance, sorry I haven't called for –'

'Dickhead,' a male voice interrupted. 'Call this number again and you're dead. Didn't you get the message the first time I gave it you?'

'Carl?'

'Fuck off.' The man hung up and Nick put down his handset. Carl. She'd never stopped seeing Carl. It hadn't occurred to him that Carl was responsible for the beating he had received back in March. But what other 'message' could he have been talking about?

Did Carl do it himself? Hardly mattered. But why hadn't he let on who it was earlier, if he wanted Nick to stay away? Because the message was more for Nancy than it was for Nick. Carl didn't want to get arrested. Now Nick knew why Nancy had only come to visit him once while he was laid up in hospital. She was seeing Carl all that time. Still getting drugs off him.

What about the planted bag of crack, was that Carl too? Nancy said she'd seen a black guy, but she could have been covering for him.

One thing was certain. He and Nancy were over.

*

The train gets in at twenty past ten. You bought a London A–Z at Nottingham station and worked out where to go. It's walking distance. You head out into the streets, pulling the hood up on your anorak. That way, people can't easily tell your age. But it's no good. Even before you leave the station, there are approaches.

'Hey, pretty girl, looking for a place to stay?'

Your hand grips the shaft of the blade you always carry with you, better protection than a rape alarm. So this is London. It could be Hyson Green or the run-down roads leading out of Nottingham, to Mansfield or Alfreton. Only difference is there's more traffic; the roads are wider. You don't see the attraction. In the short walk during which St Pancras turns into King's Cross, you're twice asked for business. You keep your head down, squeeze the handle of the knife. Soon, you will be with him.

Absence sharpens love, you read somewhere. He won't be able to turn you away. He said he wants to wait until after the exams before seeing you. Okay, the exams aren't over yet, not quite. You'll go along with whatever plans he has. Just as long as, tonight, he lets you be with him.

His building isn't hard to find. You expected somewhere smarter, like his place in Nottingham, but Pentonville Road is full of gaudy, cheap shops. Girls younger than you are plying their trade. You know your lover wouldn't be tempted. He's never paid for it in his life. Men who use prostitutes see women as objects. He loves women. He loves you.

His flat is dark, empty-looking. There are only two doorbells. You try them both, twice. No response. You'll have to wait. There's a shop doorway opposite, but that's too obvious. You're bound to be moved on. You don't want anyone to think you're on the game. You can't go into a pub, either. Close up, you don't look anywhere near eighteen.

He'll be home soon. There's a phone box. You can see his flat from there. You'll pretend to be making a call.

There are glossy, coloured cards pasted onto every surface, each decorated with near-naked women and a mobile number. You pick up the phone and pretend to talk to him. He has told you so much about his life. How he was brought up in a home much like yours, went through the whole drugs thing, got married early, then went to university, began to see the world in a new way. He knew he had to make a difference to people who lived like he used to, people like you. If I can make it, you can, he told you. You believe him. But you can only do it with his help.

A taxi pulls up on the corner outside his building. He gets out and your heart leaps. Then someone else gets out of the car. A woman. You recognize her from the TV news, when she talked about the Power Project. You don't know what your lover's London job is. Even so, you tell yourself, the MP's there for something to do with his work. Because it can't be what it looks like. It can't be. They go into the building. A light goes on inside. You stare in disbelief, the situation starting to sink in. Not long afterwards, a light goes out.

A light goes out in you, too.

Nick walked off his anger. After a while, he started to get some perspective. He'd been a fool for a woman, but he'd done that before and doubtless would again. Nancy had cheated on him. That hurt. He wasn't used to being cheated on, but it wasn't like when Sarah cheated on him, during their break-up, fifteen years ago. That was cataclysmic and had taken him years to get over. Tonight, by comparison, was a minor insult to his pride.

Three or four weeks ago, he'd told Chantelle that he was disentangling himself from Nancy, but he hadn't followed through and called her. Why not now? She might be flattered. And he had her number in his wallet, left over from work. He had found it after she gave him that lift home and had written it down.

He focused. It was all right. He'd not had so many drinks that he was likely to make an idiot of himself. He dialled her number.

'Hello?' Her voice sounded posher on the phone, almost BBC.

'Chantelle, it's Nick. I hope you don't mind me phoning at this time.'

'I was wondering if you were ever going to call me.'

'Sorry it's been a couple of weeks but . . . can I come round and see you?' Nick asked, presumptuously.

'Are you a little drunk? Is this a booty call?'

'I guess it is, yes.'

'No three-course meal and an after-dinner drink first?'

'Not unless you haven't already eaten.'

'I have. And I have an early start. But you can call me another time, when you're not in such a hurry, boss man.'

'I certainly will.'

She hung up before he could think of anything else to say. Nick kept walking. He passed the Forest recreation ground, where the football team of the same name used to play. Some of the trees were old enough to remember those early games. Nick saw movements in their shadows. Boys barely in their teens were waiting for trade. They would give a punter a blow job for the price of a ten pound bag of crack, take it in the arse for double or treble that. The police did nothing to stop the trade. The boys would only go somewhere else, they argued.

Opposite the Forest was the High School, which had educated ministers in this government and the last. At the end of its tall stone walls, a girl who couldn't be more than seventeen asked Nick if he was looking for business. He told her that he wasn't, then, fleetingly, felt tempted. She was fit-looking. He had money in his pocket, could take her back to his. He craved the feel of flesh on flesh, the oblivion of orgasm. But he had never succumbed to paying for it, no matter how drunk or horny he was.

If he kept walking along this road, he would find himself opposite Alexandra Park, where Jerry would have just finished her exams. Alice might be on shift. She no longer used the drop-in centre, so he hadn't seen her for a while. He liked Alice. And she'd made it clear that she liked him. Hell, she'd even gone to Jerry's parents' evening for him. If he turned up at the hostel, she might invite him to her room when the girls had all turned in for the night.

But something had happened to Nick this last three months. He had become a professional again. Jerry and Alice were entwined in the world of his work. He could not turn up at the hostel, half cut, bent on seduction and still retain his sense of pride.

Then he remembered that Alice had quit her job. She was backpacking in India. Nick used to dream of going on the road. Lately, he didn't look more than one day ahead.

He turned on his heels and headed home.

39

S arah opened the blinds and stood at the window, trying to choose her words. The street, so busy last night, was quiet now. There was a light rain. The few people on the pavement walked rapidly, on their way to work. Only a girl in a black cagoule lingered near by, perhaps waiting for the phone box to be free.

'Babe?' Paul was awake. His bare chest gleamed in the morning light. He sweated in his sleep. The few times they had spent the night together, she had woken to find him clammy beside her. He didn't snore, but he'd often woken her up by talking in the early hours. Sometimes he had nightmares that made him writhe or cry out, but, in the morning, he never had any recollection of what he had done or said.

'I've put the kettle on,' she told him. 'I'm going for a shower.'

When she got back, he had made coffee. They drank in what should have been companionable silence.

'I bumped into Annette in the constituency last week,' Sarah said. 'I asked how you were. She said you were fine, but the kids weren't seeing enough of you. She said it sometimes felt like you were separated.'

'She doesn't like to admit what's going on,' Paul told her.

'You can imagine how shitty I felt. I don't want to be the cause of pain in a marriage, Paul. I don't think you've been entirely honest with me.'

When he didn't answer, she left the table and began to dress, with her back to him. Only then did he begin to speak.

'It's not easy for me to leave Annette. She put me through university. She knows me inside out. It's more like we're brother and sister than a married couple. She knows I see other women. She accepts that I have another life in London. But we've not talked about divorce, or a legal separation. So, to that extent, yes, I misled you. I'm sorry.'

'Apology accepted,' Sarah said. She felt humiliated. Served her right for breaking one of her own rules. She needed to leave – now – but hadn't done her make-up. That was okay. She could stand the scrutiny on the morning train to Nottingham. 'I'm going. I don't want you to call me again. I'll see you at the ABC committee next week but, from now on, we keep it strictly professional. Agreed?'

'No.'

'Then, tough, we'll have to disagree. It's over. Try to make things work with Annette. She deserves better.'

'I know, but –'

Sarah didn't want to hear the rest. She wouldn't hang around and wait for a taxi. If necessary, she would walk to St Pancras in the rain.

'Wait!' Paul called as she left the flat, shutting the door behind her. She hurried down the stairwell and let herself out into the street. Somebody pushed past her into the building, but Sarah didn't pause or look round, not even when she was on the street and heard Paul, from the outside door, yell his last words.

'Sarah, wait! I need you!'

Need, she thought, walking as fast as two-inch heels would allow, was not the same as love. She had never come close to loving Paul. Last night, after they got back, she had tried to talk about the play with him, to use it as a launch for discussing their relationship. His every response was either trite or irrelevant.

Loneliness and lust, that was all she'd felt. She walked faster, head down. Had she ever got anything out of the relationship beyond the physical? Even that had never been particularly good.

There were no other MPs in the first-class carriage to Nottingham. With luck, she would manage a doze. She needed to catch up on her sleep.

This Friday was Nick's last morning at the Power Project. He showed up before nine, determined to finish things properly. There would be no leaving do today, no farewell drink. He was the only worker left. If he wanted to he could spend the day using the project's phone, internet and stationery to pursue his next job.

Instead, he tied up loose ends. There might be no new career in prospect, but he had lived cheaply and managed to put a bit away during the last six months. He still had most of the five grand Andy Saint had given him last year. Guilt and gratitude money, for Nick had never mentioned Andrew to anyone, even though he had given him the contacts to get started in the wholesale cannabis game. Tall Paul, whom they had discussed last night, had worked for one of those contacts.

Curious, Nick loaded the page for the search engine, Alta Vista. Andrew said that Paul's surname was 'Morris'. He typed in the name. Thousands of them. Could he narrow it down? He tried adding 'Nottingham' and it worked. Nick was directed to BBC Radio Nottingham's website, where there was a short item about his leaving the city.

Mr Morris, who has been chair of the police committee for two years, is stepping down from the County Council in order to take up a special adviser job in the Home Office.

Wow. Andrew was telling the truth about Paul's rise. It was possible to move from dealing drugs to advising the government, at the highest level. Provided you'd never been caught. Provided your past never caught up with you. Provided a dealer from your old world didn't identify you to an MP in your new one.

The failed bust had nothing to do with Jerry, or Beany, or Carl. The person who planted the crack was Tall Paul.

He clocks you at the top of the stairs and stops. He blinks. You still have the hood of your cagoule up, to protect you from the rain, but he recognizes you. 'Jerry! What are you doing here?'

'I had to see you.'

'How did you –?' He stops himself. 'You'd better come in.'

You are getting angrier by the second, but you follow him into the flat. The place is like nowhere you have been before. His house in Nottingham is ordinary, the sort of boring home you see on TV soaps. This place is in a different class. Big African painting on the walls. Bare, polished boards, glass dining table. Books with dust jackets. A wooden wine rack, every space full. He took you to shabby hotels for a screw when he could have moved you in here.

'Why don't you take your anorak off?'

You shake your head. 'How long have you been with that MP?'

His eyes dart from side to side. He didn't expect you to recognize her and doesn't know what to say, so you say it for him.

'Why don't you tell me what the pimps tell their whores? You can love two women at once, more than two if you want. User.'

'It's not that way. Listen.' He takes a step forward and you take a step away from him, so he stops, reconsiders. 'You're right. I am a user. I'm ambitious. But it wasn't you I was using, it was her. You know what I like. You think I enjoy doing it with an old woman like her? She's not just an MP, she's a minister. A high flyer. She can protect me, promote me. And, in return, she gets a taste of me, that's all, a tiny piece compared to what I give to you. It's just the game, sweetheart. You and me, we're the real thing.'

For a moment, half a moment, you let yourself be convinced. Then you remember that he told her he needed her, yelled it across the street. You remember how he hasn't called you once to ask how your exams went, or talked to you about the flat that he promised to move you into. He's a liar. He's always been a liar.

'It's me you're playing games with.'

He pleads. 'No. I love you. I don't want her, I want you.'

You stare at him, rage building up inside you. Everything he's said to you was a lie. You're his dirty, underage bit on the side. Not even the side. The side of the side.

'Where did you sleep last night?' he asks in a fake, caring tone.

'I didn't. I went to an all-night caff after I saw her come in with you.'

'How did you get this address?' His front has gone for a moment and he's treating you like a child again.

'Your wife gave it to me.'

That gets him. The panic in his eyes is sweet to see. You're tempted to take the lie further. Your lover wants to keep it all: you, his wife, that MP woman. There'll be other girls you don't know about. He holds his breath.

'It's all right,' you tell him. 'I pretended I was delivering a package for you. She doesn't know.'

He smiles. 'I need a shower,' he says. 'I'll bet you do too.'

You stand, stern-faced, enjoying the power you have over him. He breathes out. He thinks you're going to forgive him. He thinks you have no choice, that he's the only thing you have going in your life.

'I'll join you in the shower,' you say.

He turns his back on you. He's never done that before. You hate it. Full of rage, you reach into your pocket, grip the shaft of the knife. But then your brain kicks into gear and you remember to think. Only a fool uses their own knife that way, gets blood on her clothes. You check out his kitchen. Then, when the sound of water starts, you begin to undress.

The Nottingham train was delayed by signalling problems but Sarah was still back in the city by midday, with time on her hands. She decided to stop in at the Power Project on her way through town. It was Nick's last day. She wanted to wish him well. Maybe a drink with him would help drive Paul from her mind.

The Power Project offices were almost deserted. Only Nick was inside, sitting at Kingston's old desk, writing a report. He looked up when she came in, grinned. She felt her heart begin to beat more quickly.

'Hello, stranger,' he said.

'I thought I'd see how you were, maybe take you for an early lunch.'

'That's a nice thought,' he said. 'Give me five minutes. I've nearly finished up here.'

They went down the road to the Old Angel Inn. The food wasn't up to much, but it was the sort of dingy pub where nobody recognized an MP, never mind hassled her. Nick had a pint and Sarah stuck to tomato juice.

'Any joy with finding a new job?' Sarah asked.

'No time. I've been too busy winding up the Power Project.'

'There's still plenty of money in drugs rehabilitation. Alcohol too. I'll always be happy to provide you with a reference, if that helps.'

He thanked her. 'I'm surprised you don't steer clear of me.'

'If my job forced me to abandon people I care about, I'd be in the wrong job. How are things with you and that teacher you were seeing?'

'Over.'

She made the appropriate sympathetic noises, but it was clear he didn't want to discuss it further. 'How about you?' he asked. 'Seeing anyone?'

She shook her head.

Nick lowered his voice. 'There was something I wanted to tell you. About the last time I visited your flat.'

'That was ages ago.'

'When I was leaving, this guy arrived. Tall guy called Paul.'

Sarah tried to keep her expression neutral. 'Paul Morris. I work with him.'

'So you said. And I'm not sure I should tell you this. I mean, the past is the past.'

'What?'

Nick took a gulp of his pint. 'I didn't give anybody up when I was sent down. They offered me a lighter sentence if I did, but I couldn't stomach it. Plus, the dope business is full of heavy people. Chances were, I'd've been knifed in the back before any of them came to trial.'

'What are you getting at?'

'One of the guys I used to work with. A middle man. For all I know, he might have come clean and you might know about his background already. I didn't recognize him at first because he had big hair back then. Full beard too. But I used to sell to the guy you had round your flat when I was last there. Paul Morris.'

40

You get off the train at quarter past five. You can't go back to the hostel. Not yet. You don't know if you've been missed. You don't know if the police will be waiting for you. All the way home, you have been thinking about this. You need protection, now that your protector is dead. Who to turn to? Beany is just a lad, and not a very bright one at that. Talk to the police or social services and they will put you away. There is only one adult who might help. You think he likes you, even though he turned you down. You think you can trust him, but there is only one way to find out.

You have money, because you took some from his flat after cleaning up. Maybe the police will decide it was a burglary. You queue for a taxi, and give the driver Nick Cane's address. You hope he'll be in. What if he isn't? The taxi edges through the Friday rush-hour traffic. It would have been quicker to walk. The car inches along Maid Marian Way, up the hill. This city is full of hills to climb. At the top of Derby Road, with the traffic virtually gridlocked, you thrust a fiver at the cabbie and say you'll get out. He grunts disfavour, but takes the note and unlocks the door.

You dash across to the island that's called Canning Circus. Three big roads circle the island's two pubs like a medieval moat.

You get to the middle and wait again for the pedestrian lights to take you across Alfreton Road. Why would Nick be home? It's Friday evening and he's the sort of bloke who goes to the pub after work. There is no café opposite where you can wait like you waited last night. You climb the metal staircase to his flat. A window is open, which is a good sign. You press the doorbell.

When the doorbell rang, Nick was asleep. He wasn't used to drinking at lunchtime and, after Sarah had burst into tears in the Old Angel, he'd bought them both a proper drink. Then she bought a third round and told him what he had already worked out from Andrew's guess and the nature of Sarah's reaction – she was sleeping with Paul Morris. Or had been. She'd given him the chop, that very morning. Now she was in a quandary over what to do. Nick couldn't help her with the decision, not without more information. There was Home Office stuff, she said, government stuff she couldn't share. There were things he thought best not to tell her, too. Things that, so far, he only suspected, like Paul being behind the attempted bust.

He ignored the doorbell. He never had casual visitors. Probably someone selling something. In a way, he was sorry he'd told Sarah about Paul's past. Their affair was already over and Paul can't have ever been investigated, or he wouldn't have been appointed to the police authority. Six months ago, Nick would not have believed that such a transformation was possible. Now he suspected there were plenty of people in government with a criminal past they'd managed to keep quiet.

Something else bothered him. Andy's eyes when he mentioned Paul had been shifty. He knew more than he was letting on. Nick hadn't told Sarah that it was Andrew who had set up the meeting with the guy who'd introduced him to Paul. Andrew, who used to be his middle man for dope deals, on an industrial scale. Andrew, who now liked to hang out with MPs.

'You know what I worked out about Paul in the end,' Sarah had told him, after her third brandy. 'He wasn't interested in me for me. He was interested because I had some power. He was after my connections. Funny thing was, I didn't do anything to help him, apart from joining the Power Project board. And I was glad to do that, because it helped you. In fact, he even got me onto . . . No, I can't tell you that.'

Sarah began to moan about how it was always a mistake to sleep with married men, especially when they claimed to be separated. Nick didn't argue, nor ask what other experience she had in that area. He didn't want to know. It was hard enough knowing that Paul had been giving it to Sarah while Nick had been wasting his time with Nancy.

Nick wasn't sure that he liked the shift that had taken place in his relationship with Sarah. He'd gone from former lover and potential future lover to old friend and confidant. Nick wanted the potential part to remain, even if the resumption of relations lay at some distant point in the future – say, if she failed to be re-elected. That was highly likely, given her slender majority. If she were still single in 2001 or 2002, and Nick had managed to remake his life by then, both of them would only be forty. Still time for a family, even.

This was a fantasy. But everyone needed fantasies to sustain them.

The doorbell rang again. It was followed by an urgent knocking. What if this was Sarah, here to see him about some fresh disaster? The thought propelled Nick out of bed, to the door, wearing only his underpants. He half opened the door and saw a girl in a black cagoule, its hood up, despite the warm weather outside.

'Can I come in?' she said. 'I don't know where else to go.'
'Course you can,' Nick said.
He pulled on his jeans and a T-shirt, then filled the kettle.

'Why don't you take that anorak off?' he suggested.

Then he saw that she was shivering. The girl looked terrified. She shook her head. 'I'm cold.'

'Take the hood down at least.'

Nick was still coming round from his alcohol-induced sleep, but he knew that the room wasn't cold. Jerry seemed to be suffering from shock. He made a large pot of tea. In Sheffield, when he was growing up, there wasn't much that couldn't be sorted out with a pot of tea. He didn't take sugar, but found some to put in Jerry's mug. He added plenty of milk so that it wasn't too hot and passed it to her. She swigged the drink like it was beer.

'Are you going to tell me what's happened?' he asked.

She nodded solemnly. 'Do you know a guy called Paul Morris?'

'I've met him, yes.'

'This morning, I killed him.'

She shouldn't drink in the afternoon, but after a couple of Solpadeines, Sarah had a clear enough head to face constituency business. She turned her mobile off. She didn't want Paul to call, or even text her. She visited a school and gave a few ideas to the city council team who were applying for funding for a new tram system. Sarah was cynical about the cost. It could only be worthwhile if it got commuters out of their cars. Unfortunately, the only route that the council could get a European subsidy for was one that passed through the area with the lowest car ownership in the city.

This was the Friday evening when she gave her monthly report to Nottingham West Labour party's general committee. Sarah didn't plan to mention that the Power Project had closed down today. There had been nothing in the *Evening Post*. Constituency activists, as a rule, weren't very interested in drugs issues, except insofar as they related to poverty. For them, illegal drugs were a weakness in society that had no ideological solution. Users with more money didn't move off drugs, they moved on to better ones.

Sarah had seen signs of coke at Labour functions in London. Young advisers sniffing as they came out of toilets, clandestine conversations followed by rapid exits and rowdy returns. Not in Nottingham, where politics retained a certain innocence, even though – according to Home Office research – the city had the cheapest cocaine in the country.

The leader of the City Council walked her out of the building. After the day she'd had, Sarah was knackered. She might cry off going to the pub after tonight's meeting. She noticed Winston, her agent, waiting by the porter's desk at the front of the Council House. He looked angry.

'Not had your phone turned on?'

She shook her head. 'Been busy all afternoon. Sorry.'

'The Home Office has been trying to get you. Riot at Wormwood Scrubs. They need you back in the city.'

'Shit. Did you tell them I need to go to the general committee first?'

'I'll give your report. Brief me while I walk you down to the station.'

'Couldn't I give media interviews from the local BBC studio?'

'No chance. They need you there. Let's get you on a train.'

'Do you think I should give myself up?'

'No,' Nick told Jerry. 'Let me think for a minute, figure out what to do.' It didn't occur to him not to help her. Jerry's age might get her a lenient sentence, but her life would still be fucked. She was over sixteen and the murder was premeditated. No way would she get the charge lowered to manslaughter.

'I want you to go through all of the details again. First things first. What did you do with the knife?'

She pointed to a carry-all by her chair. 'It's wrapped in the towel I dried myself off with.'

'Where did you get the idea to strip naked before you picked up the knife?'

'A book I read,' she said. 'Stops there being bloodstains on you. Anyway, he wanted me to get in the shower with him.'

'Did he struggle?' Nick asked.

She shook her head. 'I slashed his throat, from behind.' She said this calmly, like it was what anyone would have done.

'He didn't see you coming?'

'He knew I was getting into the shower. He was soaping himself. He said, "Hey, babe." Then I cut him. And he just fell. Like he was nothing.'

'Why? Why did you need to do it?'

'He betrayed me.'

'You've been reading too much Shakespeare. People betray each other all the time. They don't go round killing each other or . . .'

'Or there'd be a lot less betrayal,' she said.

He thought she might cry, but she remained frozen, her expression blank. He got her another mug of sweet tea and thought about what she had told him. He was less surprised about Jerry and Paul than he had been by Sarah and Paul. According to Sarah, Paul was married with kids, and had been back when Nick used to know him.

What was it with the pimps and dealers who liked to screw underage girls? Ego, probably. Guys like that needed to be unconditionally adored. Older, less vulnerable women saw the dealers for what they were: unscrupulous users, bullies who got rich off the weakness of others. Young girls took them at their own valuation: glamorous gangsters who deserved to be treated like gods.

Nick knew he'd been lucky with his contacts in the drugs trade. He'd never had any need to use violence. What divided him,

Andrew and Paul from most people in the drugs trade was that they had an alternative. They were highly educated. All sorts of careers were open to them. But nothing as lucrative as what they were doing on the side. Paul had his seat on the county council, then his government job in London. Did that mean he'd got out? Or was all that a cover, like the Crack Action Team was for Frank Davis? In either scenario, Paul would have had a strong incentive to want Nick out of the way.

The drugs business had qualified Paul to do the job that he'd been doing, just as Nick's past qualified him to work at the Power Project. Paul's shady past wasn't what had killed him. What had killed him was jealousy, a blind rage that Jerry was only just emerging from.

She slurped her tea and began to speak again.

'It was like I was somebody else. All the time I was getting undressed, and getting into the shower, and stabbing him, and clearing up afterwards, I wasn't me. I was really calm, but I wasn't me.'

Nick had heard such descriptions before. Inside, the career crims didn't discuss their crimes with the likes of Nick, only traded tips with each other. But the wife murderers, the drunken manslaughterers, all had similar stories to tell. Temporary disassociation. Ferocious passion. They either gave themselves up or left so much evidence that they were caught within hours.

'There are bound to be traces of you,' Nick told Jerry.

'I don't think so. I tidied up. There were too many papers to go through, but we never wrote to each other. Never did photos either.'

'There'll be his phone, with your number.'

'I took his phone. Anyway, he bought my mobile, paid for all the credit, so it's in his name, if it's in anybody's name. Do you think we should turn it on, see if there are any messages?'

'No!'

Nick wasn't sure how traces worked with mobiles, but he did know that they couldn't be traced when they were switched off.

'Give me his phone,' he told her. 'Yours, too.'

She did as he asked. 'I'll get rid of them. And the stuff in the bag. If you get caught, say you threw the knife and the towel into the Trent. It's a five-minute walk to Trent Bridge from the station. You went there as soon as you got off the train from London.'

'They're bound to catch me, aren't they?'

'Not necessarily. You say nobody at the hostel knew you were sleeping with him. Let's hope that's true. But you'll need an alibi for last night.'

He could lie for her. She was over sixteen now, so it wasn't a crime for them to be lovers. But chances were Jerry would be caught by forensics, or CCTV. Nick's fake alibi would be exposed. Then he would go back inside, serve his remaining three years plus whatever they gave him for being an accessory. That was too big a favour to offer.

'Nobody will have noticed I wasn't home. Things are dead slack there. The only warden who took any interest in me was Alice, and she's left.'

Nick thought for a moment. 'Okay. Here's what I want you to do. Go back to the hostel. Make sure you're seen. If anyone spotted you were missing, hint that you were seeing the bloke you normally see, celebrating the end of your exams. But don't tell them who it was.'

'Some of them think it's you, still.'

'Let them think that, but don't confirm it. Give me a call in a couple of hours and we'll meet. No, scrub that, best if you don't ring me. There's this drop-in centre, near the station . . .'

41

Nick decided not to wait until dark, for the days were long and twilight was still some way off. He needed to do this before he changed his mind. He took a look at the towel, covered with Paul Morris's blood. It was wrapped around the Sabatier kitchen knife that had killed him. Jerry said she'd wiped her fingerprints off the knife. Nick cleaned it again all the same. Then he put the knife back inside the towel and placed both, with a bit of brick, into a plastic bag. He planned to drop the bundle into the River Trent, exactly where he'd told Jerry to say she'd dropped it. If she were to be caught, at least her story would add up. She could argue that she got rid of the knife while still in shock. Some juries might buy that.

He turned on the Channel 4 news in case Paul's murder featured. Was a Home Office adviser and former county councillor sufficiently important for the evening bulletin? Probably, if his body had been found.

The main story was about a prison riot. Several wardens were trapped inside Wormwood Scrubs. A crackdown on cannabis use was blamed for the outbreak of violence. Prisons Minister Sarah Bone was en route to the prison, hence unavailable for comment. Her predecessor was interviewed instead.

Normally, at this point on a Friday evening, Nick would roll himself a joint, open the window and bliss out. It was tempting to do that now. The high would help him think through the trail of decisions he had to make. For instance, should he tell Sarah that her lover was dead? More critically, how far was he willing to help Jerry? He could catch a train to London, make sure that there was no evidence in the flat that would link her to him. Too far. However, he knew someone who was already in London. Someone who might have much more to lose than he had. Nick was already part of one criminal conspiracy where Paul Morris's death was concerned. He might as well make it two.

Andrew answered on the second ring.

'Nick. Nice surprise.'

'Call me back using a line you're sure is secure,' Nick said.

'Oh.' Andrew hung up immediately. A minute later, Nick's phone rang.

'What's up?'

Nick told him about the murder, leaving out Jerry's name. He didn't mention Sarah's affair with Morris. Andy didn't need to know that.

'That's very interesting,' Andrew said when Nick had finished. 'But, forgive me if this sounds rude, you're telling me this *why?*'

'The body's unlikely to have been found. I don't know if you had any ongoing involvement with Morris, but I thought you'd want a heads-up. In case there are any loose ends you need to tidy away. The girl said there was a lot of paperwork in the flat.'

Andrew changed his tone. 'There shouldn't be. What about the girl?'

'I'm trying to keep her out of it. She's just a hurt kid.'

'Noble of you, but potentially deeply foolish. Where are you this weekend?'

'Here.'

'I'll need to visit Nottingham on Sunday. I'll come to you about three.'

'You're on.'

'And thanks for the heads-up. I could always count on you.'

He didn't ask for Paul's address. Nick put down the phone, attached cycle clips to his jeans, strapped an old knapsack to his back, then hauled his brother's bike down the narrow metal stairs to the alleyway. It was downhill all the way to Trent Bridge. He would be there in less than ten minutes.

You hang out with Shaz and Beany, smoke a spliff, drink Diamond White, which is a bit dry for you. Mustn't have too much, you're seeing Nick later, but you need something to help you relax. Nobody's mentioned your being gone last night. Shaz, showing heavily now, is on about this flat that the social are getting for her. Maybe you can move into it. Yeah, right. Beany will turn it into a knocking shop before a week's gone by.

'Have they offered you anything yet?' she asks.

You shake your head. You haven't pressed for an accommodation decision because you thought that your lover was getting you a flat, though how you'd have explained that to your social worker, you never figured out.

'I think they're waiting to see what my GCSEs are like. If I'm doing A levels, they'll put me in a place nearer college, or something. I don't know.'

'It'd be all right if you lived with me,' Shaz says. 'We'd have a laugh and you'd make sure I didn't . . . you know.'

She glances sideways at Beany, who is rolling another spliff on the top of the wall, oblivious.

'You'll be all right,' you tell Shaz, convincing her even less than you convince yourself. 'I'll come and see you.'

You tell them you're meeting someone and walk down to the drop-in centre near the station. Nick's there, but he's busy. You

have to wait a while to get a word with him. When you plonk
yourself down on the chair opposite him, he looks frazzled. That's
all your fault.

'Well?'

'Nobody noticed I was gone.'

'Good. Sit tight. Don't speak to anyone else about it. Not anyone,
understood?'

'Promise.'

'I'll come see you on Sunday, probably late afternoon. Be in.'

'Okay. Did you . . .?'

He nods.

'Thank you, thank you, thank you, thank you.'

He puts a finger to his lips. 'Enough. Go.'

You go. All the money you paid him, Paul's money, a few
hundred quid at most, is nothing compared to what he has just
done for you. You want to tell him he's the best, to say that you'll
do anything for him, pay him back for the rest of your life. But
how? He doesn't want your body. He seems to be doing this
because he likes you, because he cares about you. The only way
you can repay him is by doing exactly what he tells you to do.

42

Andrew parked his four-by-four on double yellows outside the flat, with the hazards on, then phoned Nick to come and join him.

'Where are we going?' Nick asked, climbing in. Andrew moved a black briefcase from the front passenger seat.

'Not far,' Andrew assured him. 'You'll want to see this.'

He turned onto Forest Road West, then cut down Burns Street, displaying a remarkable familiarity with city short cuts for someone who hadn't lived here in fifteen years. They turned up the steep hill to Waverley Street. Below them, to the right, was the arboretum. Above were a bunch of grand Victorian buildings belonging to Trent University. The left-hand side, where they parked, was shabbier. The huge houses had once been owned by lace manufacturers and wealthy merchants, but were now either cheap hotels or divided into bedsits. Andrew took him into one of the bedsit houses, bringing the briefcase with him. He got two sets of keys out of his trouser pocket.

'I knew that you were buying up property, but I didn't realize any of it was round here,' Nick said.

'I was lying when I said I was here to look at houses. Prices in

London rise more reliably than in Nottingham. This place belongs to someone else.'

They climbed the stairs to the top floor. The first three floors were divided into two flats each, but the attic floor held just one. It was roomy in a way that modern flats weren't, with high ceilings and ornate plasterwork. There were two bedrooms, a living room with an open-plan kitchen in one corner, a separate bathroom and toilet. A lot nicer than where Nick was living at the moment.

'Why are we here?' Nick asked.

Andrew opened the briefcase. 'Have a look at these.'

Nick had once owned a flat, although he'd had to sell it. He knew what property deeds looked like. These were unusual.

'It seems to be some kind of trust.'

Andrew nodded. 'That's because you're not allowed to own property until you're eighteen. I've had it checked, though. The contract's watertight.'

The deeds related to the flat they were sitting in and the trust was in favour of a name he didn't recognize. 'Who's Geraldine Spenser?'

'Look at the address.'

Nick did. The hostel in Alexandra Park. The flat belonged to Jerry.

'Tall Paul bought it for her?'

Andrew nodded. 'Is she the girl who . . .?'

Nick couldn't lie to Andrew. 'Afraid so.'

'Quite a way to repay him. You're not . . . with her, are you?'

Nick shook his head. 'I never went for the young, impressionable ones. That was always more your thing.'

'More trouble than they're worth,' Andy said. 'As our friend Paul found out.'

'Was there anything else in the London flat?'

'There was nothing in the paperwork to tie him to her, no. But there were things it would be better if his family didn't see. Bank records under fake names, the account numbers of some very heavy people.'

'Is what he did bound to come out?'

'Hard to say. Paul covered his tracks. He paid for this place in cash, used a bent solicitor. It's not likely the police will track it down. Paul's name doesn't appear on any of the paperwork.'

'What about his connection with you?'

Andrew grimaced. 'You've probably worked out why I've been visiting Nottingham so much these last few months.'

'I suspect it has something to do with Frank Davis being out of circulation and Tall Paul getting a job in London.'

'Paul was trying to work his way out of the business, which had the unfortunate effect of drawing me back in.'

'And there was I thinking you were coming to see me.'

'I wish.' Andrew smiled. 'Noticed any changes in the drugs game since you got out?'

'It's changing all the time.' Nick thought for a moment. 'In the six months I've been doing drugs work, there are more guns in the city. Yardies fresh out of Jamaica are moving into St Ann's, Sneinton . . .'

Andy nodded. 'The traditional city crims are starting to want a piece as well. What you – we – used to do – the middle classes selling to each other, if you like – is on the way out. The city's being divided into territories rather than client groups. The estates are run by white working-class thugs. They have grow houses springing up all over the place. I won't work with them.'

'So who do you work with?' Nick asked.

'A tight unit. We've never needed to use guns. But soon, if we don't fight, with whatever means necessary, our historic customers – students, professionals, hippy types – are going to have to buy from the Yardies or the thugs.'

'Are you still just selling dope? Or everything?'

A wry smile. 'I was never *just* selling dope. Just growing dope was your contribution. As far as supply's concerned, things have changed since the early nineties. These days, the whole business is run on a cell basis. Remember that movie we watched twice in the second year at uni?'

'*The Battle of Algiers*? I'm not likely to forget it.' Nick had always thought of the film as a primer for terrorists, not drug dealers. 'How many people know who you are?'

'Now Paul's gone, there's just one. The back-up, who I've been coming to see. And you, of course. Paul only dealt with three people, including him. Each of those three . . .'

'. . . only dealt with three people.'

'And none of the cells was bigger than four. So, the question is, are you interested in a taste?'

Nick had seen this coming. 'You want me to courier gear?'

'No. Money. And most of that is done with bank transfers.'

Nick wasn't surprised by anything Andy had told him. He was only surprised that his friend hadn't made this offer earlier. Maybe he'd been waiting to see how Nick handled being out of prison. Nick was still waiting to find this out himself.

'I don't know, Andy. I'm on licence. The police probably keep an eye on me. There's something I haven't told you.'

He explained how he was sure that Paul had set up the raid because he wanted to make sure that Nick didn't tell Sarah about his past.

Andrew listened intently. 'Sounds like something Paul would have done. But the job would have been sent down a couple of levels. No way would Paul go near a bag of crack. You're lucky he didn't come after you again.'

'Maybe he figured that I'd got the message. Stupid thing was, I didn't recognize him at Sarah's. Even when I found out who he was, I didn't suspect him, not at first. Another drug dealer and my girlfriend's ex both had it in for me. So I had enough suspects to be going on with.'

'Paul couldn't be sure you wouldn't grass him up,' Andrew said. 'If he'd come to me, I'd've set him straight. But the higher up you go, the more security conscious you have to be. In his position, I'd've done the same, or worse, just to be on the safe side.'

Nick didn't ask what *worse* might mean.

'What happened to the stuff he planted?' Andrew asked.

'My ex-girlfriend's working her way through it.'

'You're well rid, then.' He was waiting for Nick to respond to his offer, but as Nick was keeping his own counsel, Andy kept talking, the way he always did. 'I've given you a lot to think about. I can promote my back-up guy, but I'd much prefer you. We have an absolute trust. Plus, you've already got respect in the city and you're smart. Sometimes we have to work with other organizations. I'd trust you with negotiations. And the rewards are immense. I'd help you to hide your assets securely, better than you did before.'

'Your back-up guy wouldn't happen to be called Wayne, would he?'

'No. Who's he?'

Nick told him about the job offer he'd received back in November.

'Do you remember the date?'

Nick told him.

'That would be just after Frank Davis was arrested.'

'I guess so.'

'The offer to you probably came from someone in Frank's operation. You should be flattered that your reputation reached them. Back then, I didn't think you were ready to return to work. But by now the police must be convinced that you're clean. In fact, you've become very well-connected.'

Nick had a few more questions. If he said no, this could be his last opportunity to find out all that Andrew got up to.

'What proportion of your business is this? Most of it?'

'You don't need to know that,' Andy said.

'Is it just Nottingham, or other cities, too?'

'Nottingham's quite enough for me, thanks very much.'

'And that currency dealing you've been getting into, that's for laundering money, isn't it?'

'More or less.'

'The property developing that the Tory MP helps you with?'

Andrew smiled. 'In the long run, property's where the big profits are. A boom is coming. I'll be out of the drugs trade before long. By the millennium, who knows? I could hand it all over to you.'

'I haven't said that I'm in yet.'

'I'm not twisting your arm. But this feels like fate to me, Nicholas.'

Andrew was the only friend who ever used his full name. He used it in a way that suggested only he knew Nick's full, true self.

'How long have I got to decide?'

'A week, tops.'

'I'll think it over.'

There was nothing else to say. Nick looked out of the bedroom window. It was an impressive panorama, with what felt like the whole city spread out beneath him.

'I've got errands to run,' Andrew said. 'Shall I leave you here or drop you off somewhere?'

Nick wanted to see Jerry, but he needed time to think first. 'I'll walk. Are you going to leave those deeds and keys with me?'

'Sure. Like I said, there shouldn't be any way this place can be connected with Paul, but there is one other thing.'

'What?'

'The boys who turned over Paul's place made it look like a break-in went wrong. They'll have been heard leaving. The body is bound to be found soon. Tell your girl to be on her guard.'

*

You sit in your room, trying to read. This has been the longest two days of your life. You can't concentrate. You can't think of anything except your dead lover. You can't believe what you have done. You dream about him. You dream of being arrested. But nothing happens.

Beany shows up on Sunday. Shaz isn't around. She's in a rented room somewhere, working for him. Some men pay extra to screw pregnant girls. Beany offers you a pill, which you refuse. You sit outside, in the sun. You take a beer off him, share a spliff. Then you let him feel you up. You can't be bothered to resist. It's only Beany. He's harmless. You let him grope your tits, over the bra, but you don't let him kiss you. Kissing means something.

'You're the best-looking girl in this city,' he tells you.

'No, I'm not. My legs are too scrawny and I've got zits.'

'You got great legs. Zits'll be gone soon.'

You hear Nick's bike coming. It has a particular squeak.

'Gotta go,' you tell Beany and jump off the wall. Only it's not Nick. It's somebody else who doesn't oil their chain. You go back to your room, wait. Somehow you fall asleep. When you wake, Nick is sitting beside you. It's like you're still dreaming.

'I don't think they've found his body yet,' Nick tells you. 'But it's probably a matter of hours. What we don't know is whether there were any witnesses. Can you remember if anyone saw you, anyone at all?'

'I sat in this all-night caff a long time. Apart from that, the only person who saw me was the MP woman. She was so keen to get away from Paul that I don't think she noticed me going in.'

Today your lover's death has become real. But you don't feel like you had anything to do with it. You feel like a victim. You look at Nick. You're good at reading people. You can tell he's holding something back.

'What else is there?'

'There is something, but I'm not sure you're ready to hear it.'

'I'm as ready as I'll ever be,' you say.

'I got some guys to search the flat, make sure there wasn't anything around that linked him to you.'

'Thanks. Thanks a lot.'

'They found one thing.' He hands you some papers. Then he hands you two sets of keys. 'Geraldine,' he says. 'That's some name.'

'I hate it. I'm going to change it when I'm old enough.'

You look through the papers. You can tell what they are. You see the address. You know exactly where it is. You remember making love there, beneath a skylight. You realize what all of this means.

'He did love me,' you say. 'He bought this flat for me.' It begins to sink in. 'No. No, no, no, no, no, no, no.' For the first time since it happened, you cry. 'He really loved me, he really loved me.'

Nick stays until the tears dry up a little. Neither of you speaks. After a while, just before the warden's shift is due to change, he kisses you on the forehead. Then he leaves quietly, leaves you all alone.

43

Prison Minister's questions were hairy. Wormwood Scrubs was the first riot since the new government's election. The opposition felt entitled to have some fun, tearing apart the minister on whose watch it had happened. Sarah was glad that she had spent the weekend dealing with the situation. By now, the prison had settled down. The acting governor had learned his lesson. The prison's previous, relatively lax regime of drug monitoring would be quietly reintroduced. This could not be said in public, which made Sarah's statement in the House problematic, but she got through it. She was learning the crucial skill of lying through her teeth without telling an outright, demonstrable untruth.

'Sarah, can I have a word?' the Home Secretary asked.

'Of course.' Sarah followed him out of the debating chamber. She was expecting her boss to congratulate her on the speech she'd just made. The riot had ruined her weekend, but at least it was over. No prison officers had been seriously hurt and the coverage hadn't been too damaging. Indeed, today's papers all reckoned that the prisons minister had come out of the situation with her reputation enhanced.

The Home Secretary, however, looked serious, as though he were the bearer of bad news. Had something happened to Mum?

Her operation was on Wednesday. Sarah had cleared her diary for the second half of the week to be with her.

'There's somebody who needs to speak to you urgently,' her boss said, when they were alone. 'Could you go with Sir Robin?'

The senior civil servant was standing, discreetly, by a large bookcase filled with the biographies of Sarah's fellow MPs. His look was inscrutable, but tense. He didn't say a word to her while they walked through the corridors, into a part of the Commons estate that she had never visited before.

'Can you tell me what this is about?' Sarah asked.

'I'm afraid not. It's an informal interview, but I would advise you to be very careful about what you say.'

Sarah began to worry. She racked her brain to think what this could concern. Presumably she had fucked something up. But what?

'An informal interview with whom?'

Sir Robin knocked on an unlabelled door. He ushered her into the tiny room. There were no windows or pictures on the walls. The office had barely enough room for her to sit on one side of a large, cheap, wooden desk.

The two men on the other side of the desk introduced themselves. Sarah was too flustered to take in names, but she got their ranks. One was a detective chief inspector, the other a detective superintendent. So this was serious. The DCI asked the questions.

'We need some sensitive information, Minister.'

'About what?'

'Your relationship with Paul Morris.'

Shit. She should have told her boss about the affair, but it was too late now. But why the cloak and dagger approach? Sarah's mind went into overdrive as she tried to figure out all the angles. Nick had told her how Paul used to be a dealer. Suppose he still was? Suppose this interview had something to do with him working with Frank Davis and the police had erroneously connected her with it?

Whatever, she'd done nothing wrong. She would talk her way out.

'I see,' was all she said.

'How would you describe your relationship with Mr Morris?' The DS had a kinder, more urbane voice. A former copper, Sarah knew this routine well. She would treat both men as equals, whom she wanted to help . . . within reasonable bounds. And she would never, ever go near a married man again.

'A professional one. We serve on some of the same committees.'

The DCI opened his briefcase and reached into it. 'Perhaps, to save time, I should show you an item we found in Mr Morris's flat. Can you confirm that these are yours?'

He held up an evidence bag containing a pair of pale blue knickers with a navy ribbon bow. Hers. No point in holding anything back, if they'd gone to the lengths of searching his flat. He must be in serious trouble. When she replied, Sarah's voice came out quietly.

'Possibly. I do own some underwear like that.'

'And can you confirm that you left Mr Morris's King's Cross apartment at twenty-five to eight last Friday morning?'

She knew then that they had a witness. This was like an old-fashioned divorce court. Was the new government so holier than thou that they were going to hound every minister who slept with someone they weren't married to?

'Yes, I did.'

'I take it you weren't there for a business meeting.'

'No, I wasn't.'

'Can you tell me what state Mr Morris was in when you left that morning?'

'Angry. I'd just dumped him. So, from then on our relationship became purely professional, which is why I characterized it in that manner just now.' As soon as she'd blurted out that bit of crappy legalese, she regretted it.

'You're sure that he was the angry one, not you?'

What was this, relationship counselling? 'I never get angry, Inspector, except for effect. Maybe angry's not the best word for the state that Paul was in. He was miffed, insulted, eager to change my mind.'

'Change your mind about what?'

'About my not seeing him again.'

The men exchanged glances. When the DCI spoke, there was a new, sarcastic edge to his voice. 'And you won't be seeing him again, will you?'

'Not outside our professional relationship, no. But I don't understand what you're getting at. What has Paul done?'

'Just to reiterate, he was in good health when you left him?'

'He was. Very good –' Sarah stopped herself. 'Wait. Are you telling me that . . .'

The superintendent took over, speaking in formal, measured tones. 'Paul Morris was murdered, Minister. Some time on Friday morning, according to the pathologist. You were seen hurrying down Pentonville Road with what passers-by referred to as a "distracted air" at around twenty to eight the same morning. Is that accurate?'

Sarah tried to keep herself together. 'Before we go any further,' she said, as soon as she was able to get the words out, 'I think I'd better consult my solicitor.'

The super gave a laconic smile. 'That's your right, Minister, but I suspect the fewer people who know about this, the better. Unless, that is, you intend to confess to murder. In which case, I advise you to speak no further and seek representation at once.'

Sarah paused to take in what he had said before she replied. 'Where and how was he killed?'

The men looked at each other again. The superintendent nodded and the DCI spoke. 'In the shower. With a kitchen knife or similar.'

'How can I be a suspect? Paul followed me into the street when I left. He was trying to get me to go back. Somebody must have seen me leave.'

'I'm afraid not,' the DCI said. 'But we will, of course, look for witnesses. Have you anything to add? Perhaps you'd care to tell us the length and the nature of your affair with Mr Morris.'

Sarah considered. She wanted to grieve for Paul, but now wasn't the time. She needed to save herself. Should she tell them about Paul's drug-dealing past? Then she'd have to explain how Nick had told her about it, the same day that she had dumped him.

She was innocent, and the police were right. She had a career to save. The fewer people who knew about this, the better. Honesty was the best policy, but she had to set a few ground rules.

'I'll tell you what you want to know. But off the record. No recording and, when you've established that I'm not responsible for Paul's murder, I need you to promise to keep my name out of it. There's no reason to upset Paul's wife and kids by telling them about the affair we had.'

The super nodded. 'If we can firmly establish that you are not involved, we'll respect your confidence. That is, after all, why we are meeting here, rather than at New Scotland Yard.'

Sarah answered their questions as honestly and as openly as she was able. She wasn't sure if they believed a word she said.

Paul Morris's murder made the Monday evening news. The body had been found the previous evening. Police were appealing for witnesses. Nick wondered whether to contact Sarah, and how much to say. After some thought, he rang her mobile. Straight to voicemail. He left a message:

I heard what happened. If you want to talk, or I can help at all, you know where to find me.

He felt bad about not telling her what Jerry had done. He owed Sarah his job, which had lifted him out of the scrap heap, and they had so much history. But it was wrong to share other people's secrets. Later, he was going to do his first shift at the switchboard of his brother's cab firm. A spliff would help him think, but wasn't compatible with the work he was about to do. Honest work. If he stayed honest, he would have to stay in this shithole of a flat for the foreseeable future. Or he could throw in his lot with Andrew and become as rich as Croesus.

Nick didn't judge people with no legitimate prospects who went into drug dealing. He didn't judge Andy, either. Like him, Nick had a choice. Less choice than when he first got arrested, but a choice nevertheless. Spend your life looking over your shoulder, respected only by people you didn't respect yourself. Or make the best of what you've got. No choice, when you put it like that. He might not get Sarah back. True love did not conquer all, if true love was what they once had. True love rarely conquered the divide between a rented Alfreton Road flat and a posh apartment in the Park. But he would never get Sarah back if he returned to drug dealing. And there was no innocence about this decision. He'd seen what crack and smack did to users, inside and out.

Andy had given him a week to think it over, so Nick wouldn't tell him his decision straight away. He didn't want to decide in haste then repent at leisure. Too much money was involved for comfort. There were bound to be more shades of grey in the argument than he was acknowledging to himself at the moment.

Only later, when he was cycling to the cab office, did it occur to Nick how Sarah could be a suspect in the murder of Paul Morris. He dismissed the thought out of hand. He knew the way the world worked. Sarah was so well respected, and was in such a position of authority, that even if she had stabbed Paul in the back, the powers-that-be were bound to let her get away with it.

44

The Home Secretary welcomed Sarah into his vast, historic office. When she'd sat down, he poured her a large brandy, but didn't have one himself.

'Have you got something to tell me?'

'Paul Morris and I were having a . . .' Sarah stumbled over her words '. . . relationship. Until Friday morning. It only started after Paul said he was getting a legal separation from his wife. On Friday, he told me that this had been a lie, so I ended the affair.'

'He was seen shouting at you in the street. You're on CCTV, leaving his flat.'

'We didn't have a row, as such, but he did try to stop me leaving. I got a train back to Nottingham. You say it's on CCTV?'

'Yes. There's a new camera outside a café that the police didn't find out about until this afternoon.'

'That means . . .' Relief began to flood Sarah's body. She felt herself shake and took a gulp of brandy. It burned her mouth, but helped. 'Has Annette been told?'

'About the murder, yes. About you, no. We'll try to keep the affair quiet, but there are no guarantees about such matters.'

'Thanks, I really appreciate that.'

'Don't thank me yet. We don't know how many members of the public saw you that morning. It only takes one to go to the press.'

'Did the CCTV show anybody else going into his flat?'

'I can't tell you any more about it. You're out of the loop now. I'm sorry for your loss but, from now on, we have to be very discreet indeed. I will represent the Home Office at the funeral. It's better if you stay away.'

'Of course.'

'And I want you to think of a good reason for resigning.'

'What?'

'When I asked you to join the ABC committee, you should have told me about your relationship with Paul Morris. That was a serious omission.'

'I didn't ask Paul to recommend me for the ABC committee!'

'He didn't. You were appointed at the suggestion of the prime minister. He thought it would be useful to have someone relatively young and connected to the issues. If Paul took any credit for your appointment, he was lying. But you still should have told me of your relationship. I'm afraid that, since you're leaving government, you'll leave the ABC committee, too. I should remind you not to mention its existence to anybody.'

Sarah began to cry. This was the second time in the last three days that she'd cried because of Paul. She couldn't believe he was dead. Unlike the Home Secretary, though, she had a good idea why he had been killed. Should she mention his drug dealing now? It could only make things worse, and expose her connection with Nick. She took another slurp of brandy.

The situation began to sink in. A tabloid shitstorm still threatened to engulf her. Which meant her boss was right. She had to resign.

'I'll go,' she said. 'But I want you to be very clear on something. I've done nothing wrong. I slept with a man who'd lied about his marital status, and I was appointed to a committee whose existence I was unaware of. It put me in an awkward position, but I certainly broke no rules, written or unwritten.'

'Agreed. And you have been an excellent minister, Sarah, as your performance in the House today amply demonstrated. If you're lucky, none of this will come out. I have instructed the investigating team to keep your involvement strictly to themselves. I told them that I would regard a leak as a demonstration that the Metropolitan Police is incapable of internal security. If you're lucky, you'll be able to return to government in due course. Can you think of a credible reason to step down from office for a while?'

'My mother's having an operation on Wednesday. I was going to take some time off to look after her. Until she's had the op, though, I don't know how serious –'

'I'm sorry to hear that,' the Home Secretary interrupted, 'but the timing is just right for this situation. We'll announce that you're stepping down of your own volition and will be replaced at the reshuffle. I suggest you go home and write a letter to Tony.'

'Will you tell him what really happened?'

Her boss considered for a moment. 'Only if it turns out that you did it.'

EPILOGUE

August 1998

For a moment, Nick did not recognize the woman who'd arrived at his door in the early evening. She'd let her hair grow longer and had more laugh lines than she had seven years ago, when they stopped being lovers, but was no less attractive for that. Her smile was still the same. He kissed her cheek and invited her in.

'How did you find me?'

'Phone book. I hope you don't mind me showing up out of the blue.'

'Not at all. You've only just caught me, though. I'm moving.'

'Somewhere nice?' Eve asked, looking at the room. Filled with cardboard boxes, it looked even smaller than it really was.

'A place near the arboretum. It's a lot nicer than this, yes.'

He'd come to an arrangement with Jerry, who had passed her GCSEs with several A grades. Social services would be providing her with a place until she was eighteen. Until then, at least, he would rent her flat from her, paying with a combination of cash and A-level English literature lessons.

'I expect you can guess why I've come round,' Eve said, almost shyly.

'Not really.'

'A few months ago, Nancy Tull mentioned you in passing. I read between the lines that you were seeing each other.'

'We were. It didn't work out, I'm afraid.'

'Pity. You two might have been good for each other. I was hoping you were still in touch with her.'

'I haven't seen her for a while. Why?'

'It's school business. I've been trying to track her down. I visited her home, but she doesn't live there any more.'

'Isn't it the summer holidays still?'

'For another week. But Nancy hasn't been in since June. Even before that, her attendance had become erratic. She'd not show up and not call in sick either. Two weeks before the end of term, she claimed to have a cold and we haven't heard from her since. Ever since summer half-term, the days when she did come in, she looked . . . gaunt, unwell. Do you have any idea what's wrong with her?'

'The guy she was seeing before me is called Carl. I know she went back to him. And I know he leads a fairly wild life. But I don't know where he lives, sorry.'

'I'd like to help Nancy,' Eve said, the deputy head disappearing from her voice. 'But I can't if . . . is it heroin this time?'

Nick tried to decide how open to be with Eve. 'I don't think so. She was using crack when I saw her last. Smokable cocaine. Very, very addictive.' When Eve didn't look surprised, Nick added, 'Why did you say *this* time?'

Eve grimaced. 'She did something similar a couple of years ago. Alcohol and cocaine were the problem, from what I gathered. She went AWOL then, too. Not for as long as this. I persuaded the head not to sack her. She agreed to have treatment. It took a while, but she turned her life around.'

'I had no idea.'

'Addicts can be very secretive. I expect you know that. Nancy said you were doing drug rehabilitation work.'

'I had a job, but the contract finished.'

'If I track down Nancy, would you talk to her?'

'I'd try, of course.' Nick would feel obliged to, since he felt partly responsible for her worsening addiction. But he wouldn't tell Eve about this, nor about his belief that Nancy was into crack well before he inadvertently supplied her. 'Only thing is, Nancy's boyfriend hates me. He attacked me once. If they're still together, I doubt he'd let me get near her. I'll ask around. How long has she got before you sack her?'

'There were a lot of parental complaints last term. She was called in for a meeting with the head yesterday, but didn't respond. Maybe she'll turn up on the first day of term, fit and well, give us her new address, apologize profusely and get back to work.'

Nick doubted this. As, obviously, did Eve. 'I wish I could help more, Eve, but we only went out for a few weeks. She turned out not to be the person I thought I knew.'

'You didn't . . .?' There was a slight uncertainty in Eve's voice.

'Tell her about us? No. I never told anybody. Did you?'

'Only my husband. You can't start a marriage with secrets.'

'I suppose not. I'm pleased to see you looking so well on it.'

'You're looking good too. How shall we stay in touch?'

'I haven't got a new phone number yet,' Nick said. He had no plans to get a landline. Too public. 'Why don't you give me yours?'

The conversation might have continued, but for the sound of feet on the stairs. In came Chantelle, wearing jeans, trainers and a vest that left little to the imagination.

'Are you ready, lover?'

'Just about. Let me introduce you to Eve, who I used to work with.'

The two women appraised each other. Chantelle saw an older woman who was no threat, and, more or less correctly, assumed something professional. Eve saw a confident, lively woman half her age, and gave Nick an approving nod.

'I'll bet you're not here to help Nick move boxes,' Chantelle said.

'That's not why I came, but I'm happy to lend a hand,' Eve said.

The next hour and a half was strange, but not in a bad way. The two women – the oldest he'd ever had feelings for and the youngest – helped him move into his new flat, which had been bought by a dead man for the girl who'd killed him.

'Is your mother really so ill?' Eric asked Sarah, over dinner in her flat. This was the first time that she had entertained him there.

'It's serious, yes. She has to have another operation because they don't think they got everything the first time. I need to spend more time with her.'

'I didn't think you were the sort of person who gave up power easily.'

'I talked it over with my boss and I only have to let them know when I'm ready to return. I'm still in the PM's good books.'

'It must hurt that you were replaced by the young woman who criticized you in a debate. What was her name?'

'Ali Blythe. No, we're friends. I congratulated her when I heard.'

Sarah's resignation had been little discussed in media coverage of the reshuffle. The main focus had been on the dismissal of the secretary of state for social security, whose career had been fatally undermined by the single parent benefit fiasco.

'There's something you're not telling me.'

'And there's something you're not telling me. I'm out of the loop since I left the Home Office. Who killed Paul Morris? You must have heard.'

Eric shrugged. 'I'm afraid not. Strictly between us, his wife thinks he was having an affair with one, possibly more than one, woman. But the Met have no leads. They can't rule out aggravated burglary. The angle of the blade suggests that his assailant was smaller than him. There was nothing useful from forensics or CCTV. The one curious thing about the case is that there was a burglary – maybe a second burglary – at least thirty-six hours after the killing. Not much taken, but without the noise the burglars made, Paul's body might not have been found for several more days.'

There was no suspicion in his eyes. The Met had kept their word and not leaked Paul's relationship with Sarah. She changed the subject.

'I saw your big drugs bust on the news.'

'Yes, that was a real result.' Nottingham police had finally caught the former head of the Crack Action Team red-handed with large quantities of cocaine and heroin. Frank Davis would receive a long sentence. 'And, this time, it wasn't a set-up. We think his bosses – whoever they were, our intelligence is mixed – cut him loose after he got released in April. So he sold off most of his property in order to fund going back into large-scale dealing, which was the only game he knew. Stupid. We were all over him with surveillance. It was just a matter of time.'

He went on. 'A pity that the Power Project had to be closed down, but it was too soon after the Crack Action Team fiasco. What's your friend Nick doing these days?'

'I wouldn't know,' Sarah said. 'I helped him out, but we don't see each other socially.'

In fact, she had tried to reach Nick, only this week, for a catch-up, but his phone was disconnected and there was a 'For Rent' sign outside his flat. They had spoken only once since her resignation, by phone. He'd asked if it had anything to do with the affair with Paul. She'd told him the truth. She trusted Nick to keep her secrets. But neither of them had suggested that they meet. She would never love anyone the way she had loved Nick, but seeing him only reminded her that, when she was with someone new, she was settling for second best.

'Forgive me for asking this,' Eric said, topping up her glass, 'but I know you met with Cane when he was winding up the Power Project.'

'I did. Forgive you for asking what?'

'You didn't hint that we had an officer inside the project, did you? He wouldn't have a clue about our friend? It's a matter of great delicacy.'

When the Power Project was set up, following the corruption of the Crack Action Team, the police had insisted on having someone on the inside. A young, over-qualified woman from out of the area had applied for the job of receptionist. Unsurprisingly, Kingston appointed her, though he was never privy to the subterfuge.

'Nick had no idea about her. He was pissed off when Chantelle left suddenly, because it meant more work for him. The only people that knew who she really was were Suraj and me. Is she still working undercover?'

'You don't need to know that.'

'Don't I?' Their eyes met, each amused at the game they were playing. Sarah wondered how hard Eric would try to persuade her to let him stay the night. His glass was nearly empty. 'One of these days,' she said, opening a second bottle of Montepulciano, 'I'll work out the difference between the things I need to know and the things I don't. That would make my life a lot simpler. Can I pour you another glass?'

'I don't mind if I do.'

You got away with it, but you did not get away. Your new flat is only a few minutes' walk from the hostel. You share it with a trainee nurse and another sixth-form student. It's too soon to say whether you'll be mates with either of them, but you try to be sociable. You could do with a new friend.

Your social worker sees you once a fortnight. You have chosen your A levels and been to an induction afternoon. You are not ready to study but Nick says you have to. He says you will move past the guilt. He says that when good people do bad things, they want to punish themselves, especially if they haven't been found out, officially punished. But that will pass, he says. He gives you books to read. He insists on giving you rent for the flat that you never want to go back to.

You miss your old mates. Even the ones you thought you never wanted to see again, like Shaz. The Saturday before term starts, you bump into her on the same old wall. First time you've seen her in weeks. She weighs a ton, waddles when she walks. Shaz takes you to a big old place that Beany owns, or rents. It's on the smarter side of Woodborough Road, in a tree-lined street called Corporation Oaks. Beany doesn't screw her very often these days. Worried about hurting the baby, he says. Plus he's got a new piece he's more interested in, someone he used to deal to.

'But she's old. He'll come back to me, you'll see.'

Shaz has good clothes, good weed too. You're starting to float when you come out of the living room and see Beany on the stairs. He's in a hurry, so he only strokes your cheek, says, 'You know where to find me, girl.' In a weird way, it's good that he still wants you. There's a shout from up the stairs.

'I know what you're like. Don't forget!'

'I won't forget,' Beany shouts back, then flashes you a grin. 'Gotta go.'

You glance at the woman on the stairs. She wears only a bra and knickers, but she looks familiar. The bra is a good one, you recognize the make, but the knickers are starting to sag. She stares back at you with the otherworldly gaze of the crackhead. Soon, she will have that grey pallor, too, and her price will go down. The woman speaks and you're sure it's her.

'Who's your friend, Shaz? Is she holding?'

'No, Pops. She's just passing through.'

The woman goes back up the stairs.

'Pops?' you say to Shaz. 'I thought her name was Nancy.'

'The guys call her Miss Popularity,' Shaz says. 'Pops for short. *Miss* because she used to be a schoolteacher, can you believe that? Beany says she gives the best blow job on the planet, says I ought to take lessons from her.'

'How long's she been working for him?'

'She's not, yet. But she loves the pipe so much she'll do anything for anyone who gets her high.'

Shaz says this as though it's worse than being paid for it. Maybe it is.

'You're not hitting the pipe too hard, are you?' you ask.

Shaz says she's not. 'It does my head in. Then there's the kiddy on the way. Are you going to give me your new address?'

You hesitate. Shaz understands what you're thinking.

'You're right,' she says. 'Don't. I can't tell Beany what I don't know.'

Outside, the sun beats down. The sweet buzz from the skunk suffuses your mind. For a few minutes you are, if not happy, not unhappy. You're not scared of the future. You're not scared of anything.

You're stoned.

ACKNOWLEDGEMENTS

The Nottingham storylines in this novel were inspired by, but are not directly based on, real events in 1997–98. I am indebted to Nick Davies's *Dark Heart: The Shocking Truth about Hidden Britain* (Vintage, 1997) and Carl Fellstrom's *Hoods: The Gangs of Nottingham* (Milo Books, 2008) for background on the Crack Action Team. My thanks to both authors, and to everybody who helped me with research for this novel. You know who you are.

ABOUT THE AUTHOR

David Belbin is the author of more than thirty novels aimed at teenagers and his work has been translated into twenty-five languages.

He was born in Sheffield but has lived in Nottingham since going to university there; he now teaches Creative Writing at Nottingham Trent University. This is his second crime novel for adults.

For more information visit www.davidbelbin.com

BONE AND CANE

DAVID BELBIN

The first in the bestselling Bone and Cane series

SHE THOUGHT HE WAS INNOCENT

During the 1997 Election, Labour MP Sarah Bone campaigns for Ed Clark to
be released from prison, convinced he was wrongly accused of murder. But,
at the party to celebrate his freedom, Ed reveals his true nature and Sarah
sees she may have made a terrible mistake.

SHE SET HIM FREE

Desperate to find out the truth, Sarah joins forces with Nick Cane, an ex-
boyfriend just released from prison, and they begin their own investigation
into Ed Clark's murky background. Soon they find that they've gone too deep.

THEY WERE WRONG

Now Nick risks going back inside and Sarah could lose her seat in the General
Election. And Ed Clark is about to get away, again.

A number one bestselling ebook, *Bone and Cane* introduces an original
partnership for a major new crime series that moves between inner-city streets
and the corridors of power.

'A gripping and grown-up page-turner' – *Tablet*

'A compelling story that threw me right back to the 1997 election.
Spare, uncompromising and very well written' – Nicola Monaghan

978 1 906994 26 6
Published by Tindal Street Press · £7.99